MISSING the BOAT:

the offered salvation and inevitable demise of the CHuRamane

Silverline™
BOOKS

MISSING THE BOAT
ISBN: 978-1-58240-015-4
First Printing, December 2008

Published by Image Comics, Inc. Office of publication: 1942 University Avenue, Suite 305, Berkeley, California 94704. Copyright © 200
Justin Shady. All rights reserved. MISSING THE BOAT™ (including all prominent characters featured herein), its logo and all character
likenesses are trademarks of JUSTIN SHADY, unless otherwise noted. Image Comics® and its logos are registered trademarks of Imag
Comics, Inc. Silverline Books and its logos are ™ and © 2008 Jim Valentino. All names, characters, events and locales in this publication are
entirely fictional. Any resemblance to actual persons (living or dead), events or places, without satiric intent, is coincidental. No part of th
publication may be reproduced or transmitted, in any form or by any means (except for short excerpts for review purposes) without th
express written permission of Mr. Shady.

PRINTED IN SOUTH KOREA

•WRITER: Wayne Chinsang|Justin Shady
•ILLUSTRATOR: dwellepHant
•EDITOR: KRis Simon
•PUBLISHER: Jim Valentino

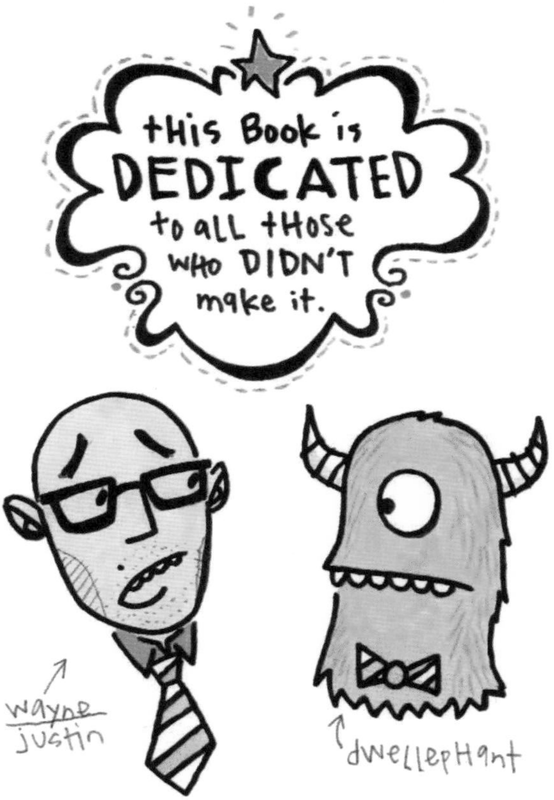
this Book is DEDICATED to all those who DIDN'T make it.
wayne
justin
dwellephant

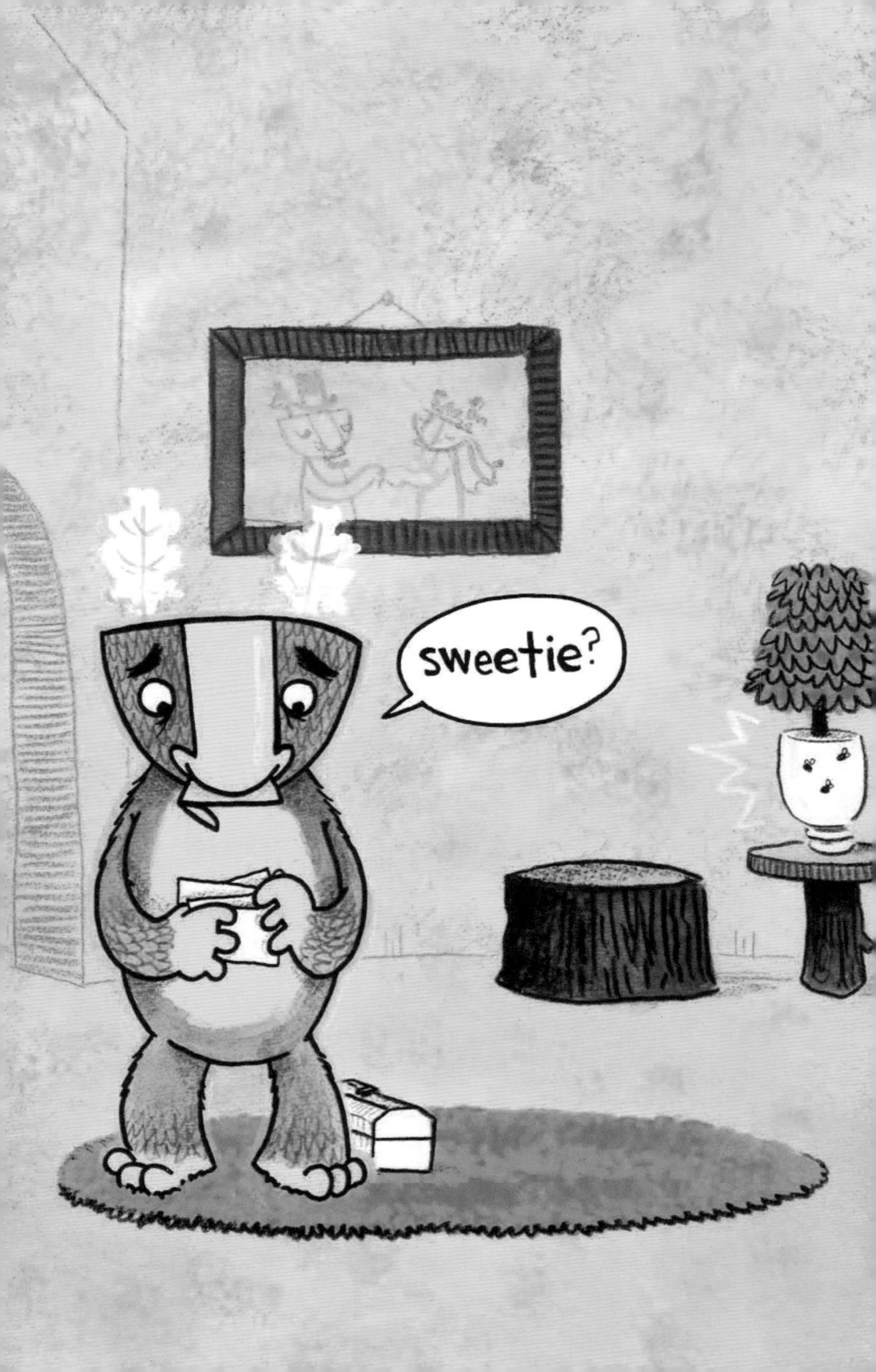
sweetie?

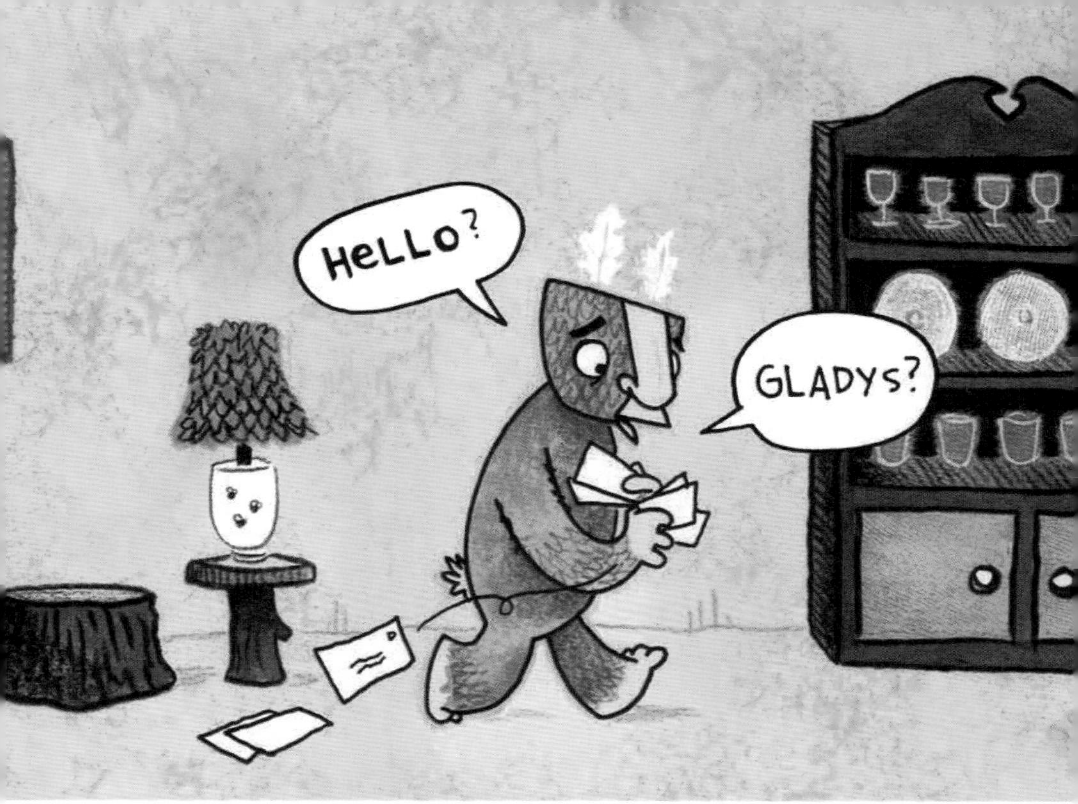
HELLO?
GLADYS?

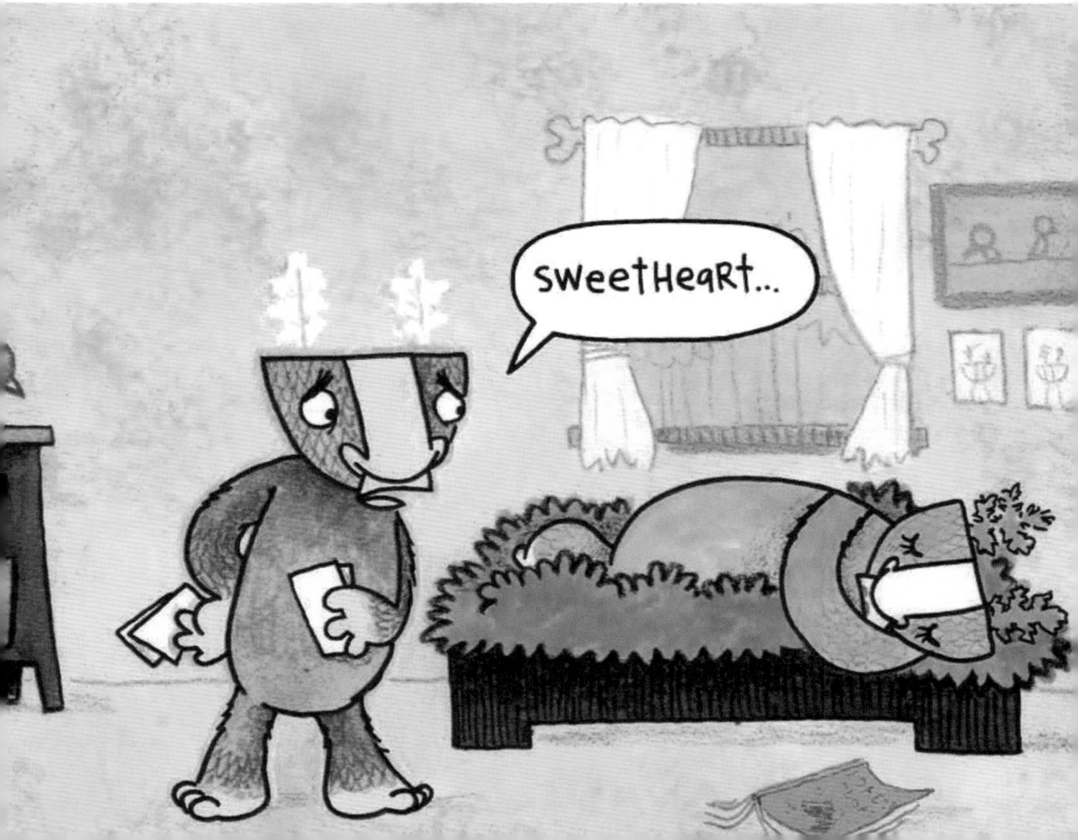
SWEETHEART...

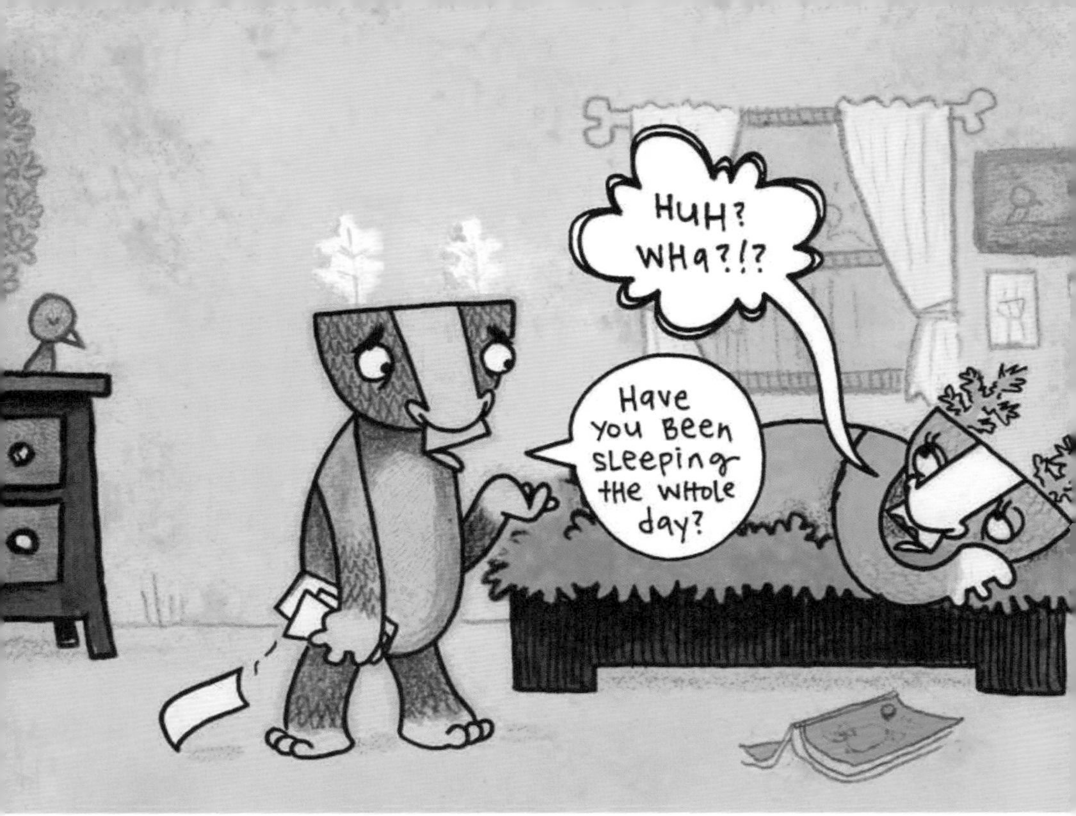
HUH? WHA?!?
Have you Been sleeping the whole day?
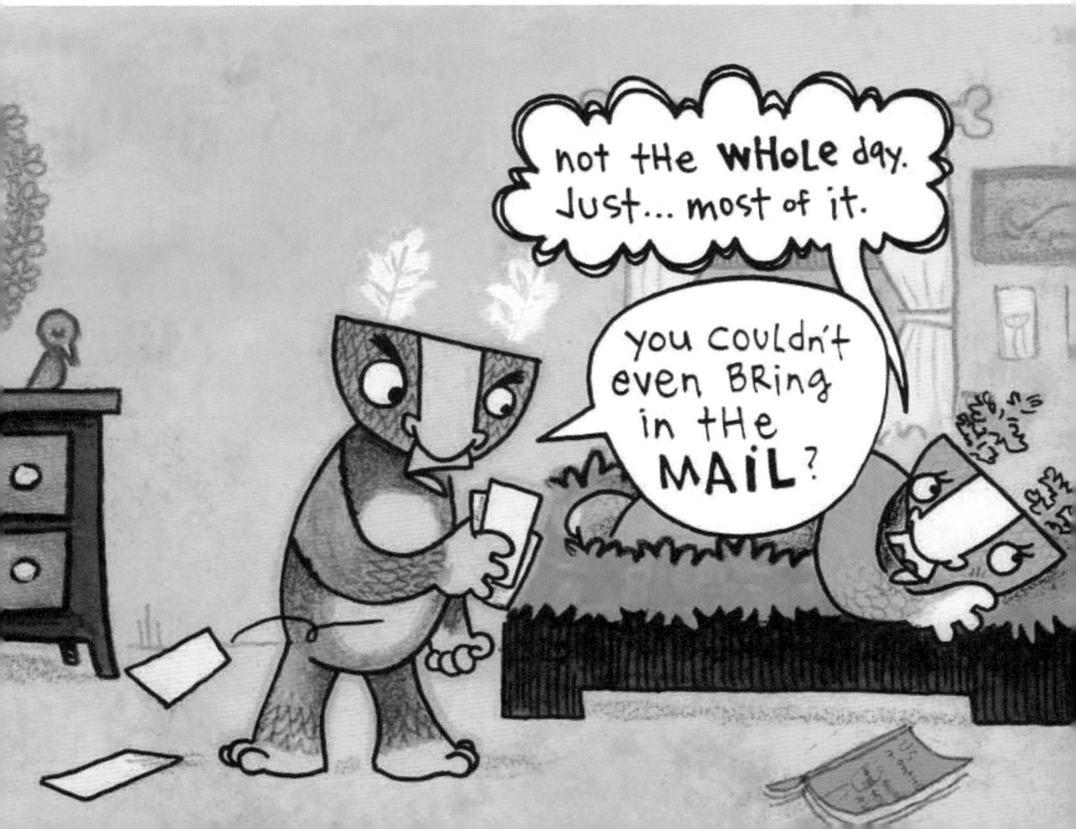
not the WHOLE day. Just... most of it.
you couldn't even Bring in the MAIL?

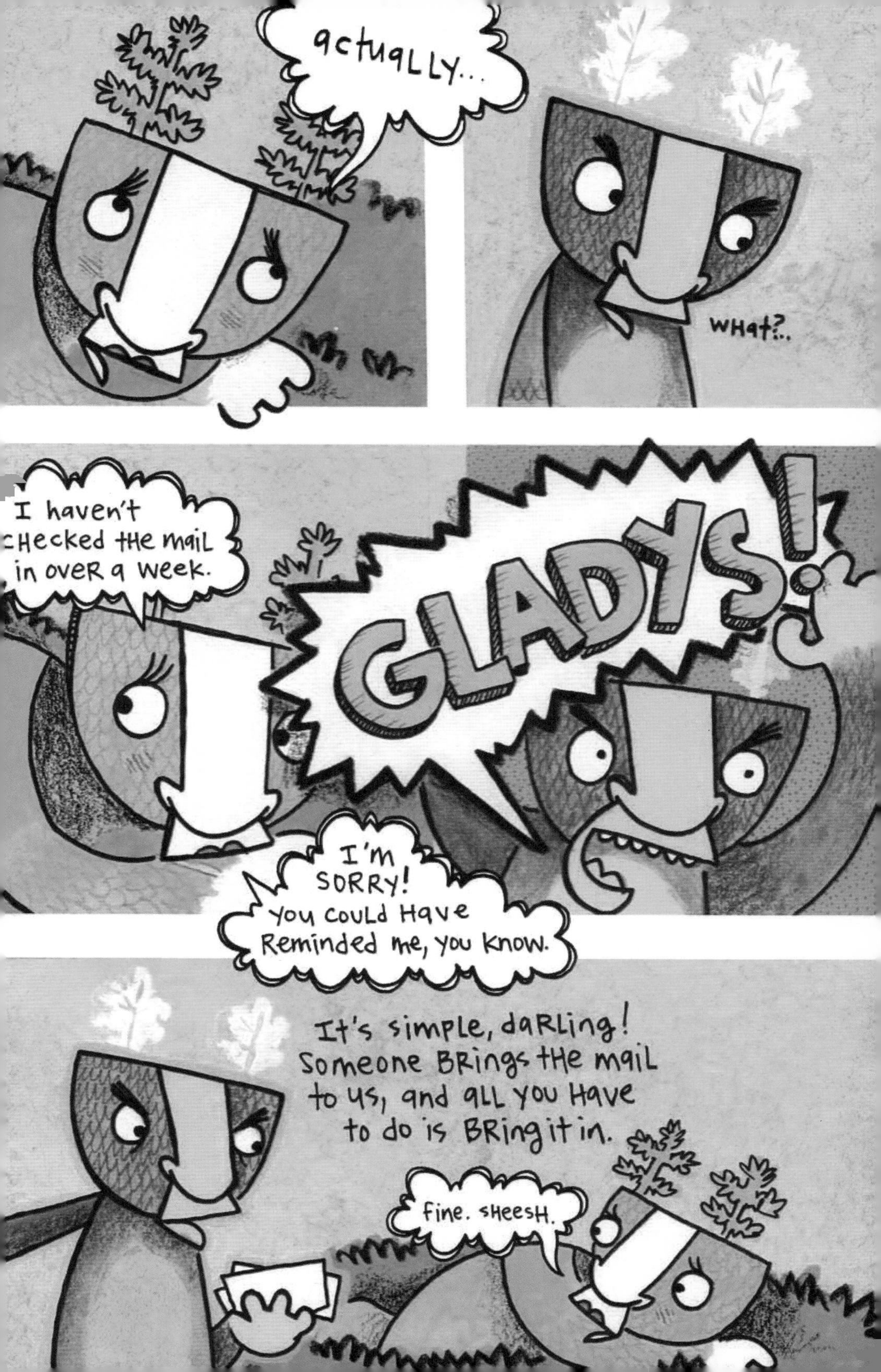
actually...
what?..
I haven't checked the mail in over a week.
GLADYS!
I'm SORRY! You could have reminded me, you know.
It's simple, darling! Someone brings the mail to us, and all you have to do is bring it in.
fine. sheesh.

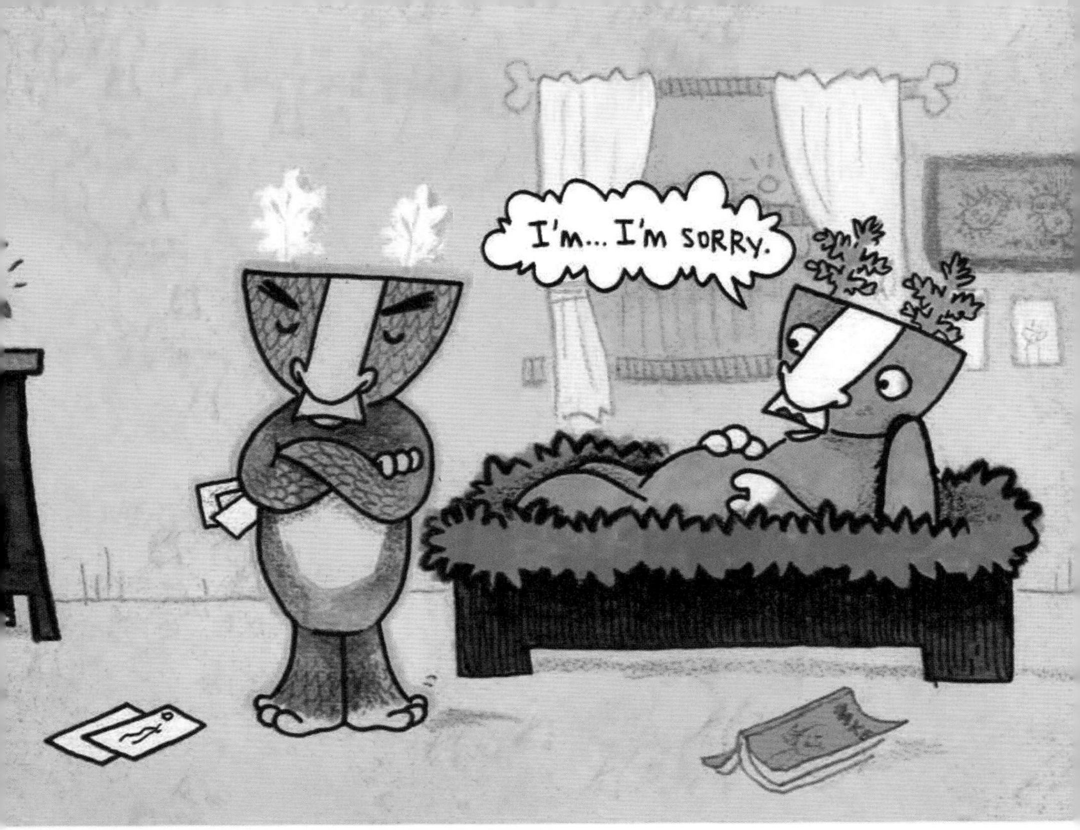
I'M... I'M SORRY.

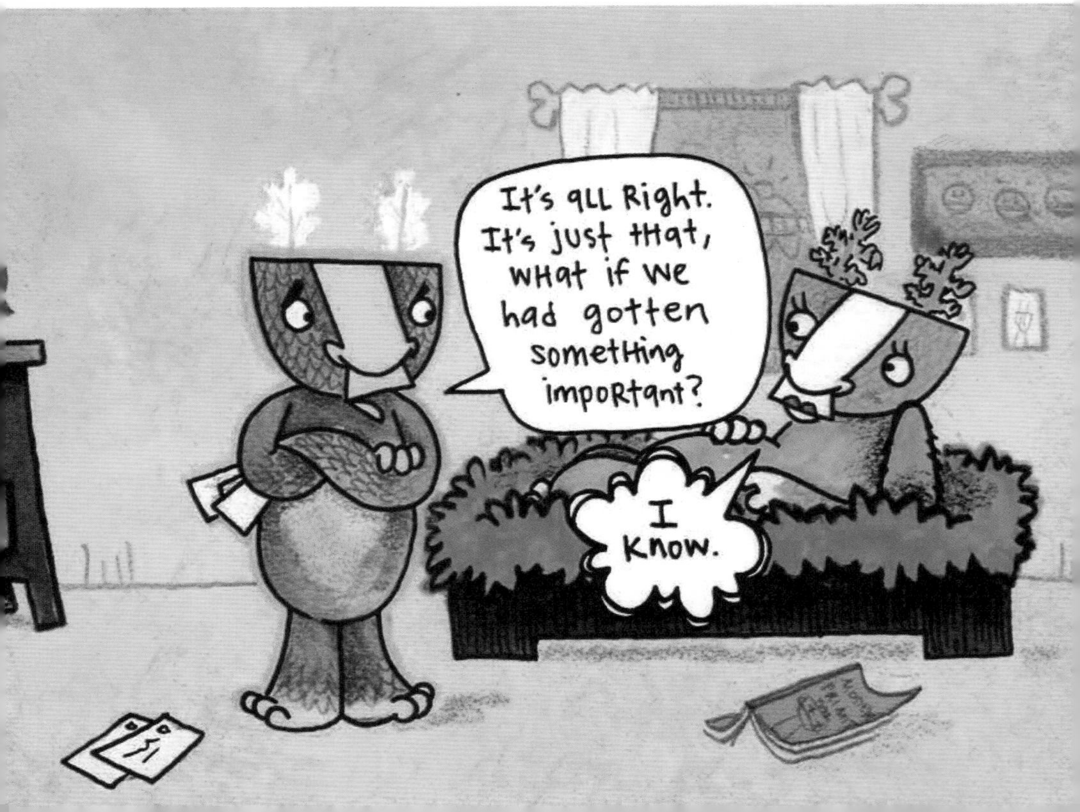
IT'S ALL RIGHT. IT'S JUST THAT, WHAT IF WE HAD GOTTEN SOMETHING IMPORTANT?
I KNOW.

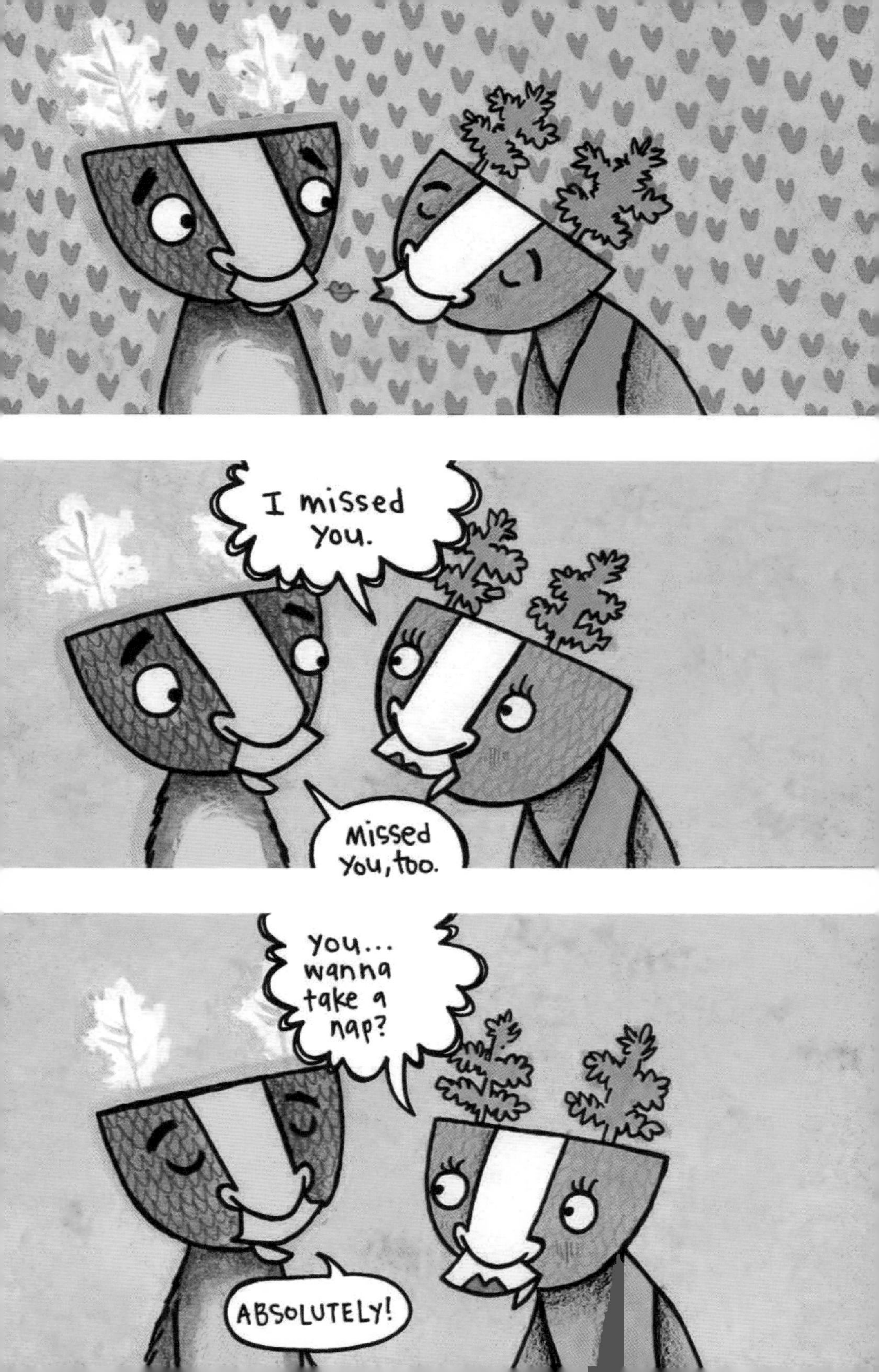
I missed you.
Missed you, too.
you... wanna take a nap?
ABSOLUTELY!

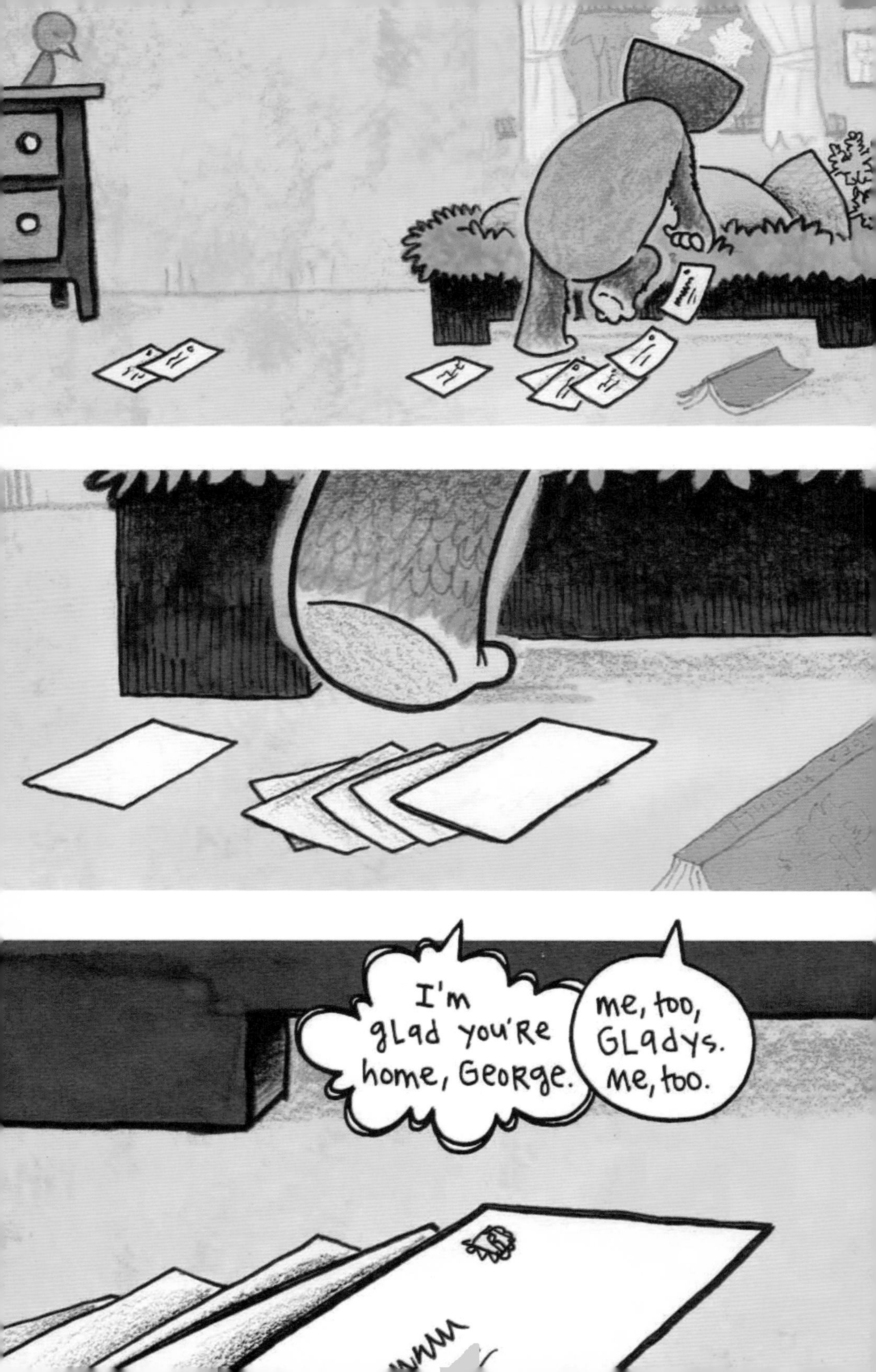
I'm glad you're home, George.
me, too, Gladys. me, too.

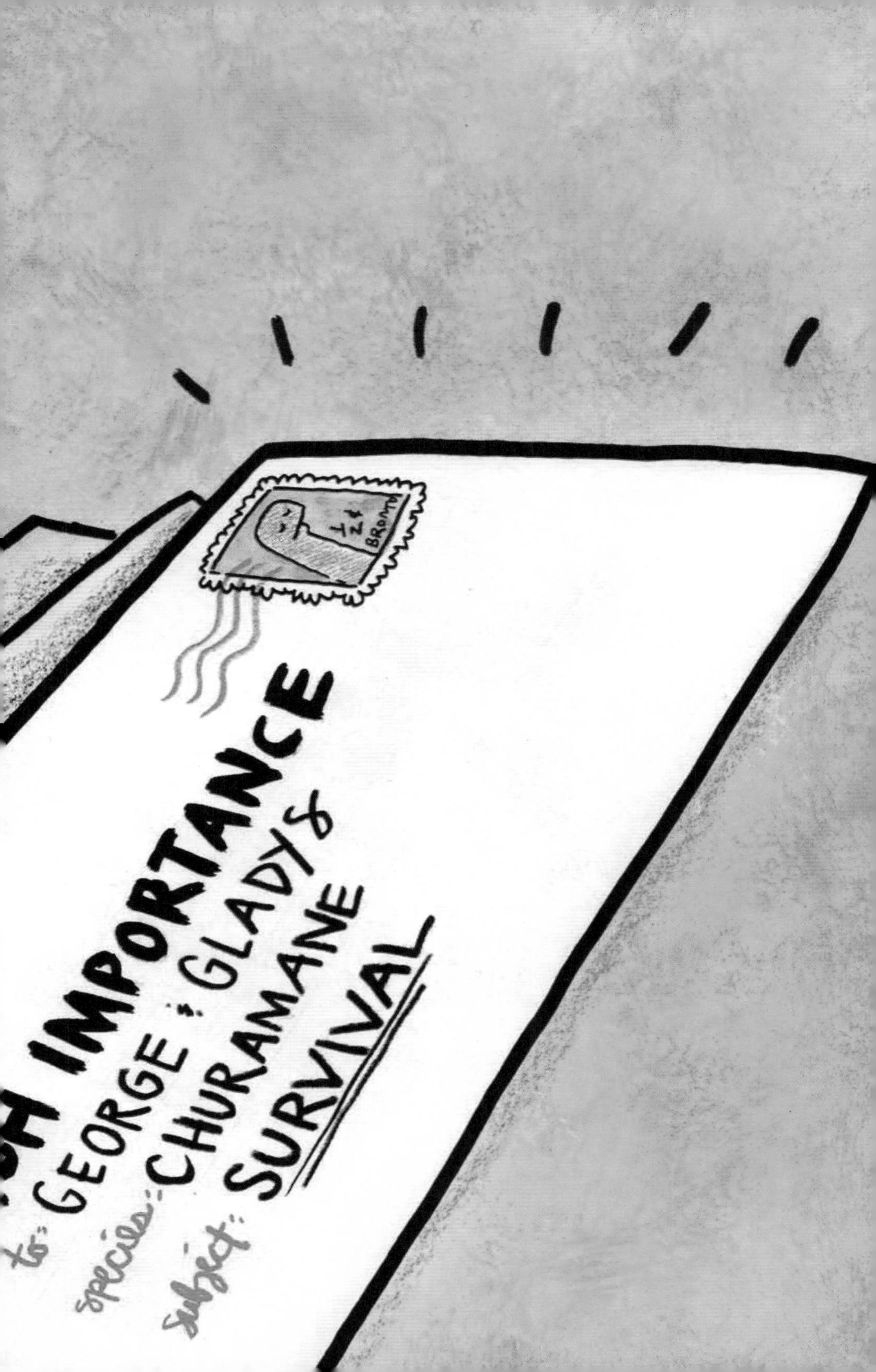
IMPORTANCE
to: GEORGE & GLADYS
species: CHURAMANE
subject: SURVIVAL
BRONTO

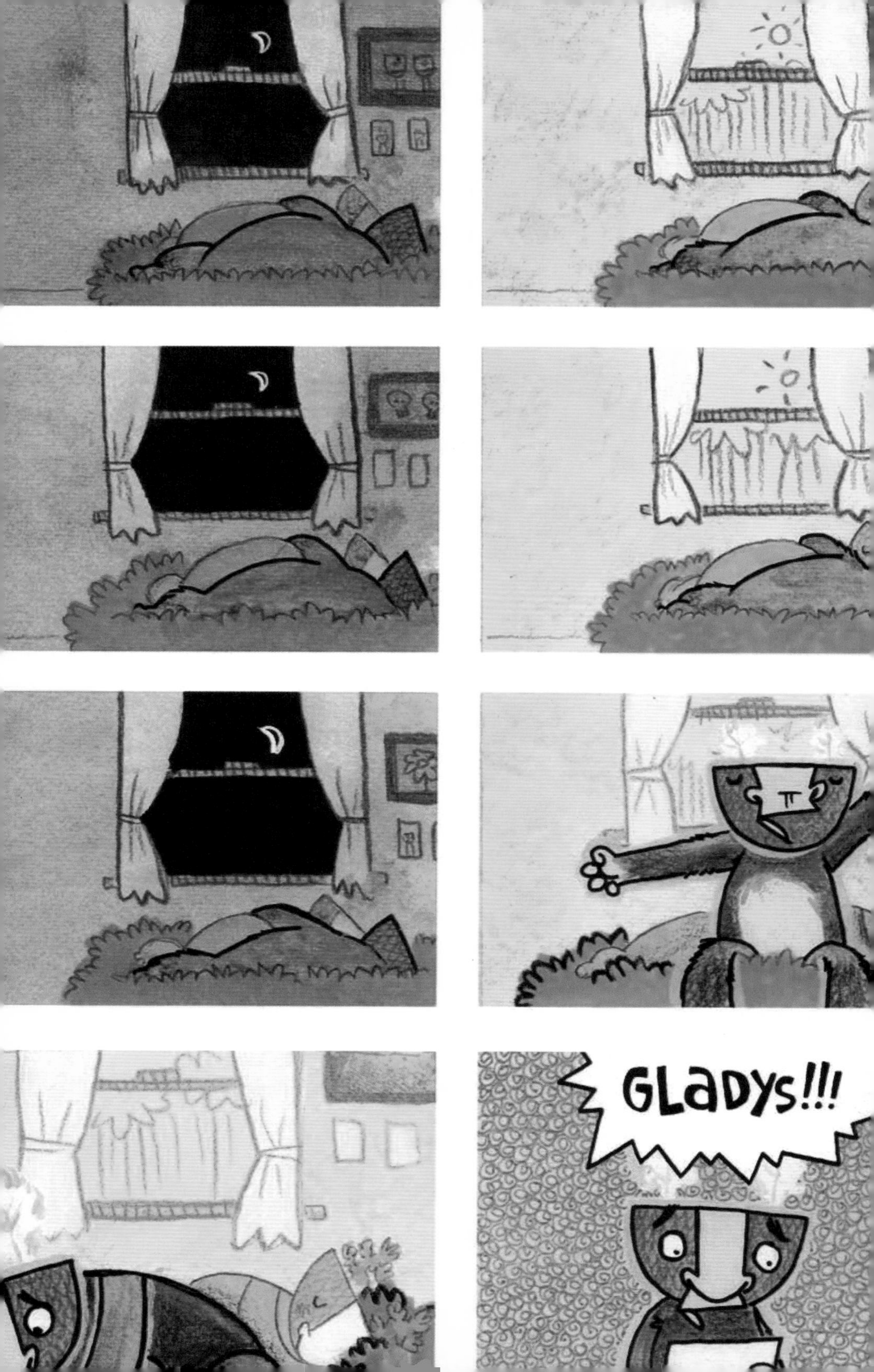
GLADYS!!!

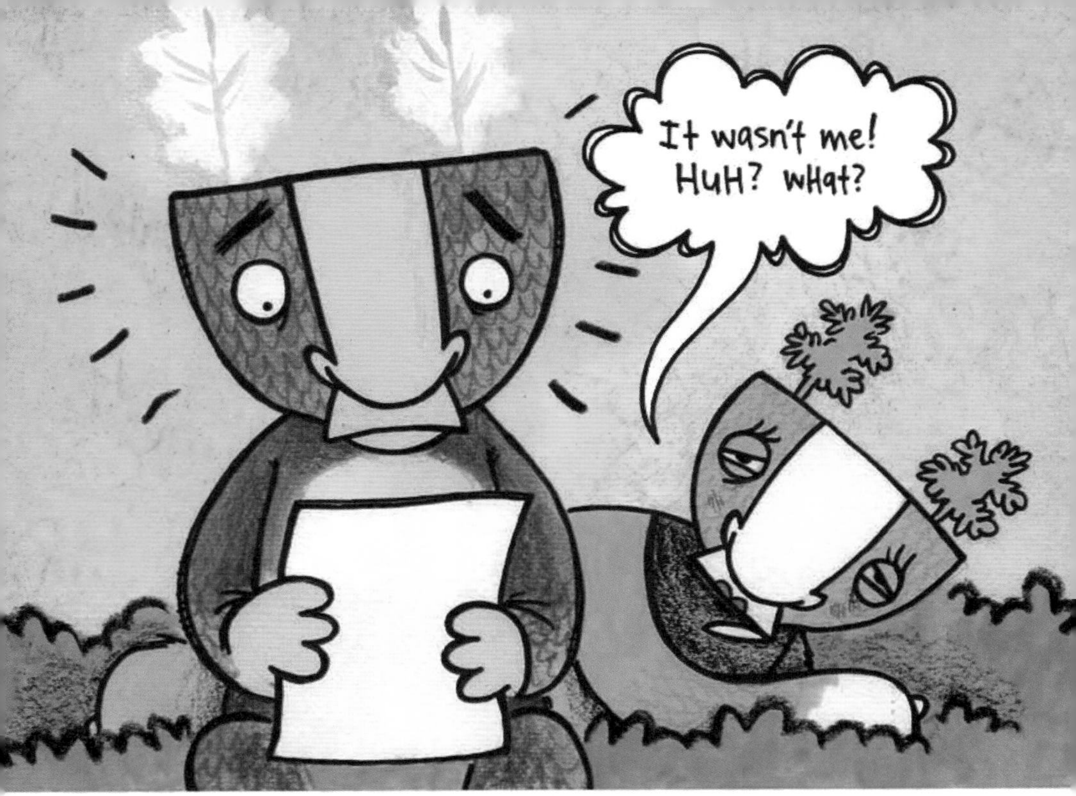
It wasn't me! HuH? wHat?
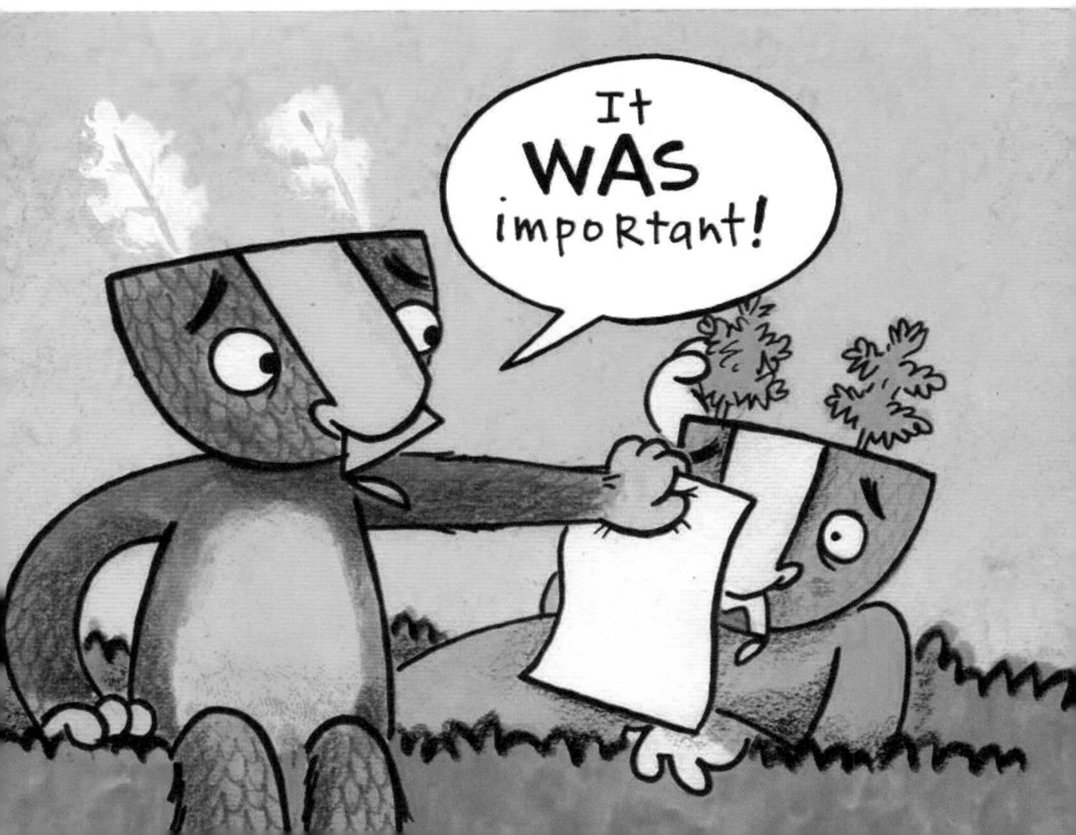
It WAS important!

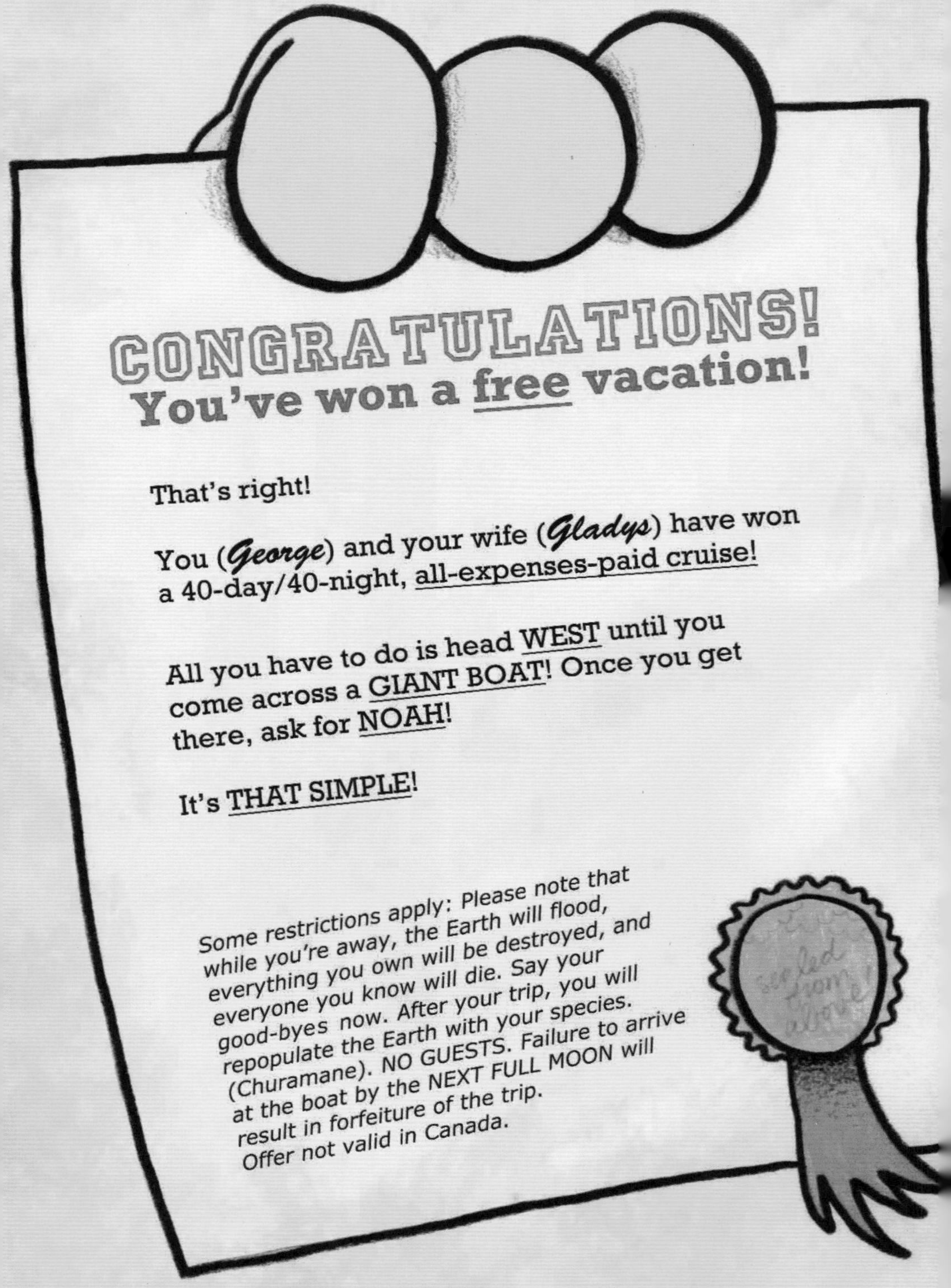
CONGRATULATIONS!
You've won a free vacation!
That's right!
You (George) and your wife (Gladys) have won a 40-day/40-night, all-expenses-paid cruise!
All you have to do is head WEST until you come across a GIANT BOAT! Once you get there, ask for NOAH!
It's THAT SIMPLE!
Some restrictions apply: Please note that while you're away, the Earth will flood, everything you own will be destroyed, and everyone you know will die. Say your good-byes now. After your trip, you will repopulate the Earth with your species (Churamane). NO GUESTS. Failure to arrive at the boat by the NEXT FULL MOON will result in forfeiture of the trip. Offer not valid in Canada.
sealed from above!

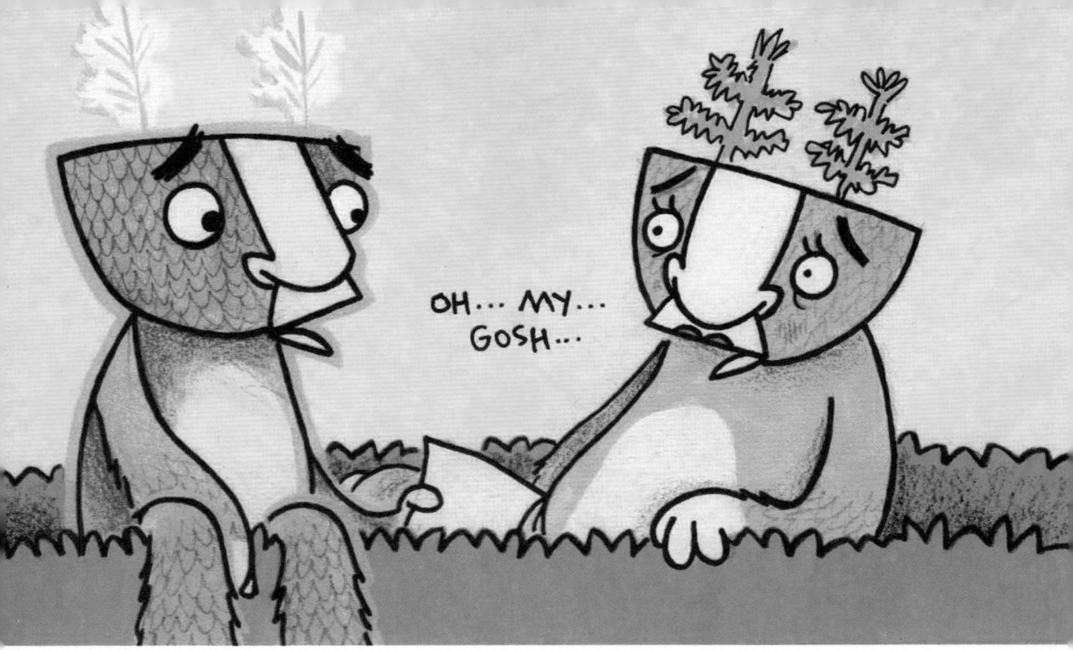
OH... MY... GOSH...

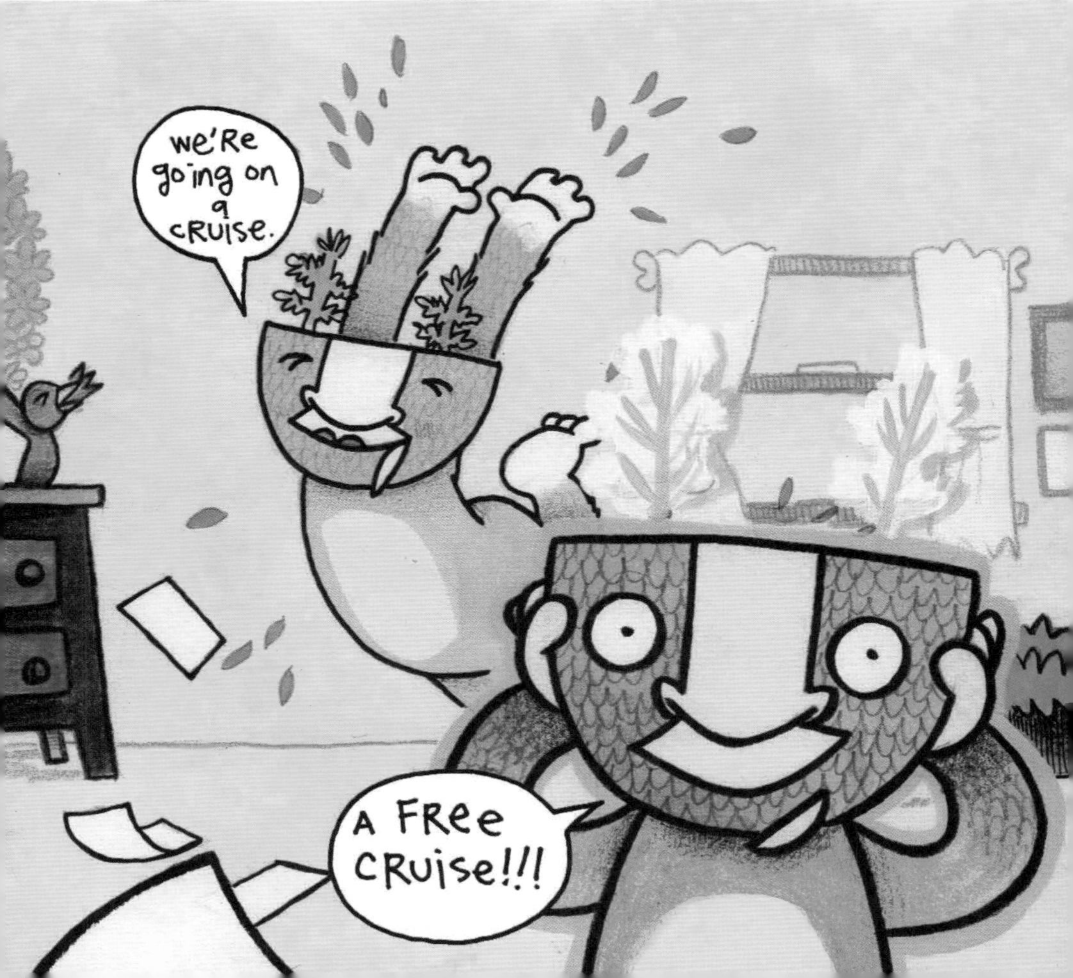
we're going on a cRUISe.
A FRee CRUise!!!

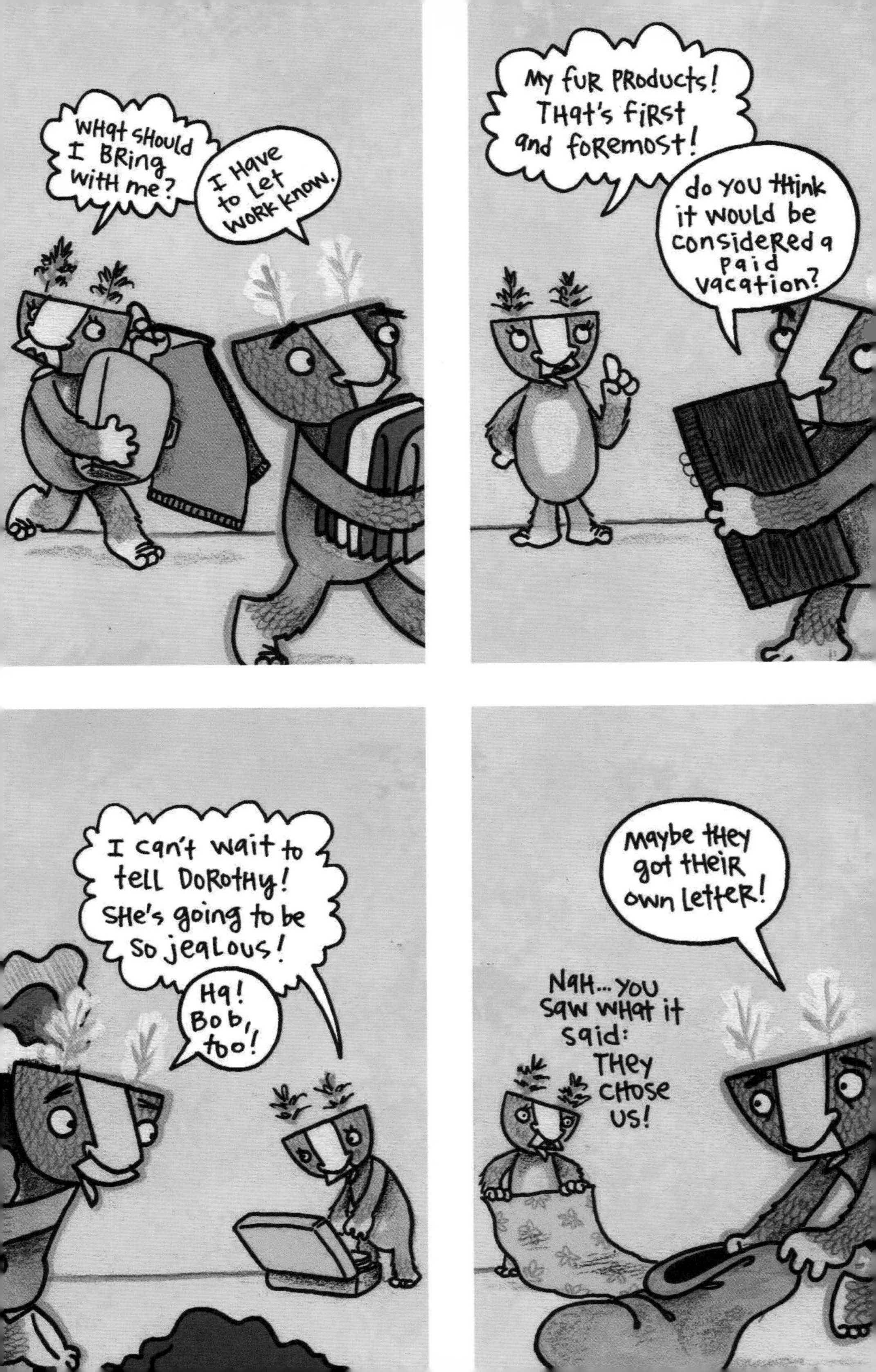

WHAT SHOULD I BRING WITH ME?
I HAVE TO LET WORK KNOW.
MY FUR PRODUCTS! THAT'S FIRST AND FOREMOST!
DO YOU THINK IT WOULD BE CONSIDERED A PAID VACATION?
I CAN'T WAIT TO TELL DOROTHY! SHE'S GOING TO BE SO JEALOUS!
HA! BOB, TOO!
MAYBE THEY GOT THEIR OWN LETTER!
NAH... YOU SAW WHAT IT SAID: THEY CHOSE US!

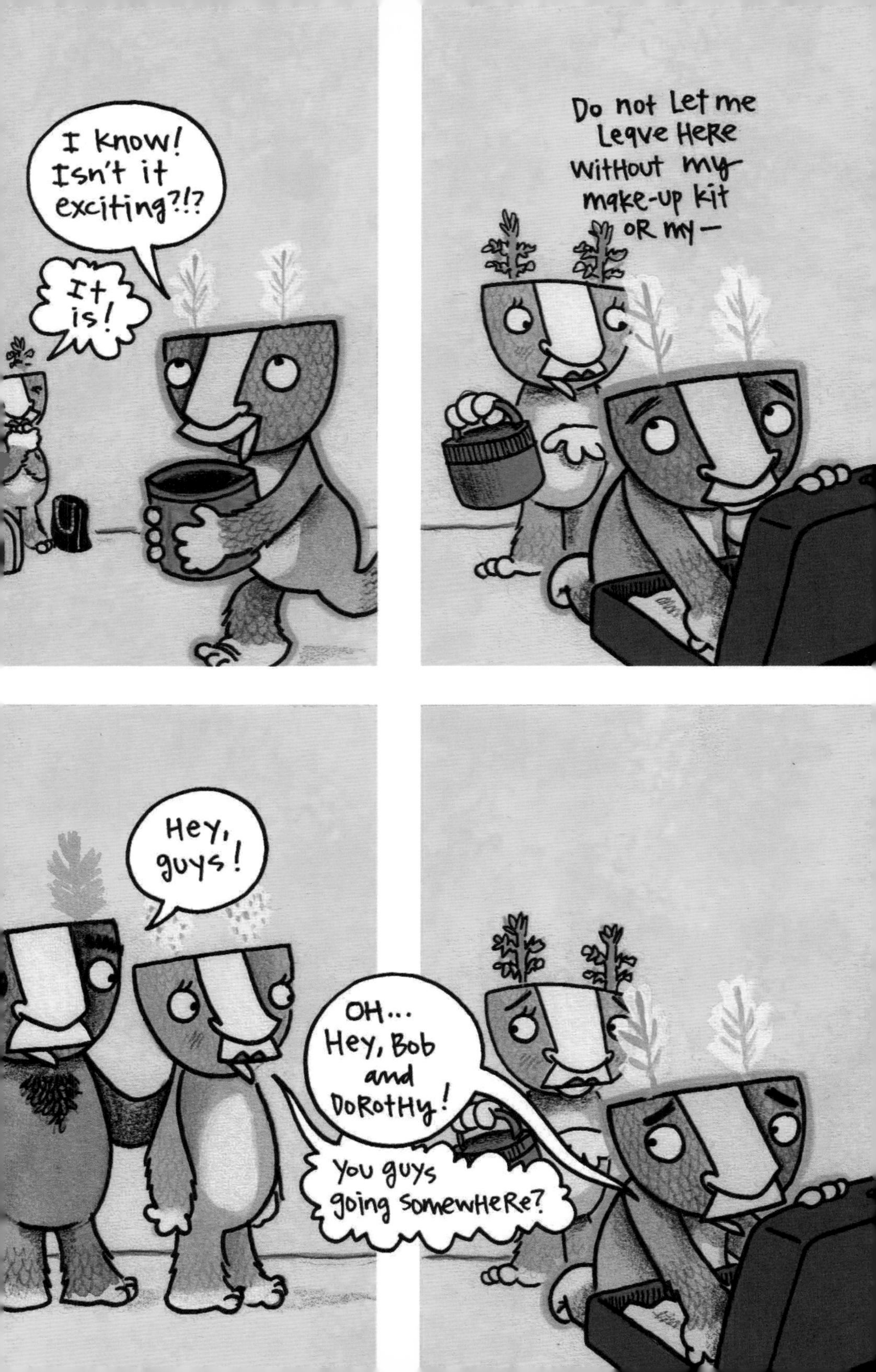
I know! Isn't it exciting?!?
It is!
Do not let me leave here without my make-up kit or my—
Hey, guys!
OH... Hey, Bob and Dorothy!
You guys going somewhere?

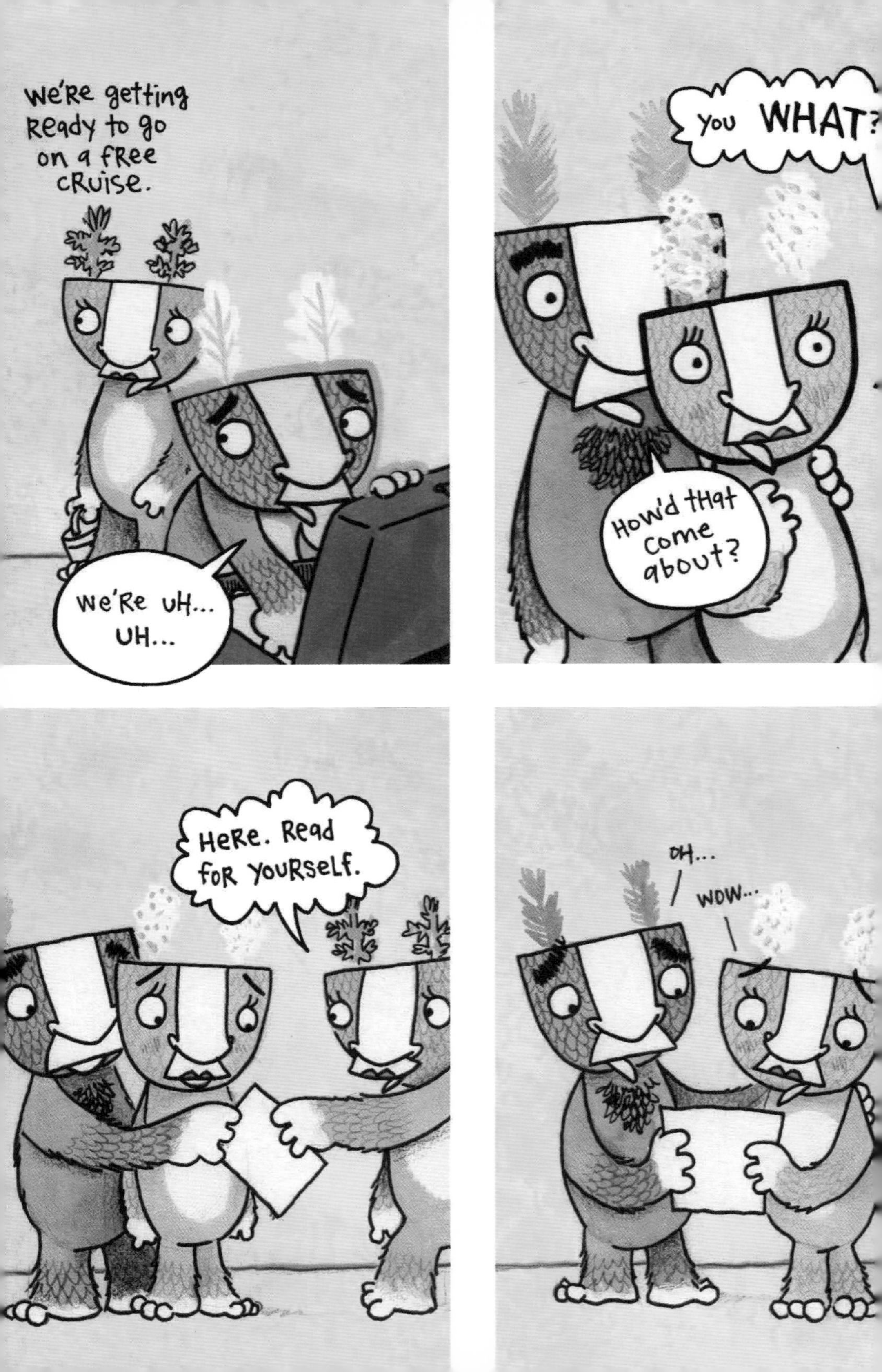
We're getting ready to go on a free cruise.
We're uh... uh...
You WHAT?
How'd that come about?
Here. Read for yourself.
Oh...
Wow...

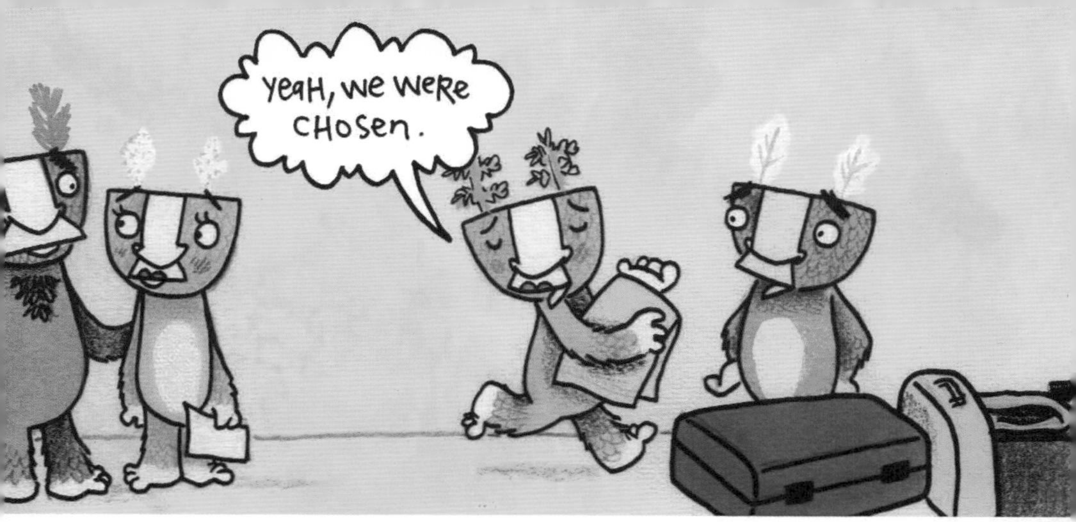
yeaH, we weRe CHosen.

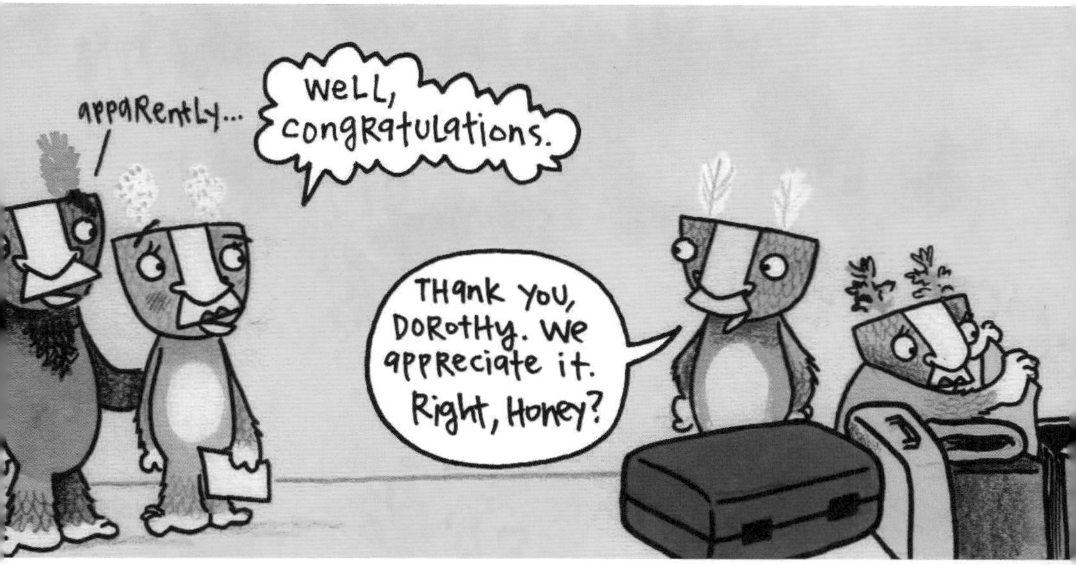
apparently...
WeLL, congRatuLations.
THank you, DoRotHy. We appReciate it. Right, Honey?

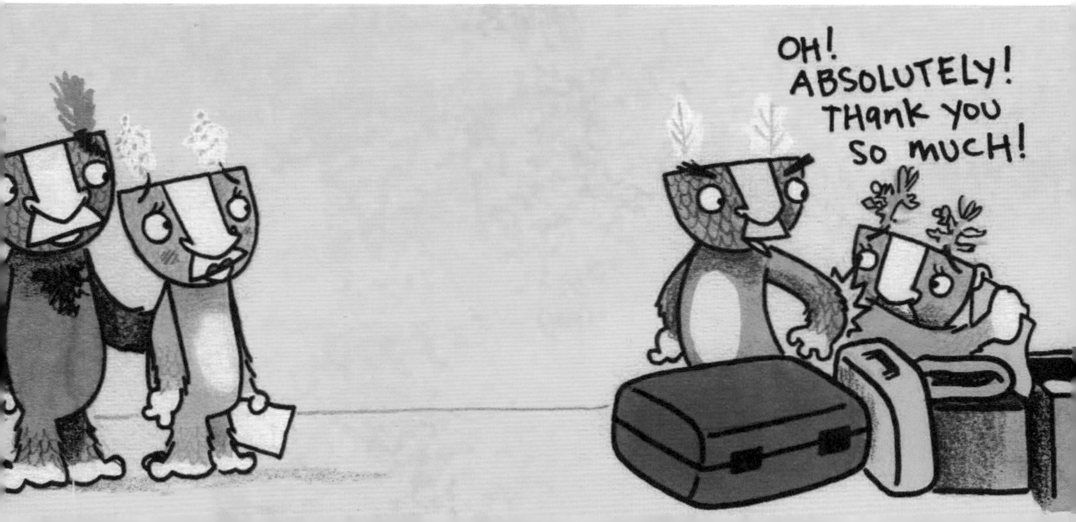
OH! ABSOLUTELY! THank you so MUCH!

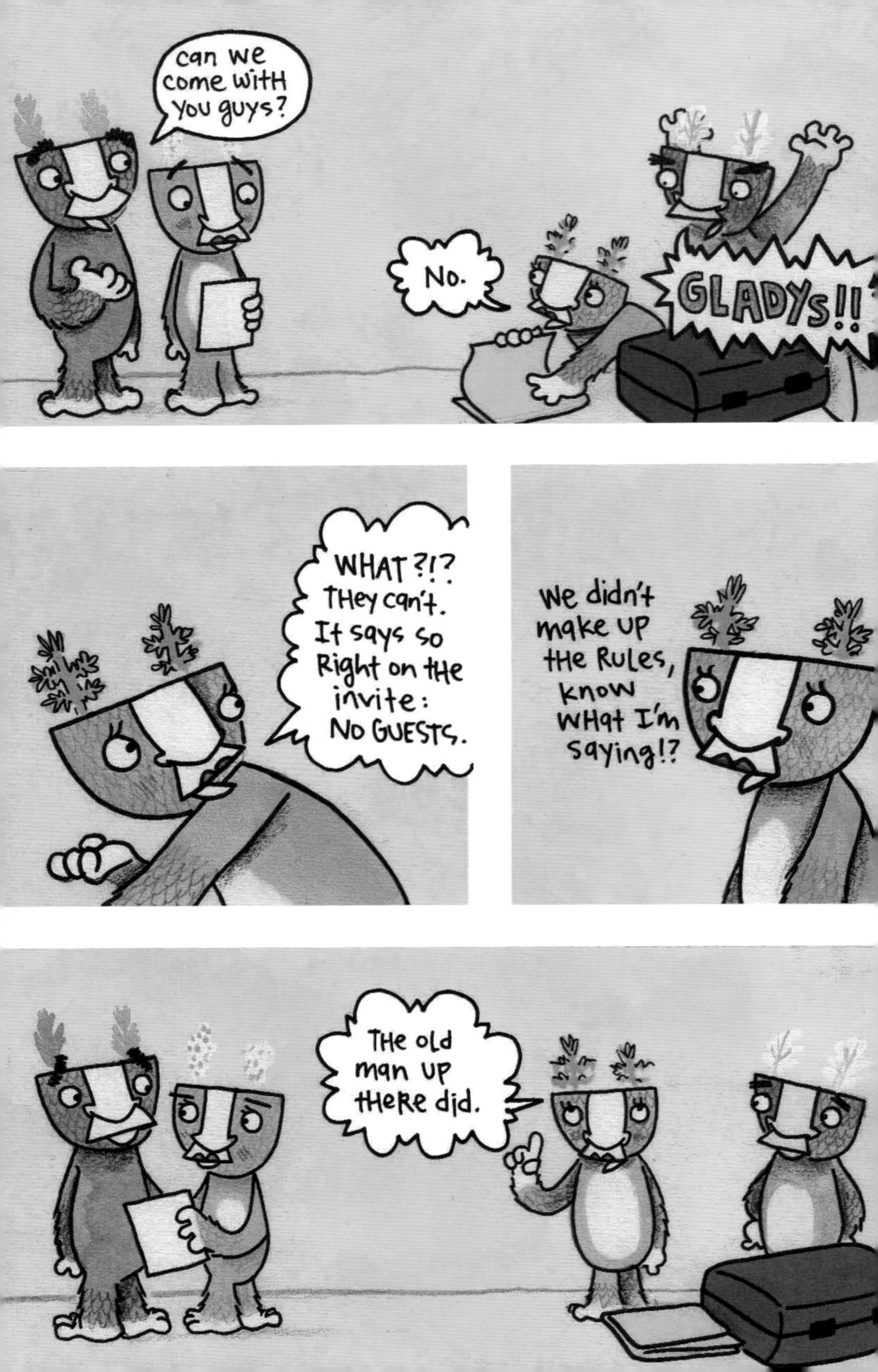
can we come with you guys?
No.
GLADYS!!
WHAT?!? They can't. It says so Right on the invite: NO GUESTS.
We didn't make up the Rules, know what I'm saying!?
The old man up there did.

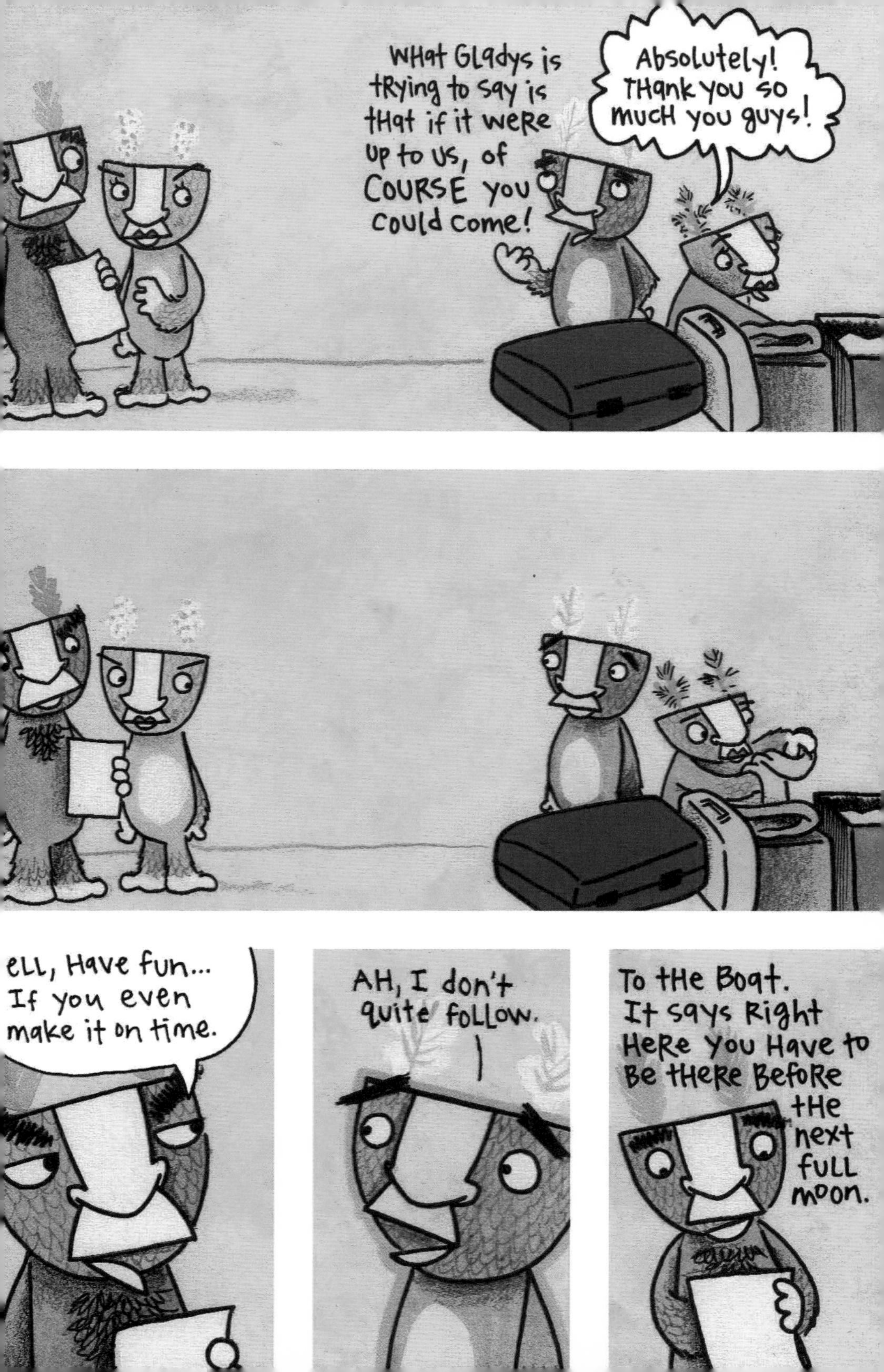
WHat Gladys is trying to say is that if it were up to us, of COURSE you could come!
Absolutely! THank you so much you guys!
eLL, Have fun... If you even make it on time.
AH, I don't quite follow.
To tHe Boat. It says Right Here You Have to Be tHere Before tHe next FULL moon.

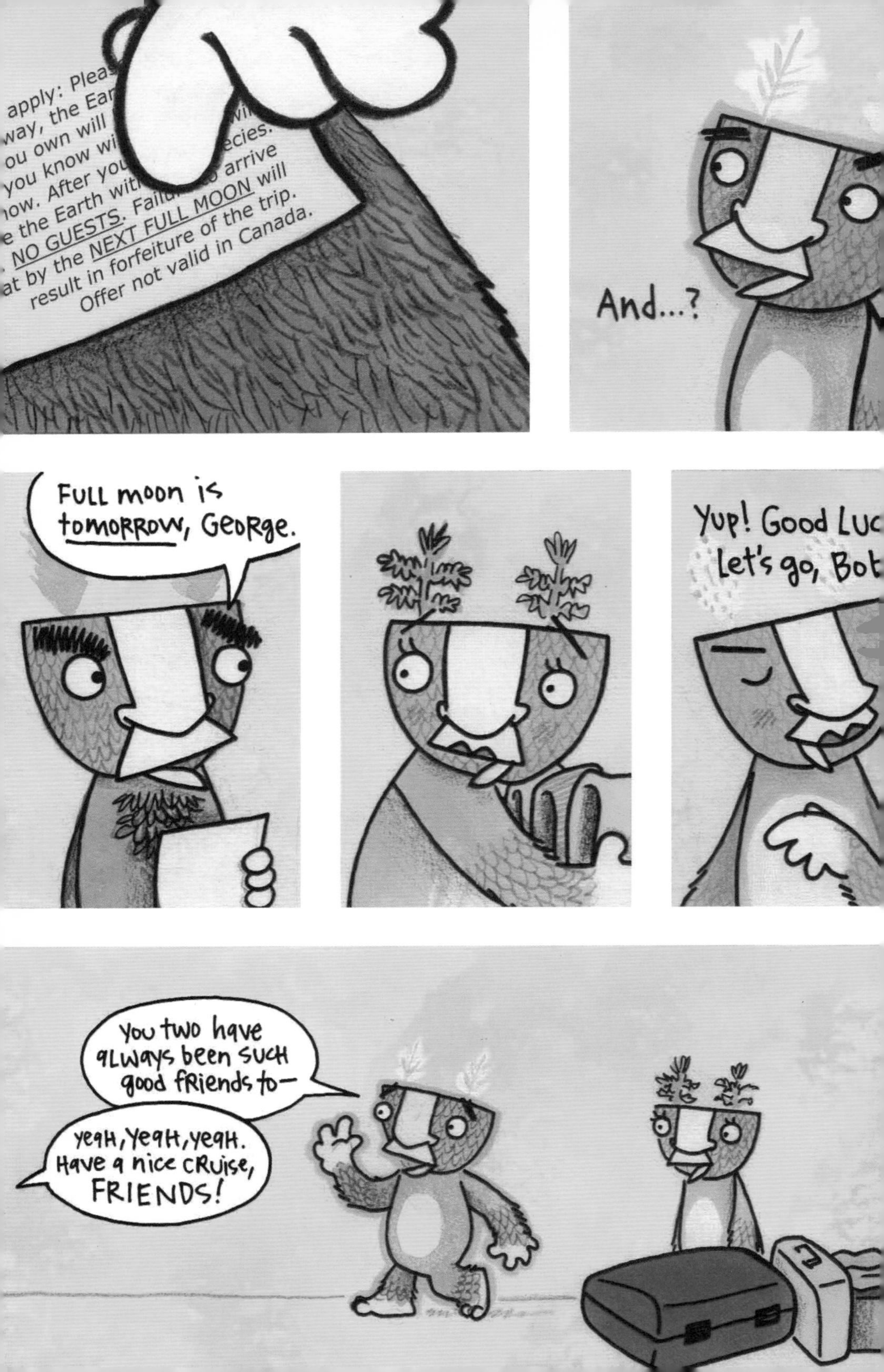
apply: Pleas
way, the Ear
ou own will
you know wi
you know wi ecies.
ow. After yo o arrive
e the Earth wit
NO GUESTS. Failu
at by the NEXT FULL MOON will
result in forfeiture of the trip.
Offer not valid in Canada.
And...?
FULL moon is tomorrow, George.
Yup! Good Luc
Let's go, Bot
You two have always been such good friends to—
yeah, yeah, yeah. Have a nice cruise, FRIENDS!

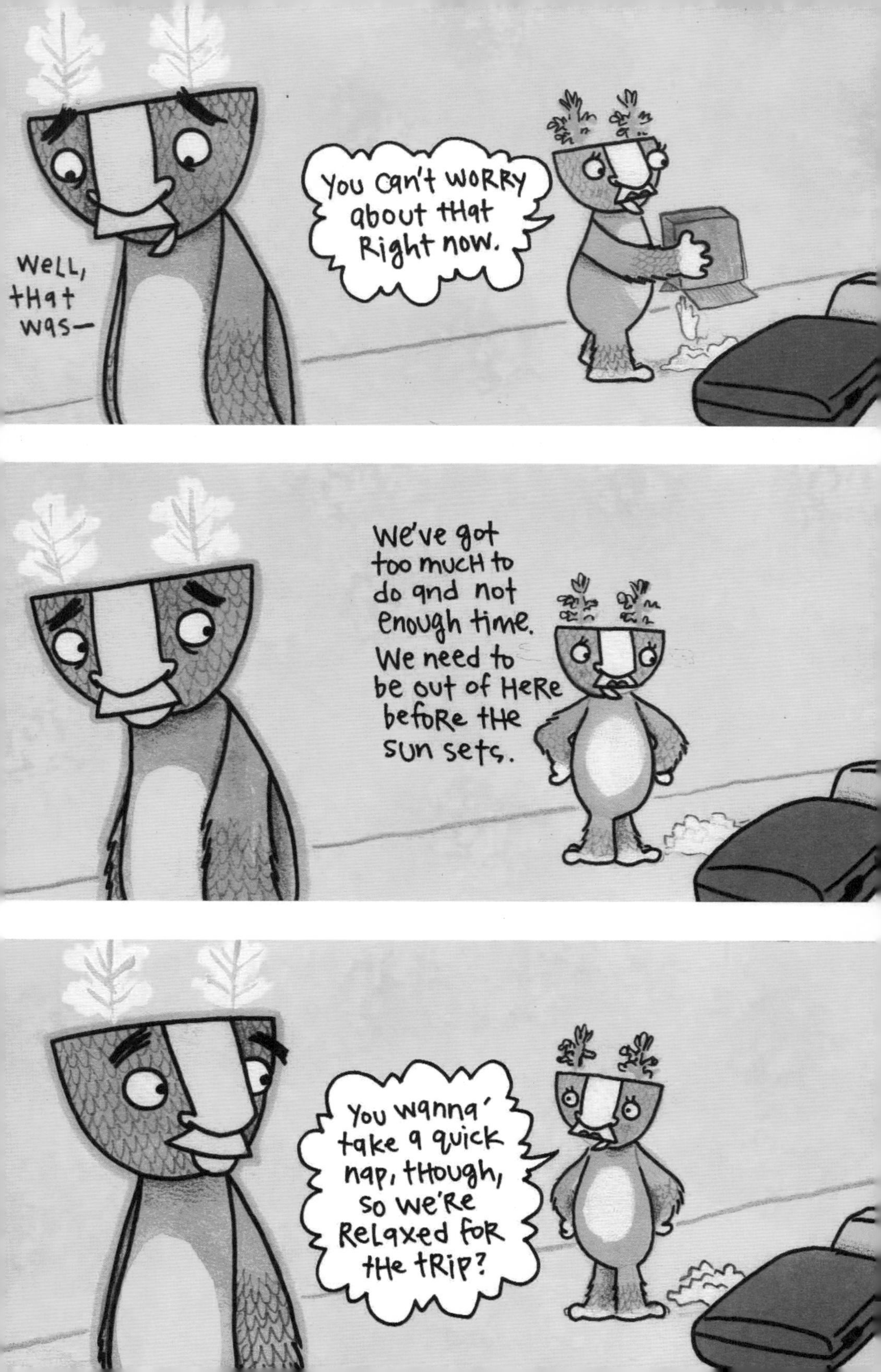
WeLL, tHat was—
You can't WORRY about tHat Right now.
We've got too mucH to do and not enough time. We need to be out of HeRe before tHe sun sets.
You wanna' take a quick nap, tHough, so we'Re Relaxed for tHe tRip?

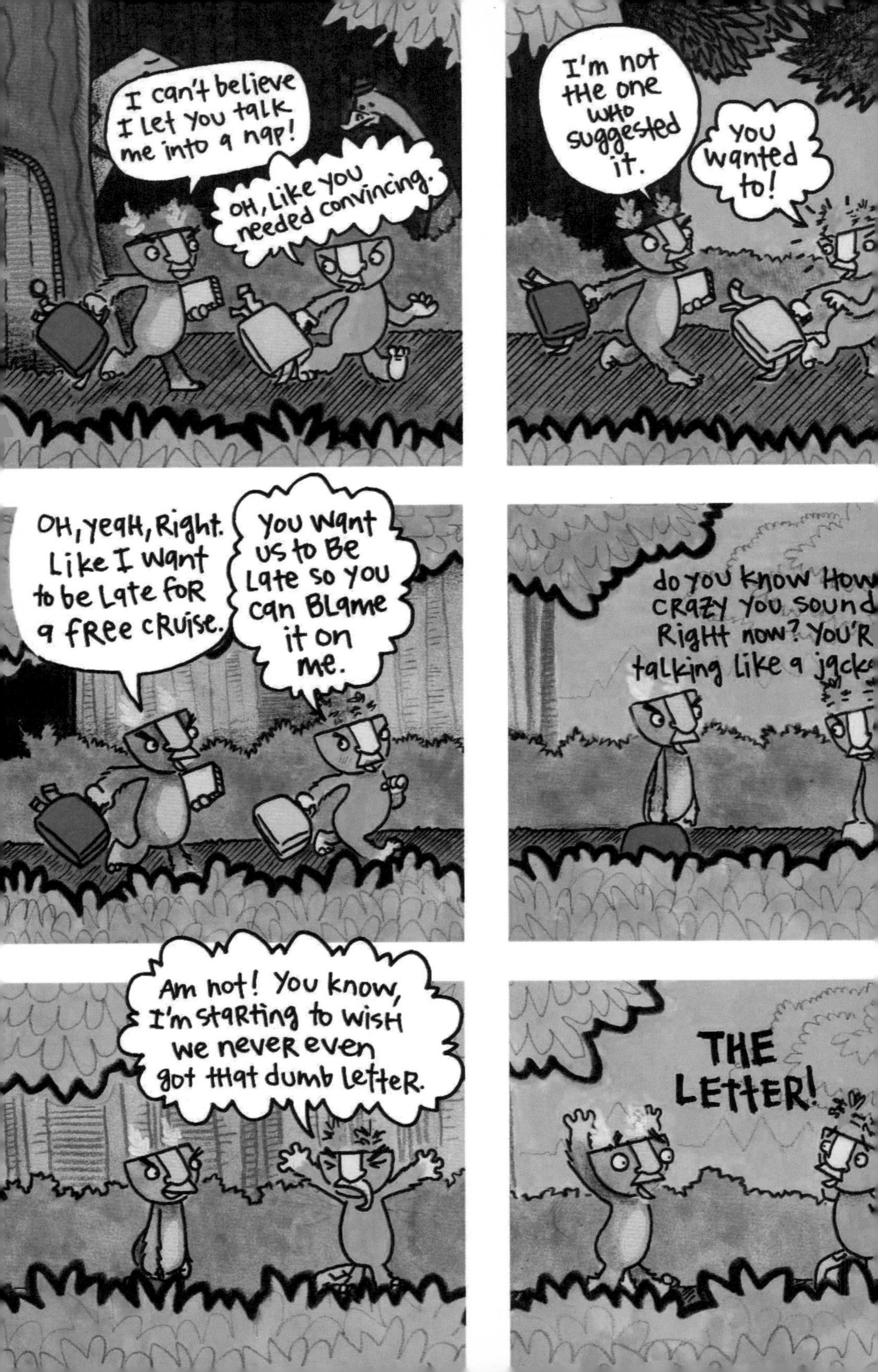
I can't believe I let you talk me into a nap!
Oh, like you needed convincing.
I'm not the one who suggested it.
You wanted to!
Oh, yeah, right. Like I want to be late for a free cruise.
You want us to be late so you can blame it on me.
do you know how crazy you sound right now? You'r talking like a jack
Am not! You know, I'm starting to wish we never even got that dumb letter.
THE LETTER!

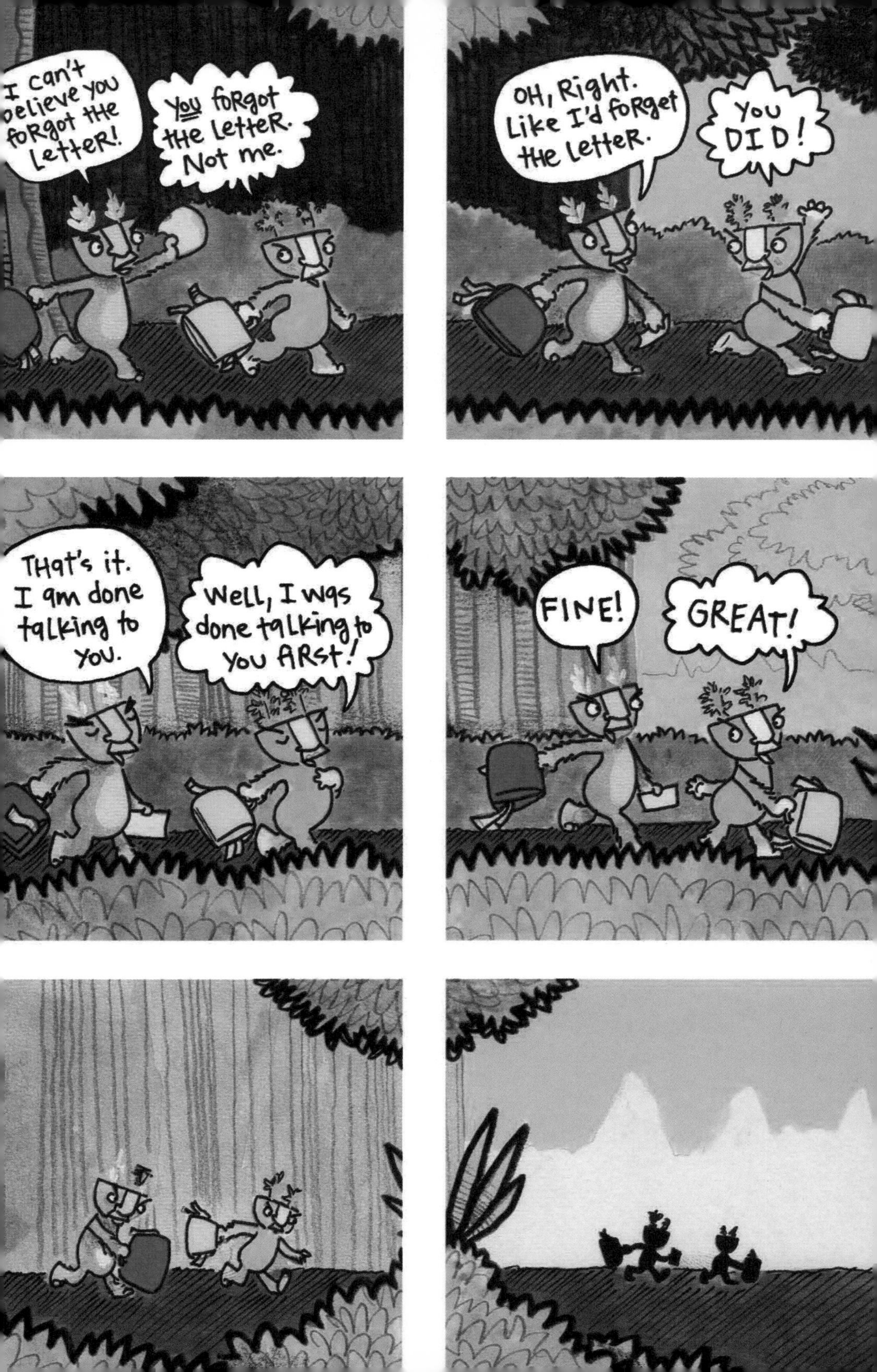
I can't believe you forgot the letter!
You forgot the letter. Not me.
Oh, right. Like I'd forget the letter.
You DID!
That's it. I am done talking to you.
Well, I was done talking to you first!
FINE!
GREAT!

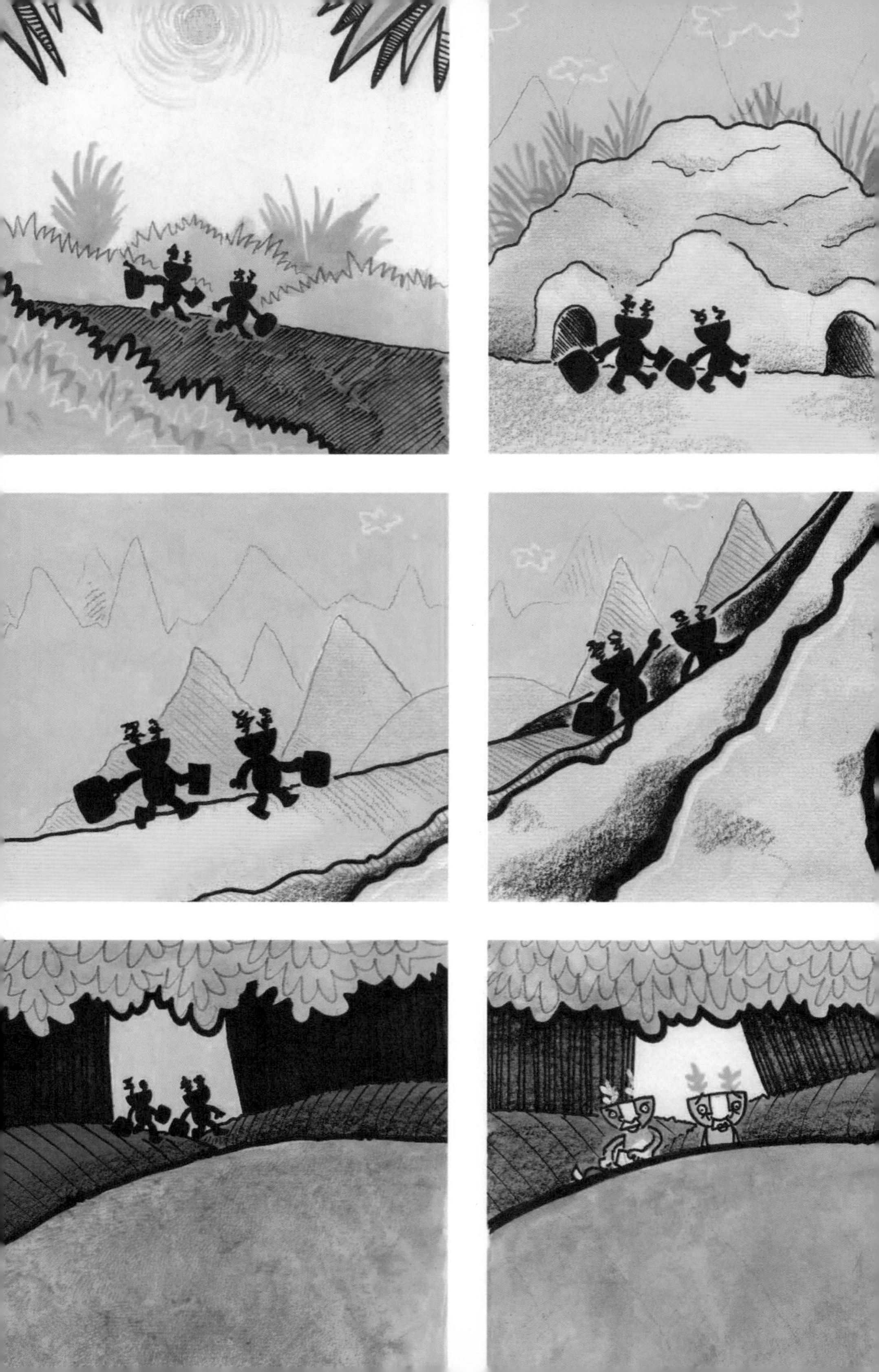

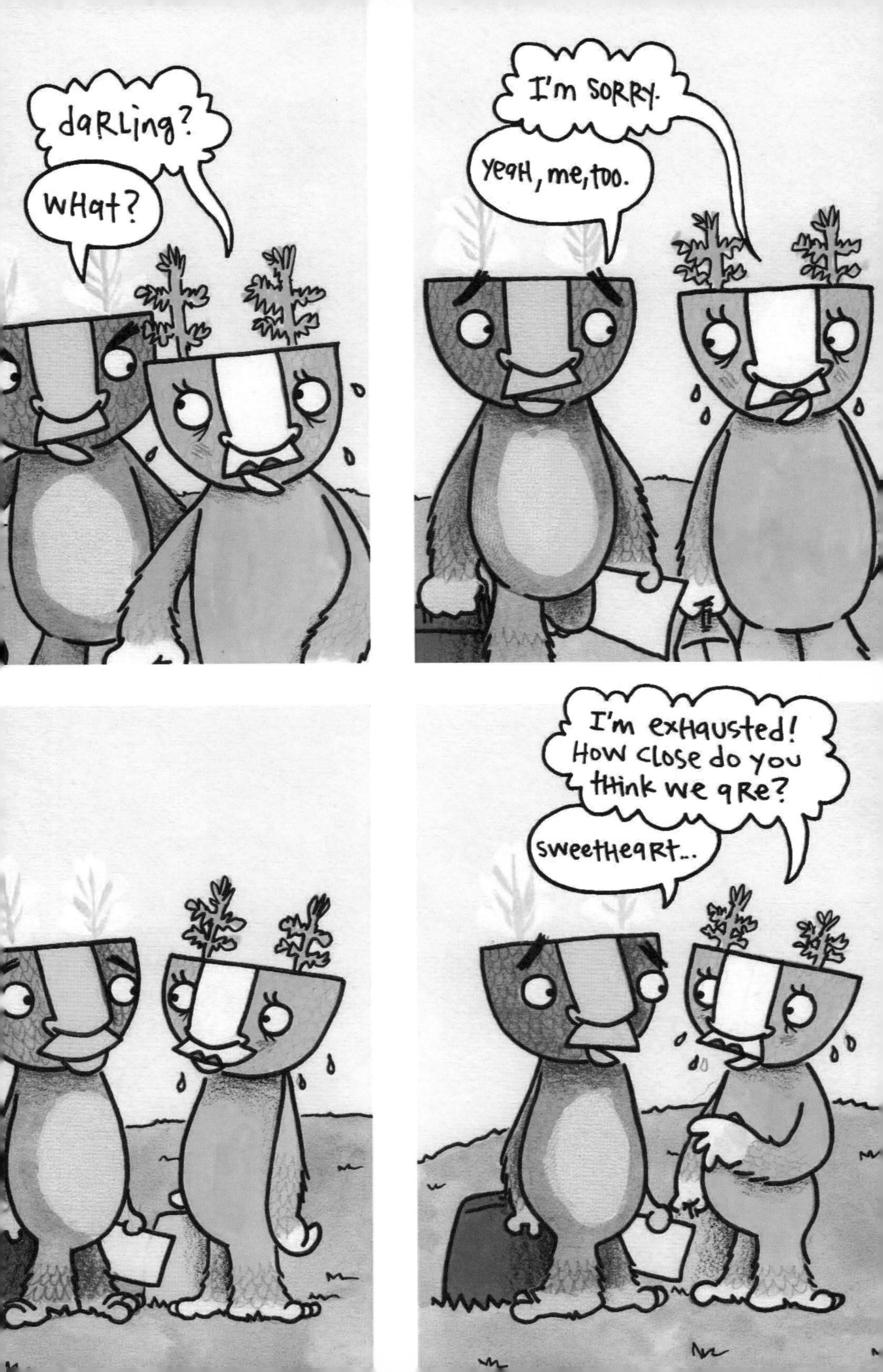
darling?
what?
I'm SORRY.
yeah, me, too.
I'm exhausted! How close do you think we are?
sweetheart...

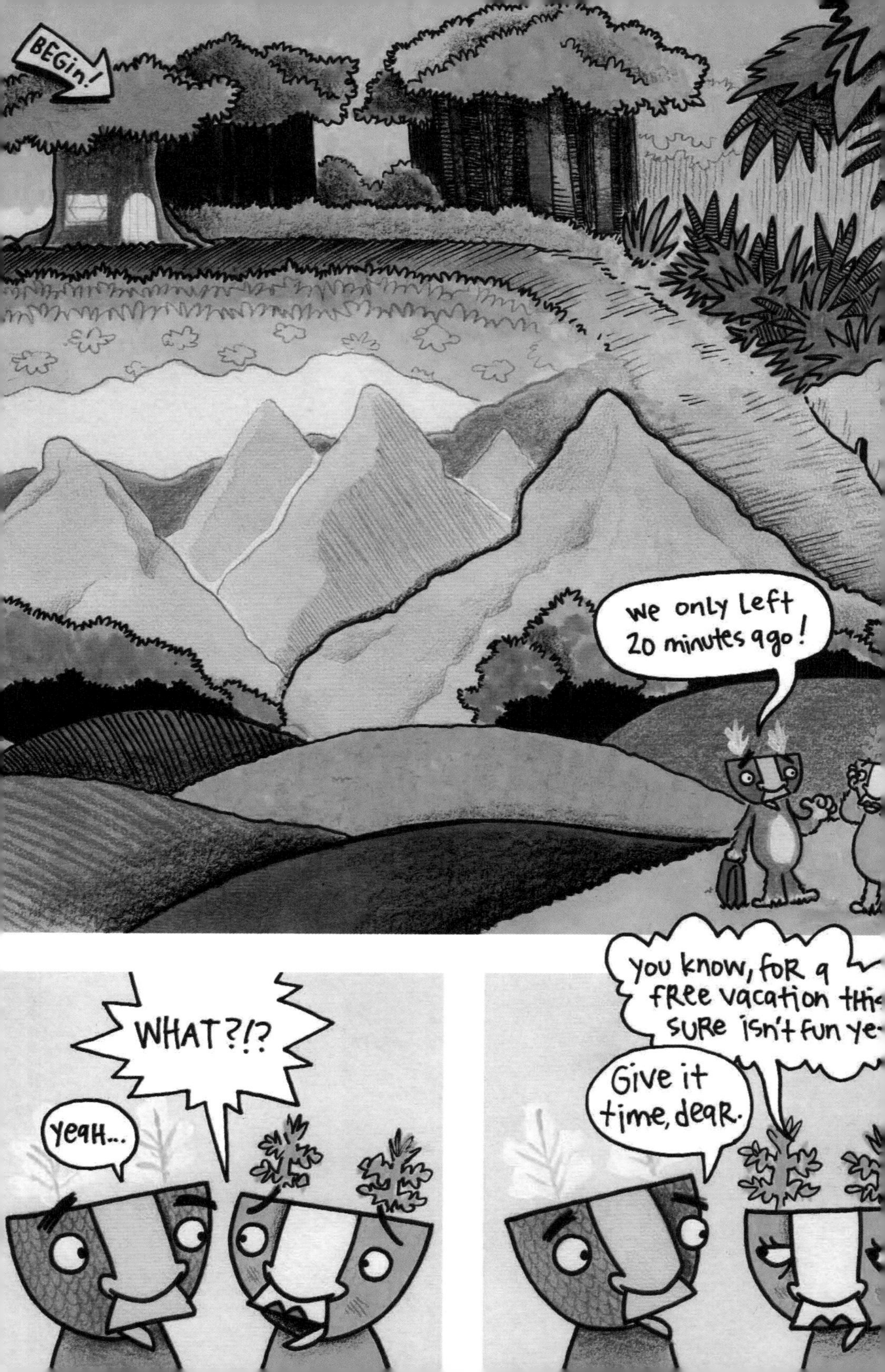
BEGIN!
we only left 20 minutes ago!
yeah...
WHAT?!?
you know, for a free vacation this sure isn't fun ye-
Give it time, dear.

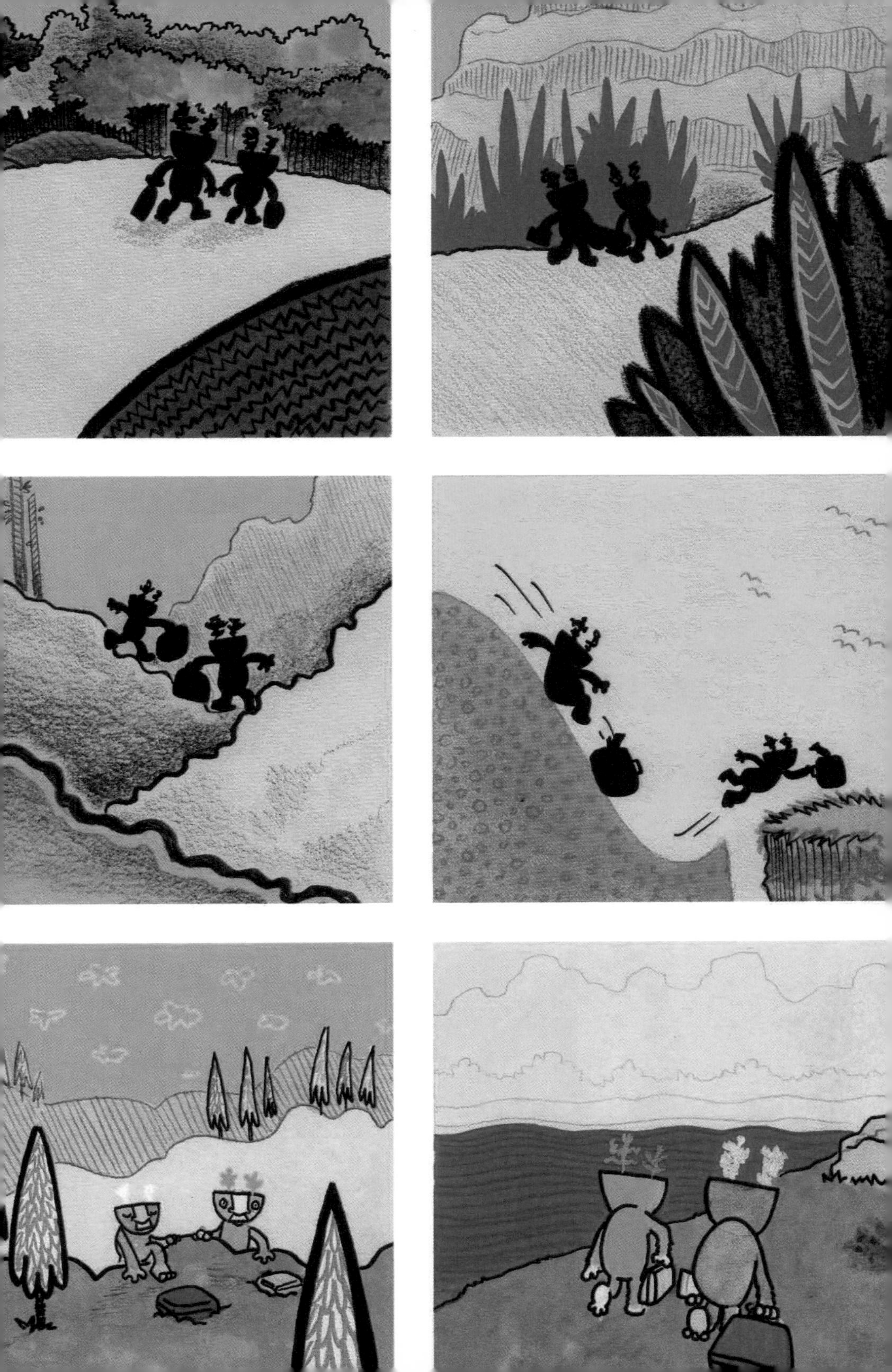

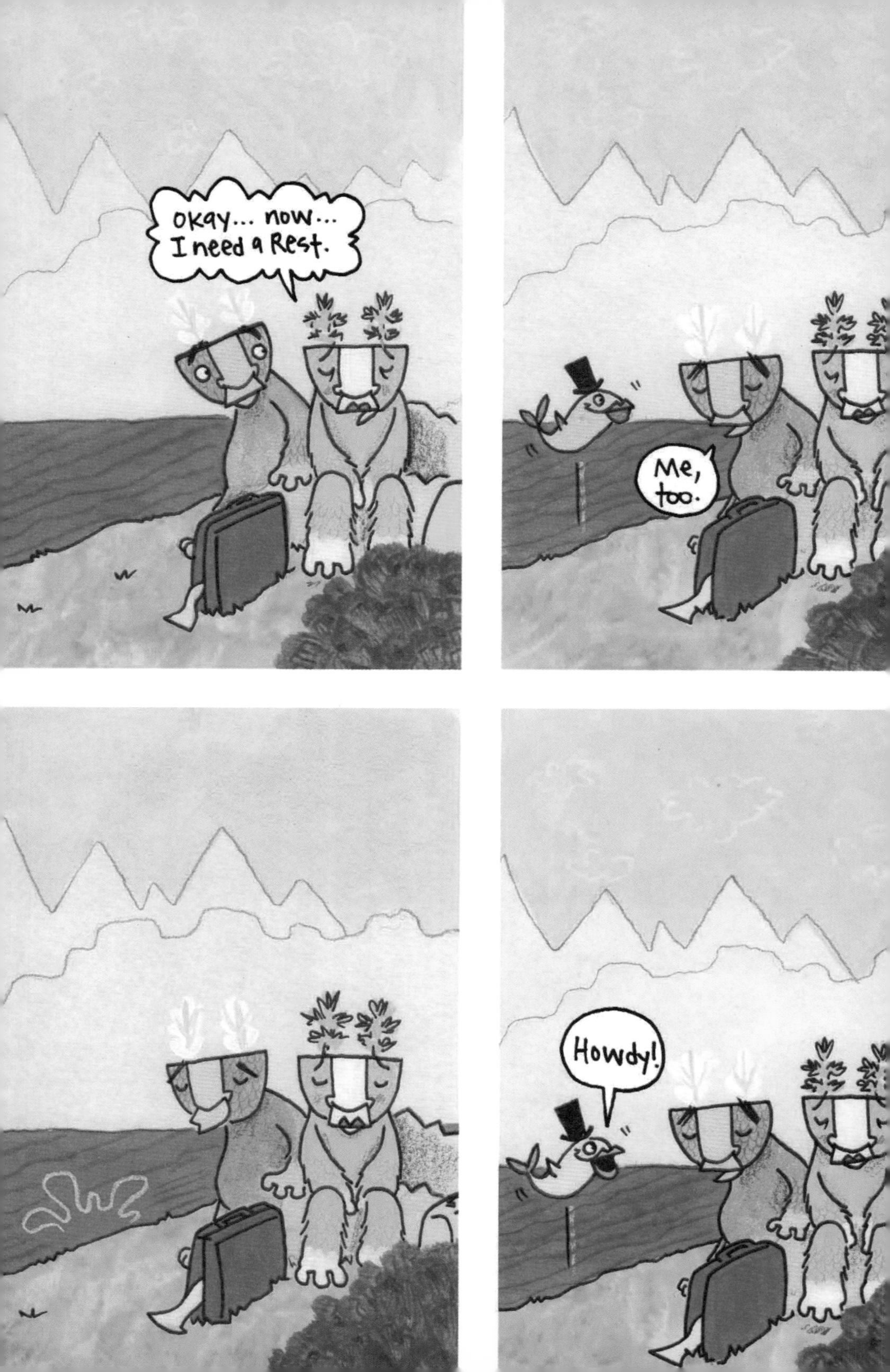
Okay... now...
I need a Rest.
Me, too.
Howdy!

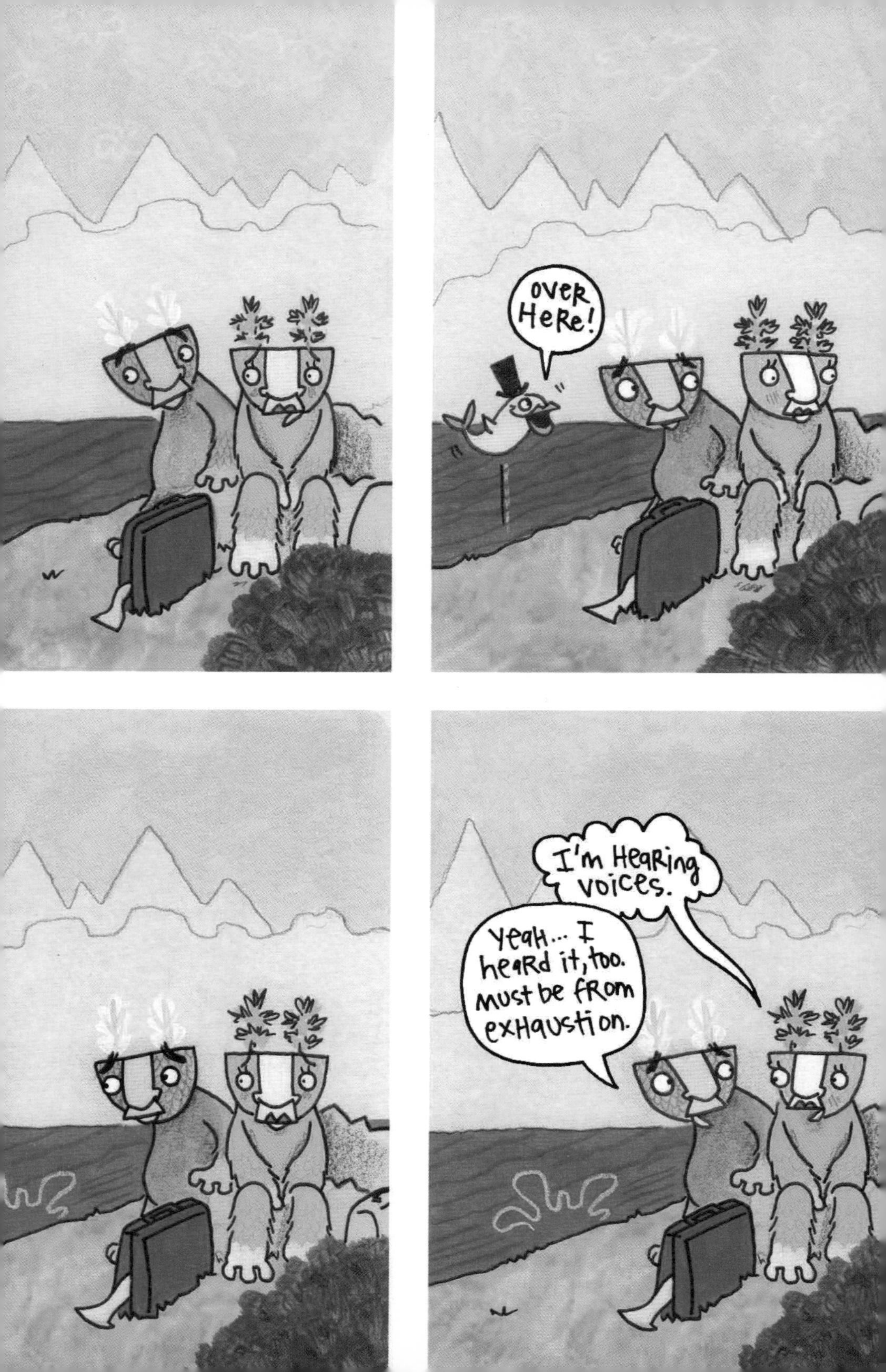
OVER HERE!
I'm Hearing voices.
Yeah... I heard it, too. Must be from exhaustion.

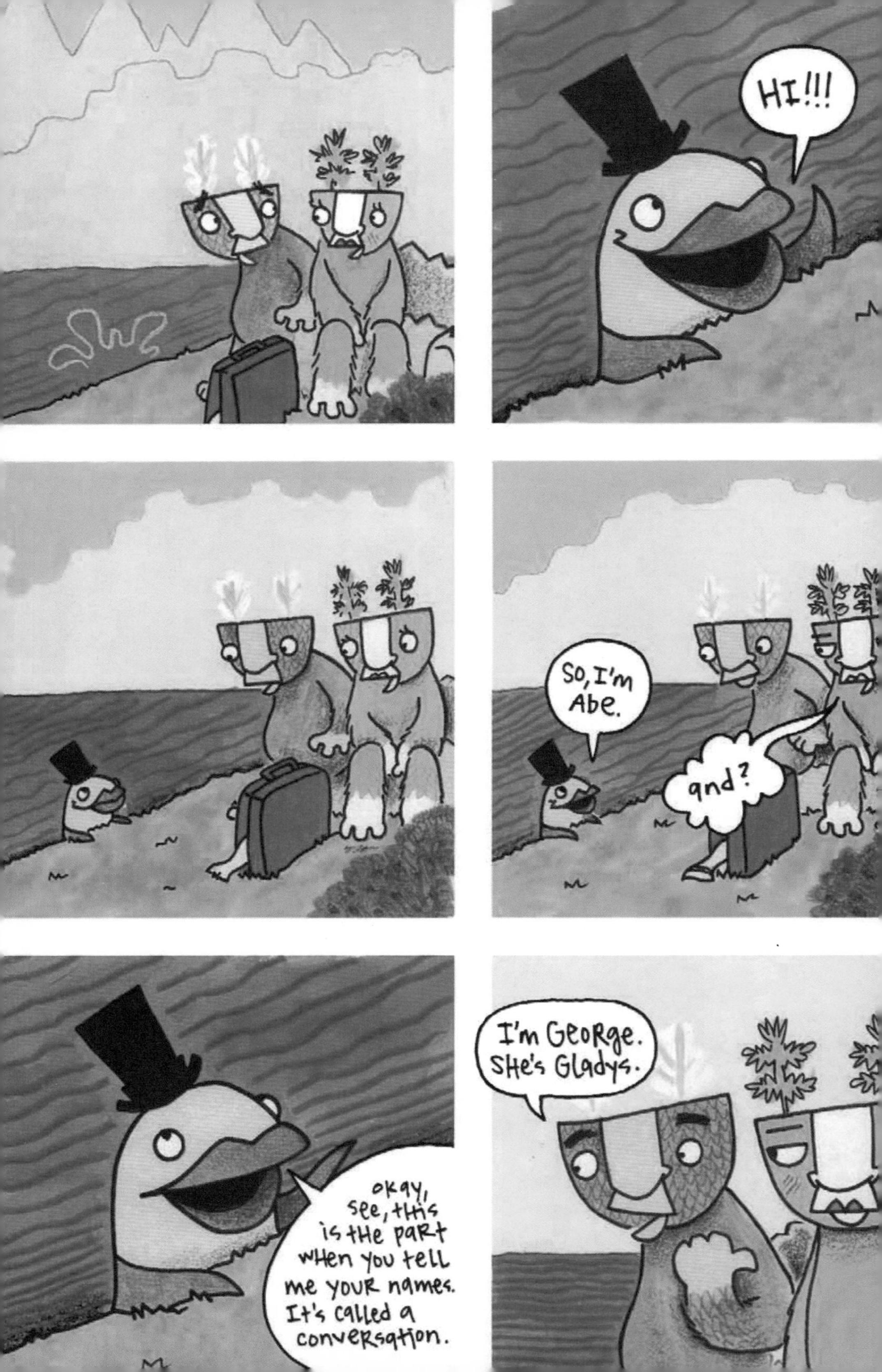
HI!!!
So, I'm Abe.
and?
okay, see, this is the part when you tell me your names. It's called a conversation.
I'm George. She's Gladys.

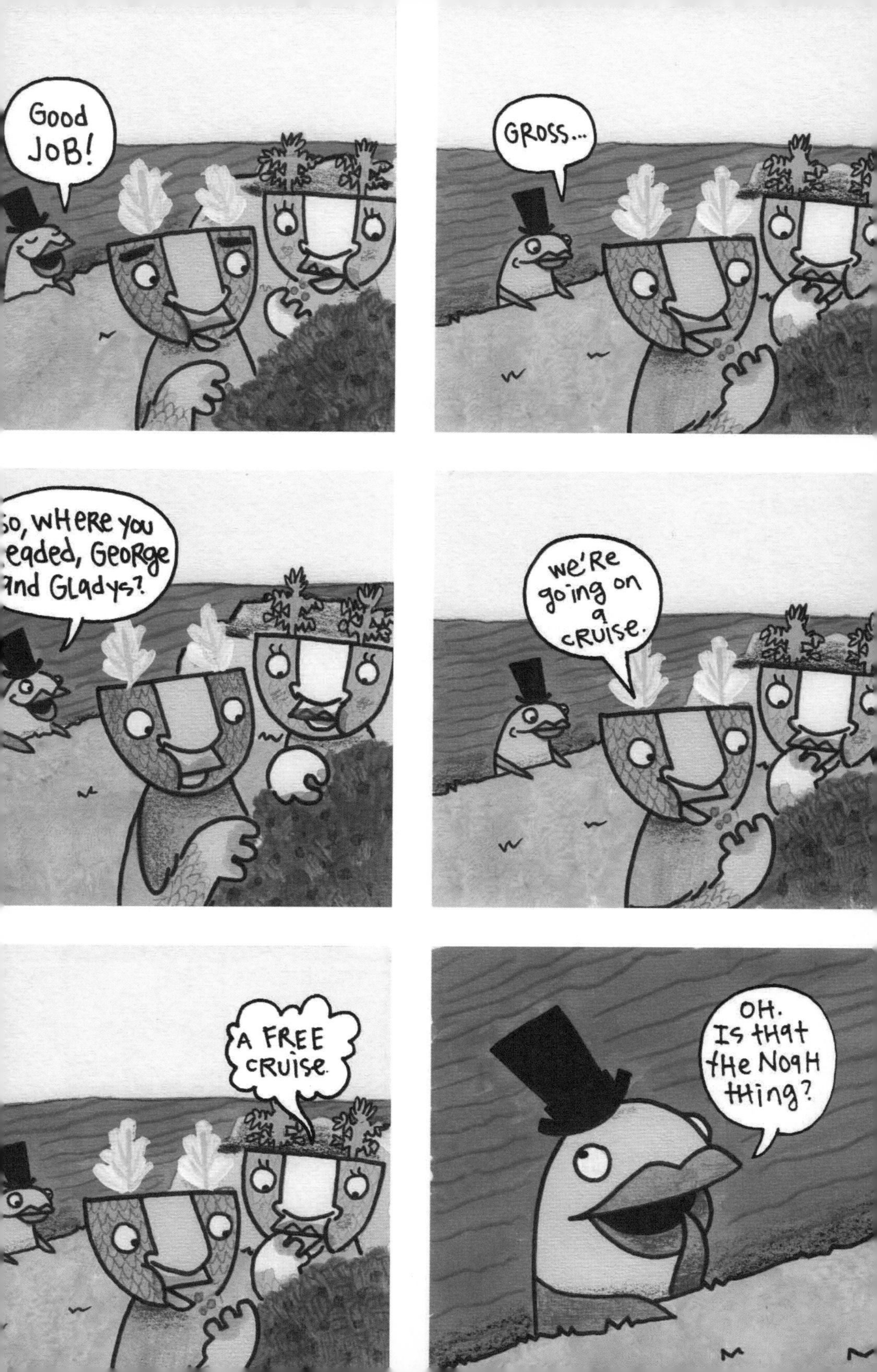

Good JOB!
GROSS...
o, WHERE you eaded, GEORGE and GLADYS?
WE'RE GOING ON A CRUISE.
A FREE CRUISE.
OH. IS THAT THE NOAH THING?

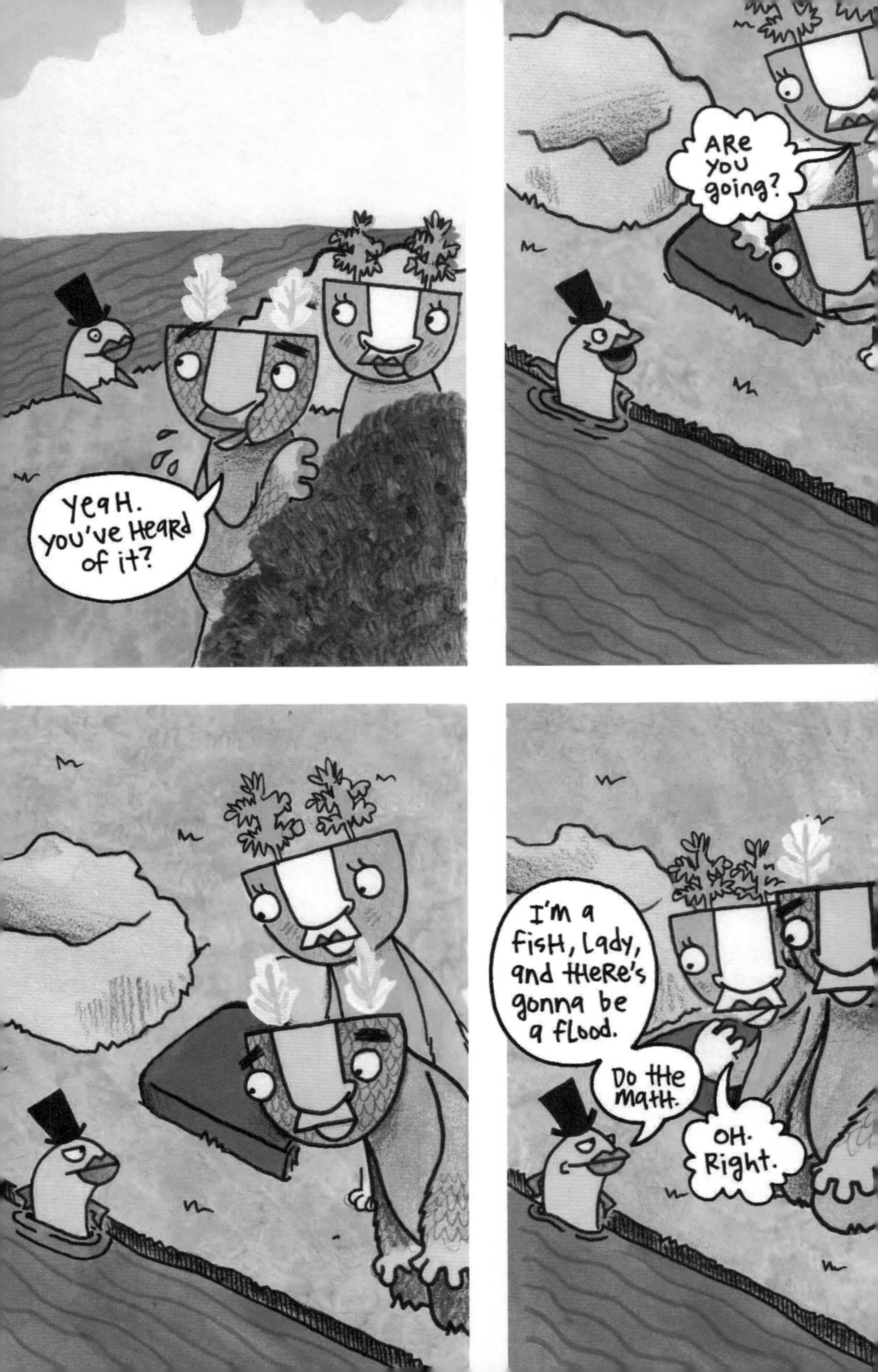
yeaH. you've Heard of it?
Are you going?
I'm a fisH, Lady, and tHere's gonna be a fLood.
Do tHe matH.
OH. Right.

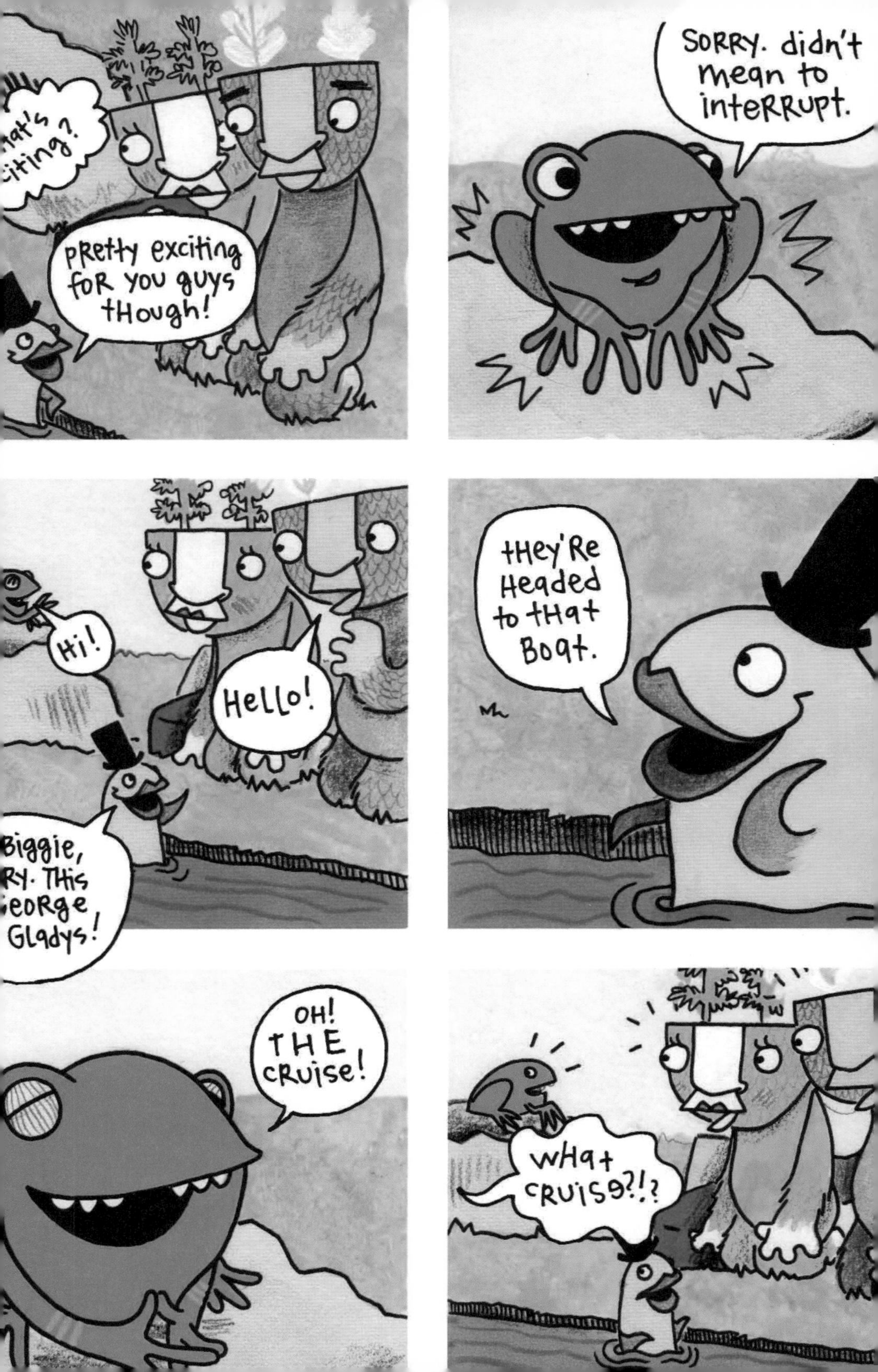

...at's ...citing?
pretty exciting for you guys though!
SORRY. didn't mean to interrupt.
Hi!
Hello!
Biggie, ...RY. THis ...eorge ... Gladys!
they're Headed to that Boat.
OH! THE cruise!
wHat cruise?!?

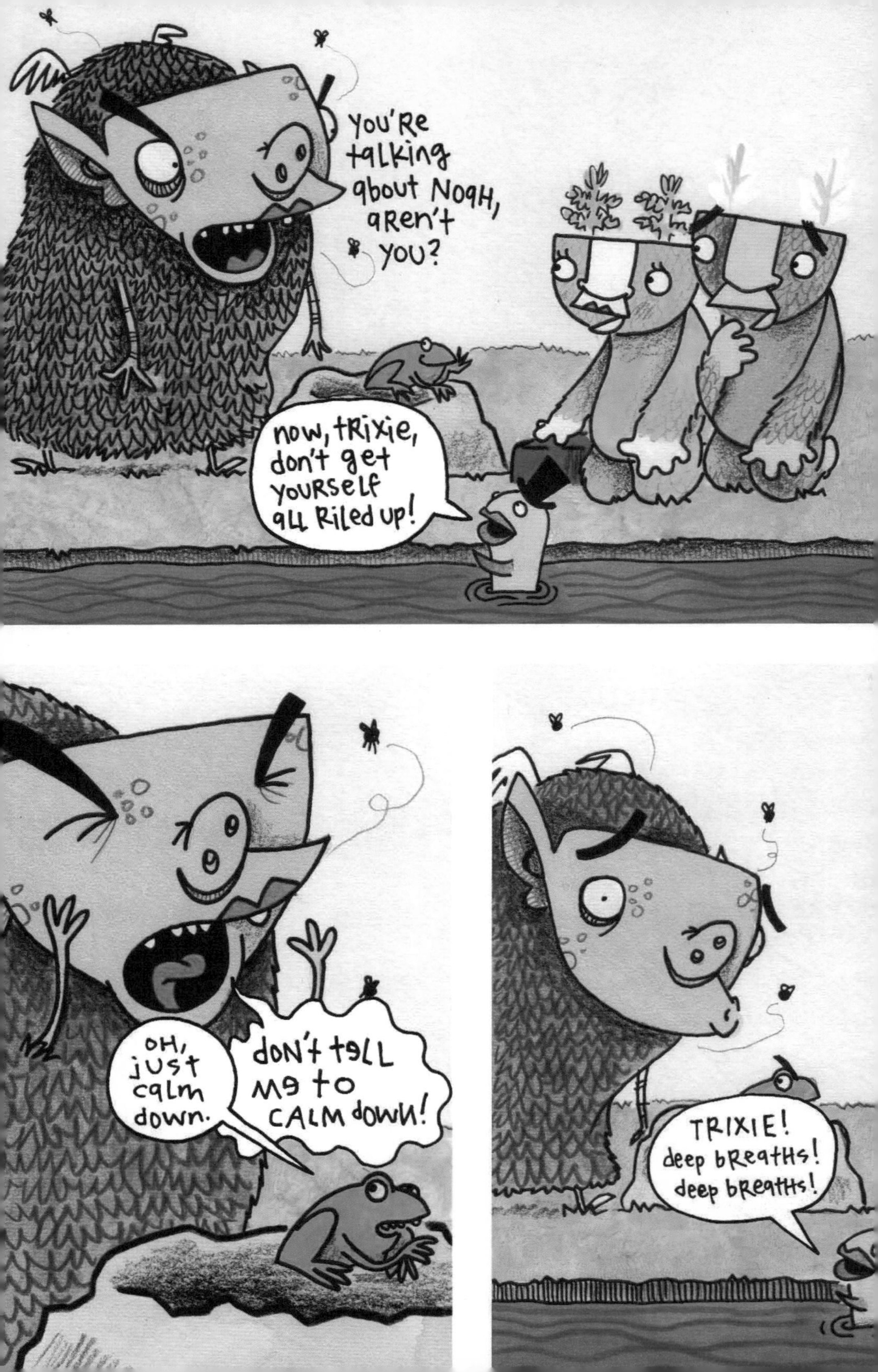
you're talking about Noah, aren't you?
now, trixie, don't get yourself all riled up!
don't tell me to calm down!
oh, just calm down.
TRIXIE! deep breaths! deep breaths!

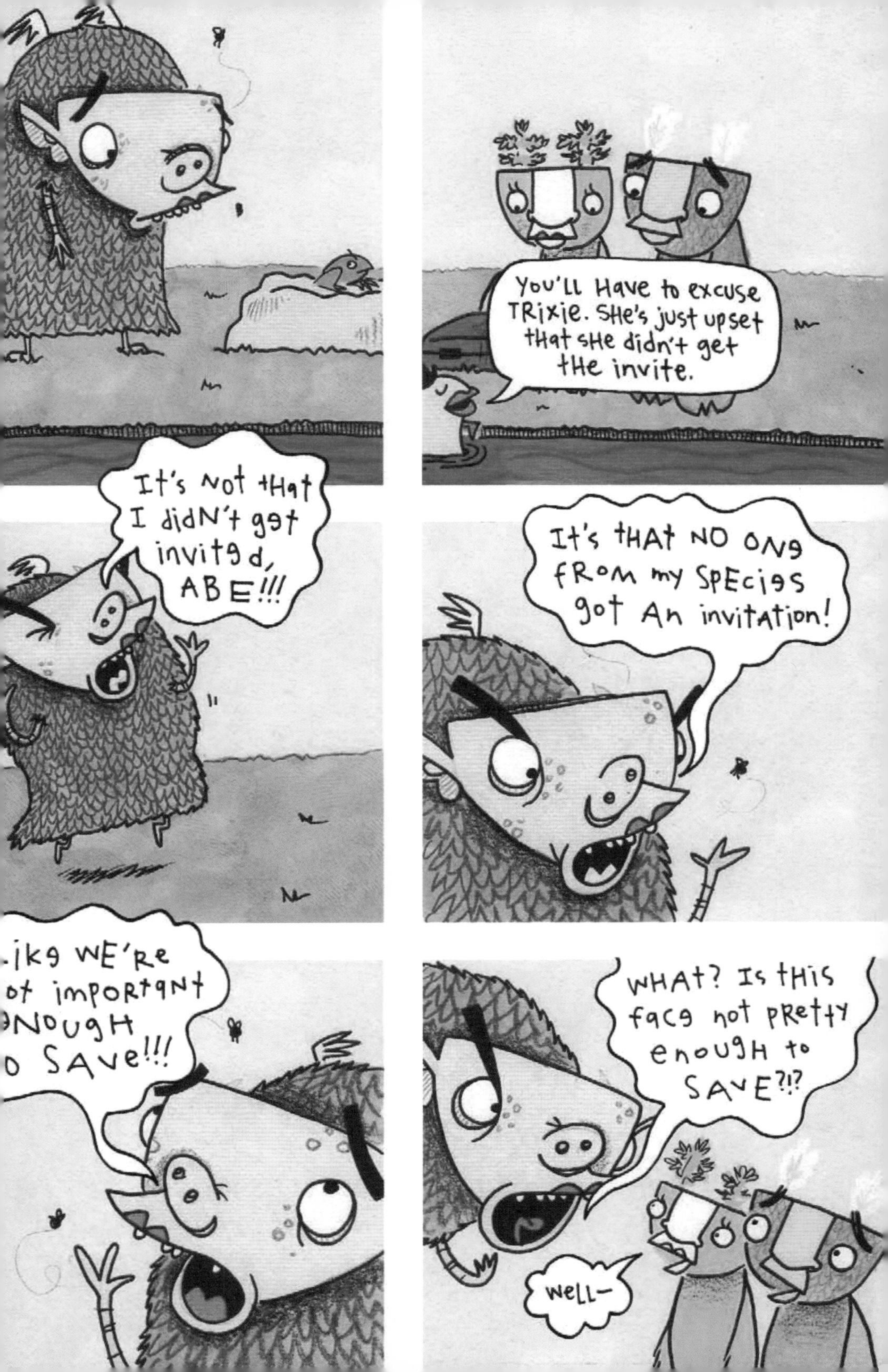
You'll have to excuse Trixie. She's just upset that she didn't get the invite.
It's not that I didn't get invited, ABE!!!
It's that no one from my species got an invitation!
ike we're
ot important
nough
o save!!!
What? Is this face not pretty enough to save?!?
Well-

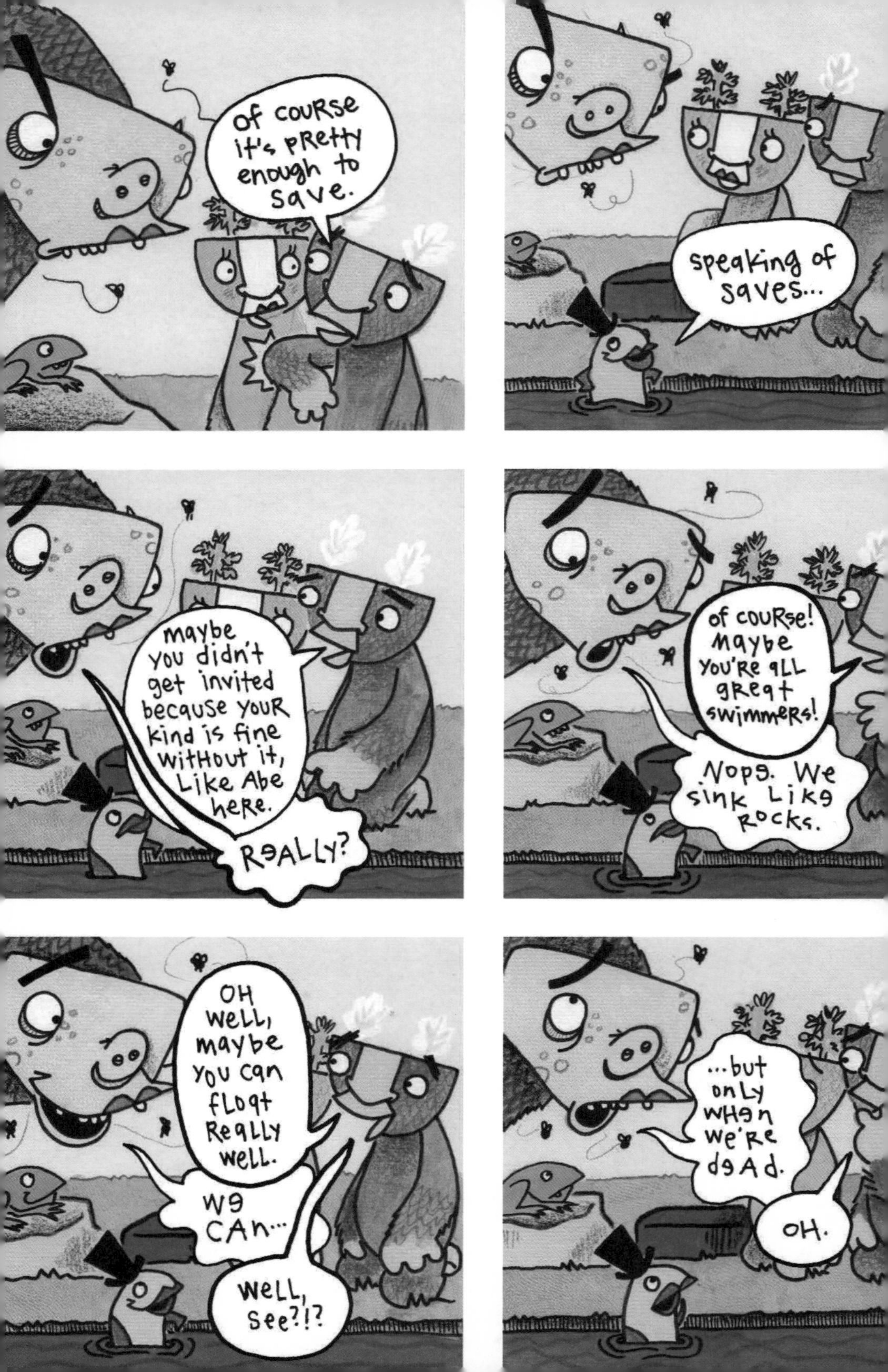
of course it's pretty enough to save.
speaking of saves...
maybe you didn't get invited because your kind is fine without it, like Abe here.
Really?
of course! maybe you're all great swimmers!
Nope. We sink like rocks.
OH well, maybe you can float really well.
We can...
Well, see?!?
...but only when we're dead.
OH.

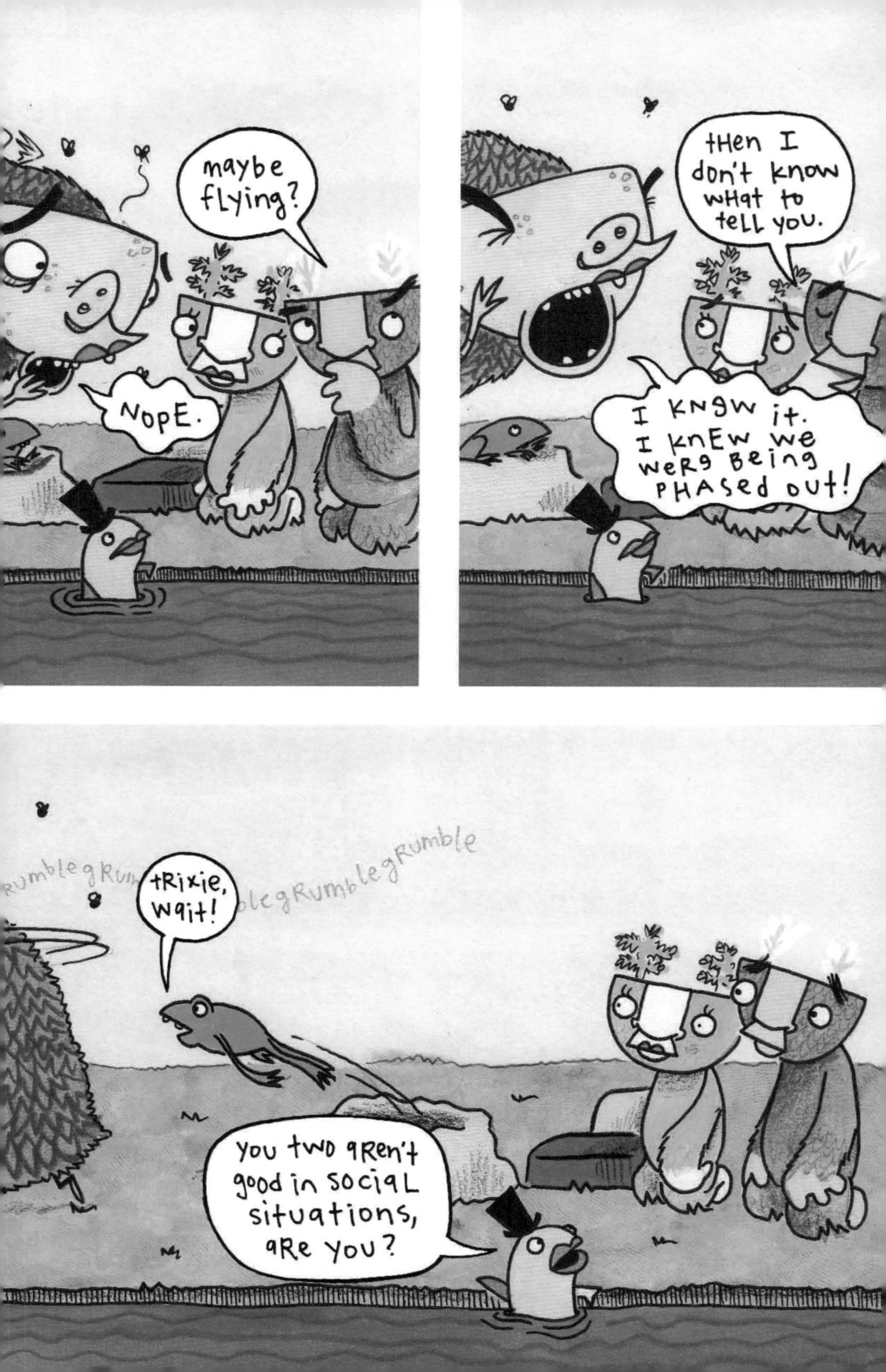
maybe flying?
NopE.
tHen I don't know wHat to tell you.
I KNOW it. I KNEW we were being PHASEd out!
RUmblegRUmblegRUmblegRUmble
tRixie, wait!
you two aren't good in SOCIAL situations, are you?

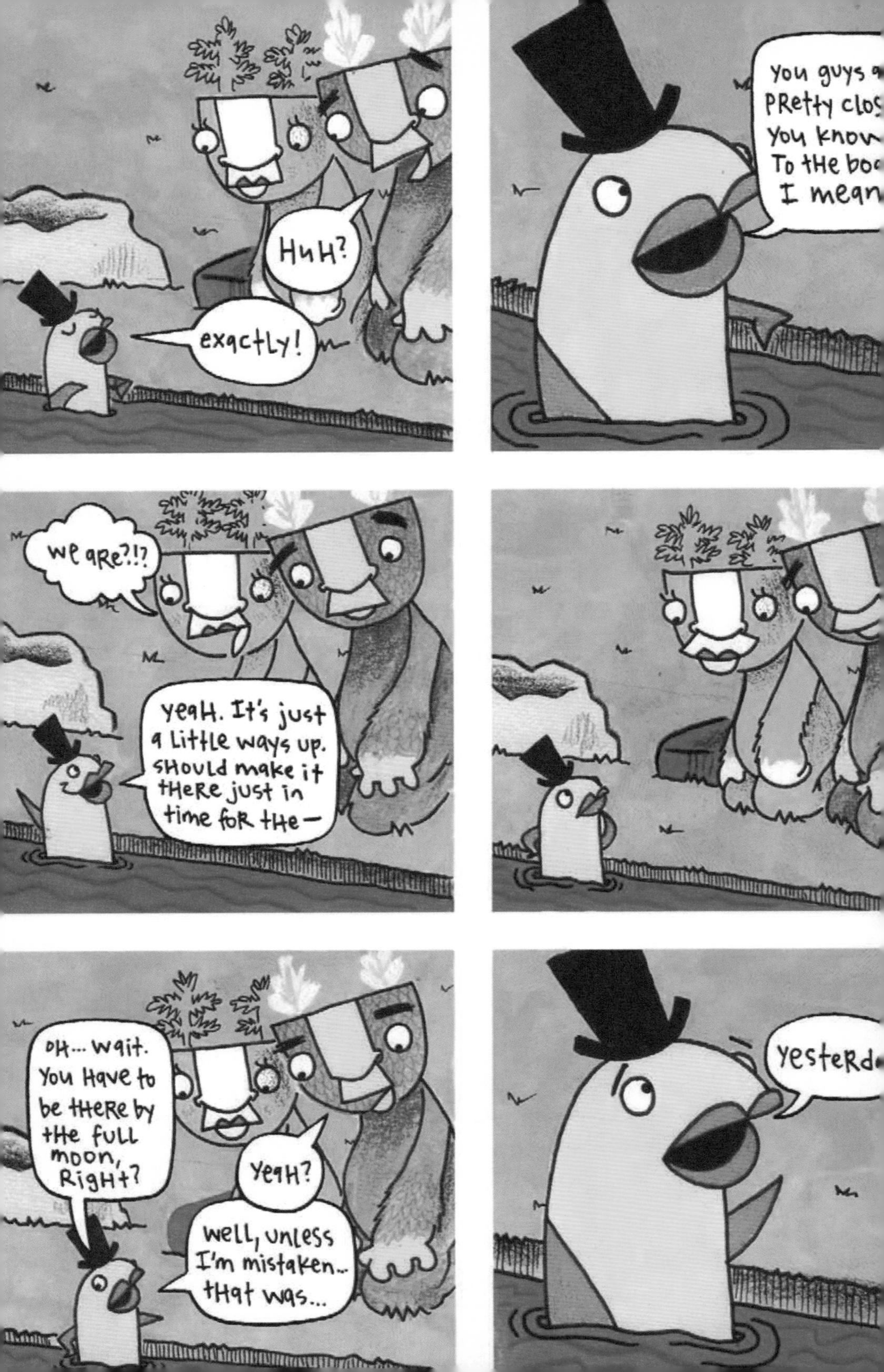
HuH?
exactLy!
You guys a
PRetty clos
You know
To tHe boo
I mean
we aRe?!?
yeaH. It's just a Little ways up. sHould make it tHeRe just in time foR tHe—
oH... wait. You Have to be tHeRe by tHe fuLL moon, RigHt?
YeaH?
weLL, unLess I'm mistaken... tHat was...
yesteRd

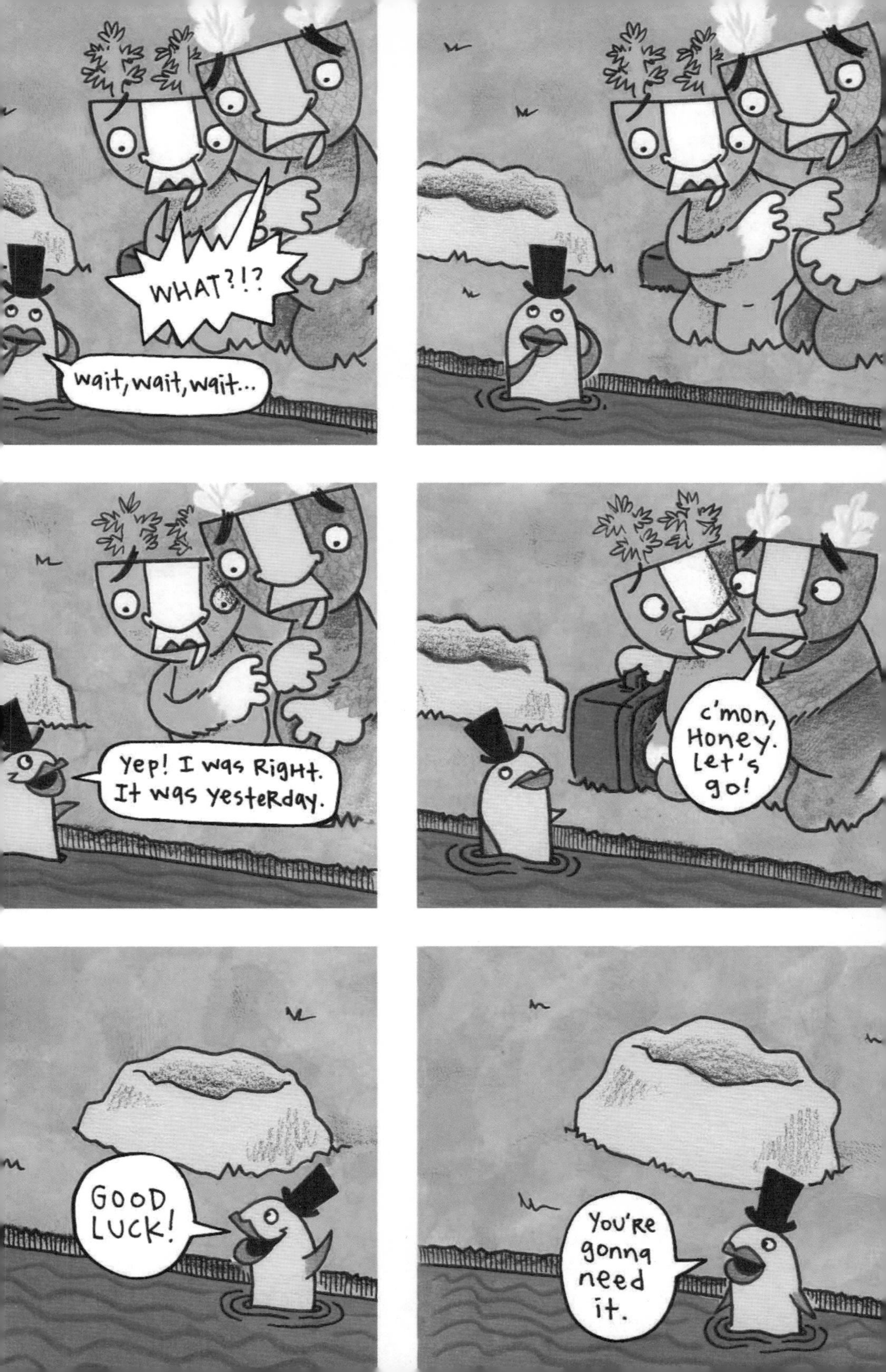
WHAT?!?
wait, wait, wait...
yep! I was Right. It was yesterday.
c'mon, Honey. Let's go!
GOOD LUCK!
You're gonna need it.

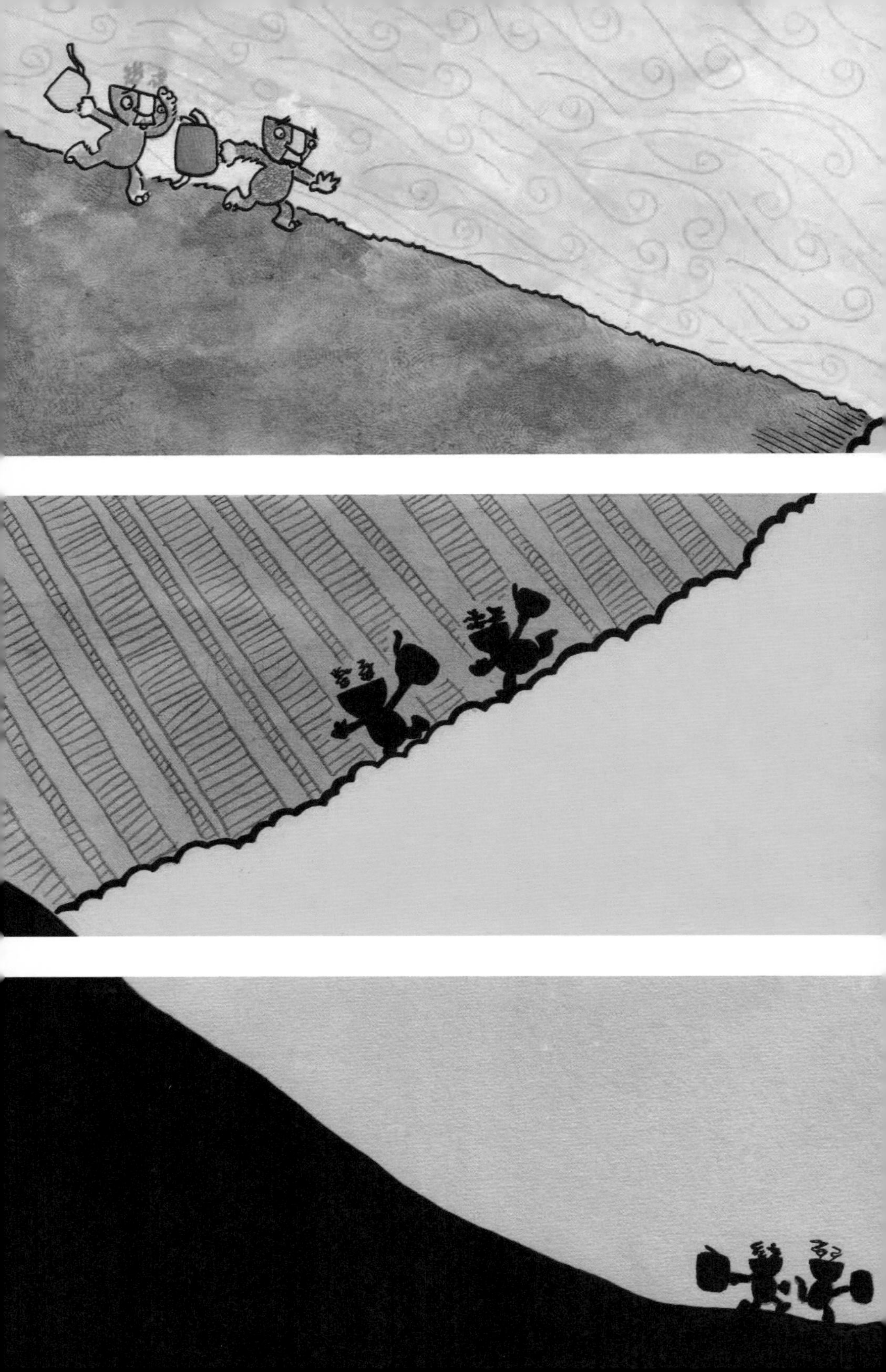

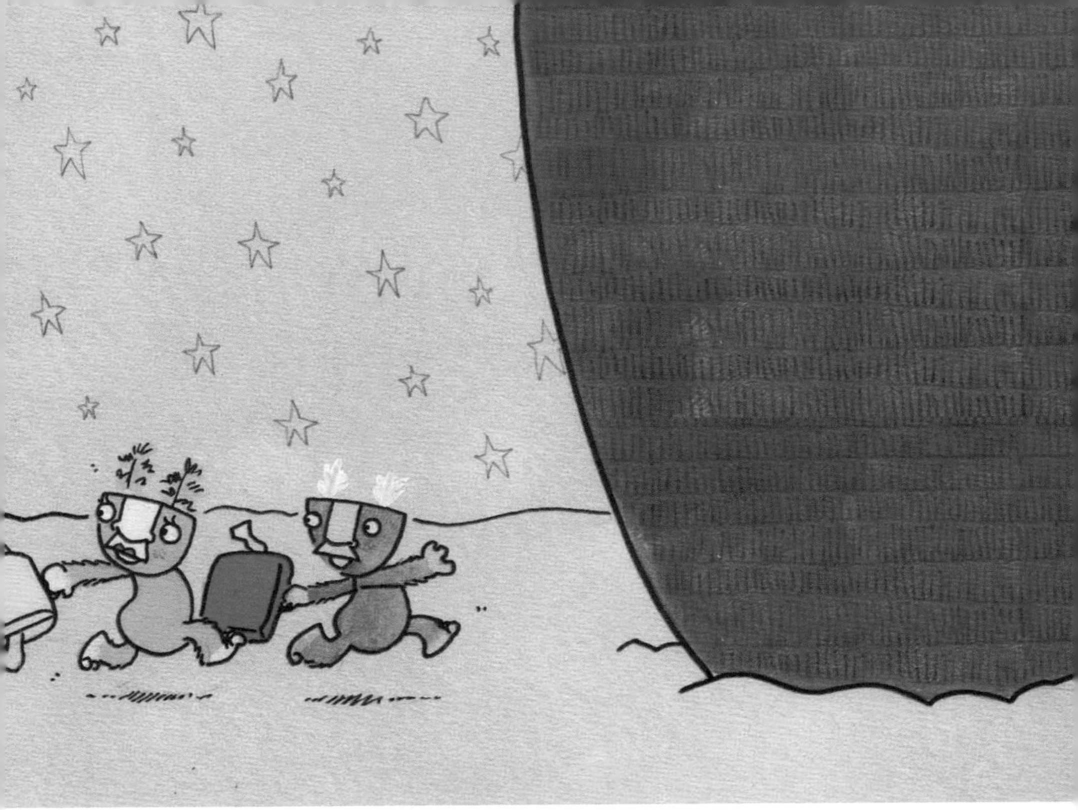

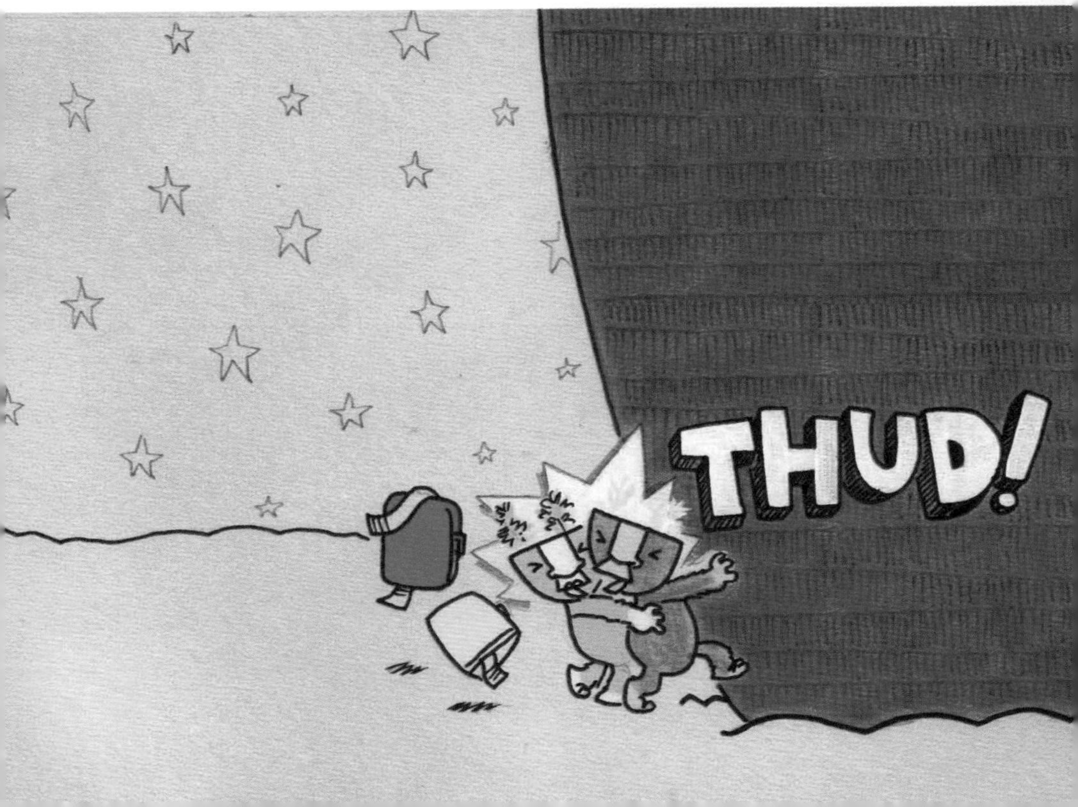
THUD!

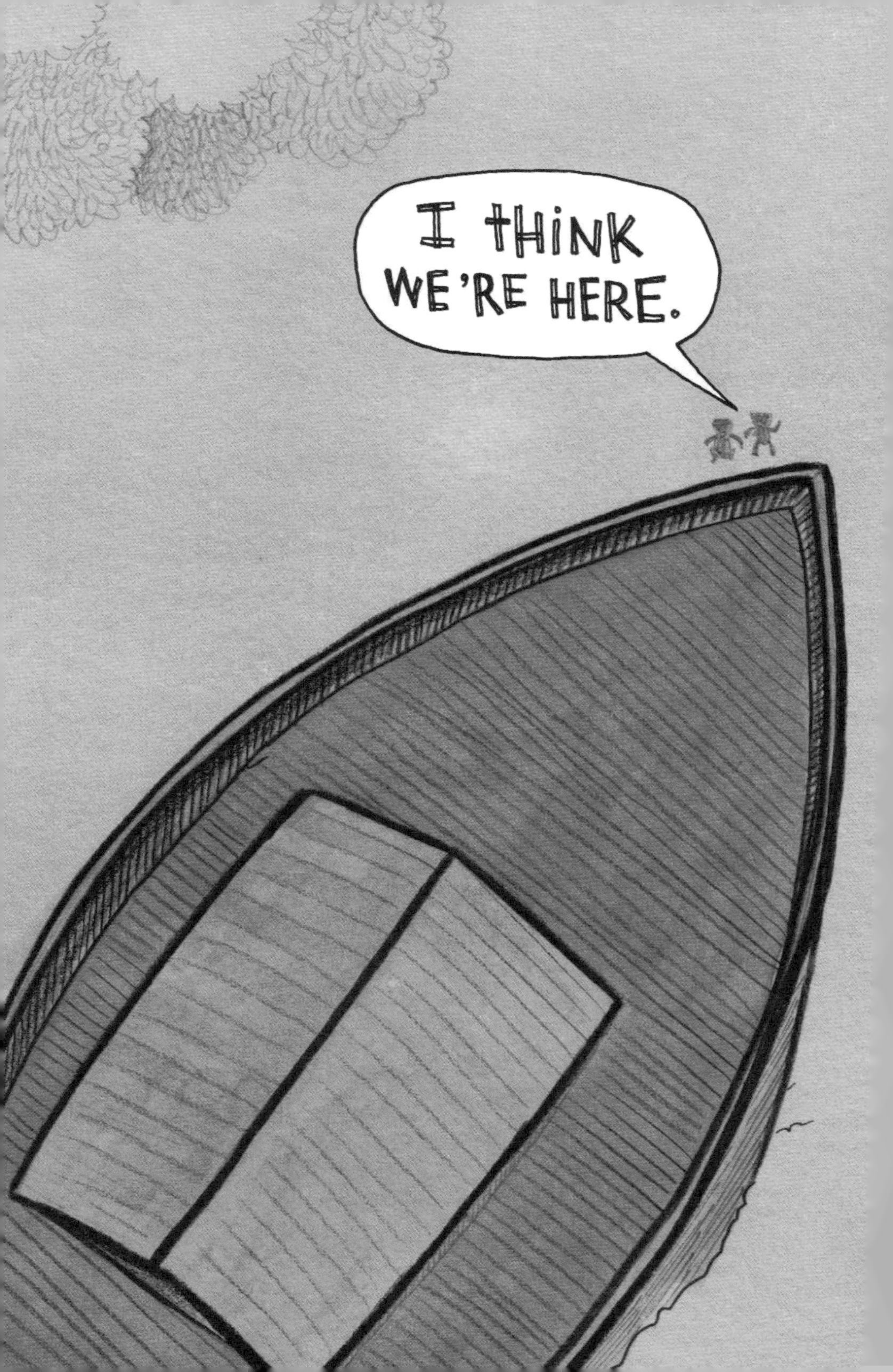
I THINK WE'RE HERE.

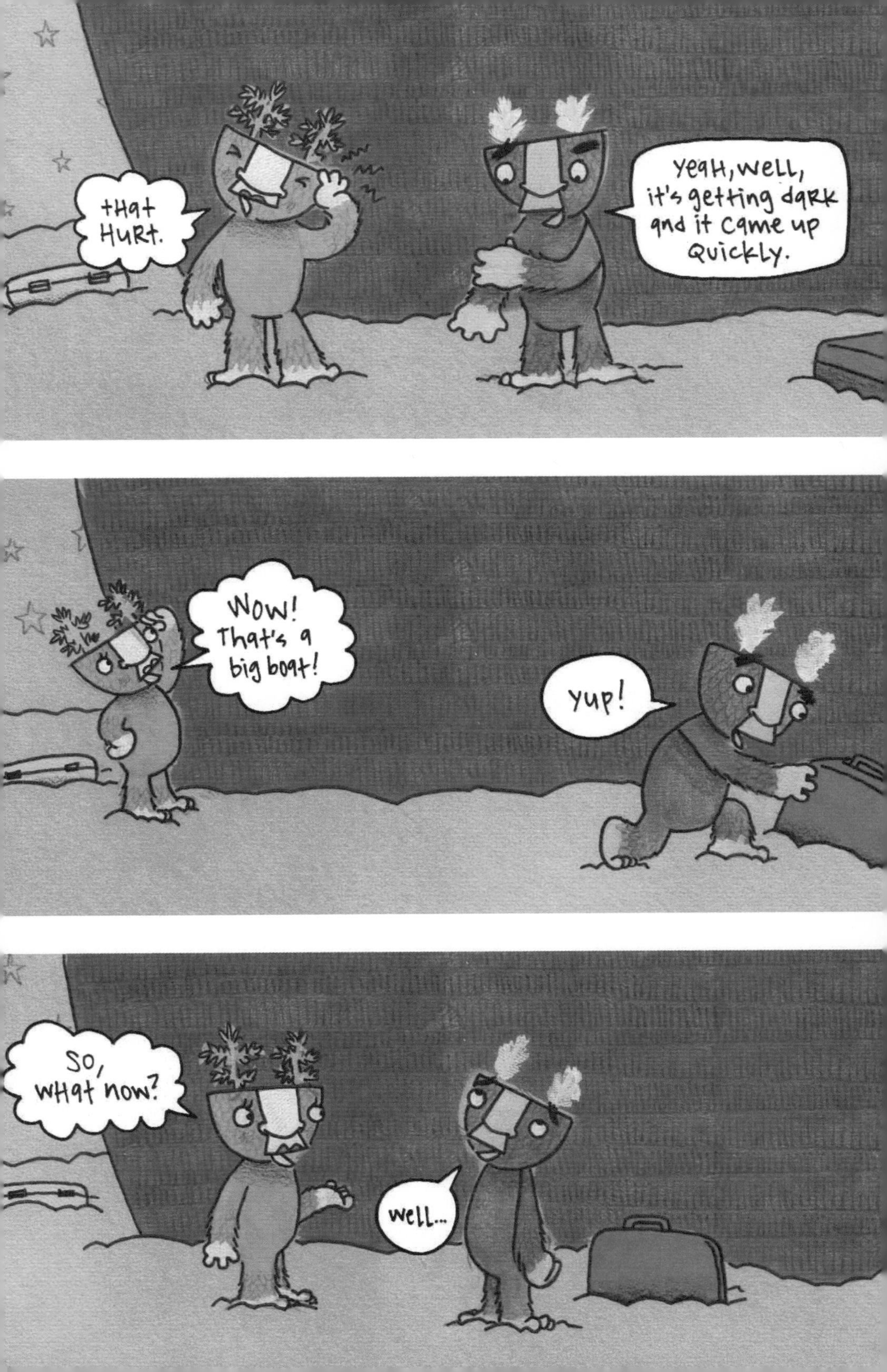
tHat HuRt.
yeaH, well, it's getting dark and it came up QuickLy.
Wow! That's a big boat!
yup!
So, wHat now?
well...

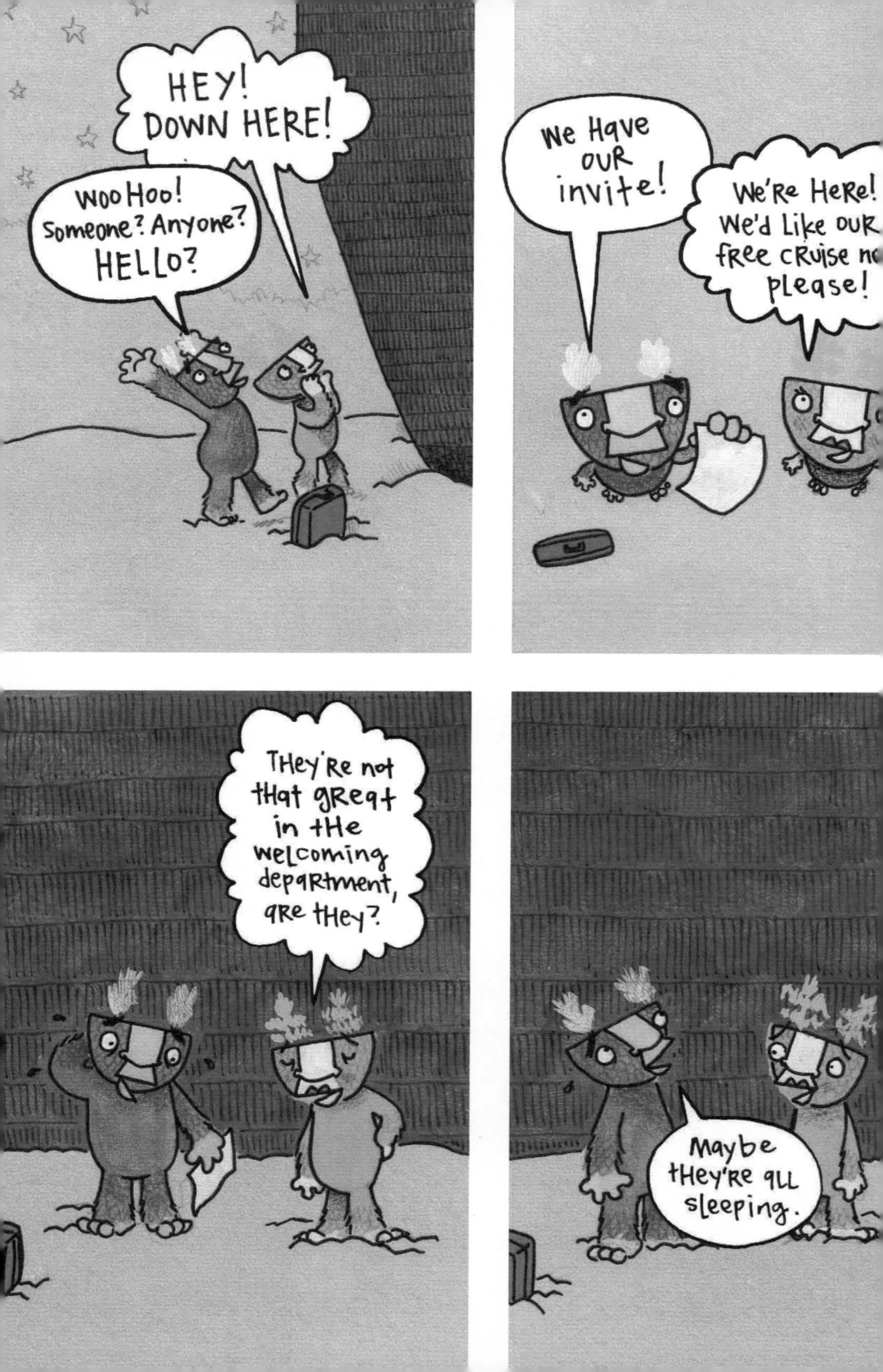
HEY! DOWN HERE!
WOO HOO! Someone? Anyone? HELLO?
We have our invite!
We're here! We'd like our free cruise
please!
They're not that great in the welcoming department, are they?
Maybe they're all sleeping.

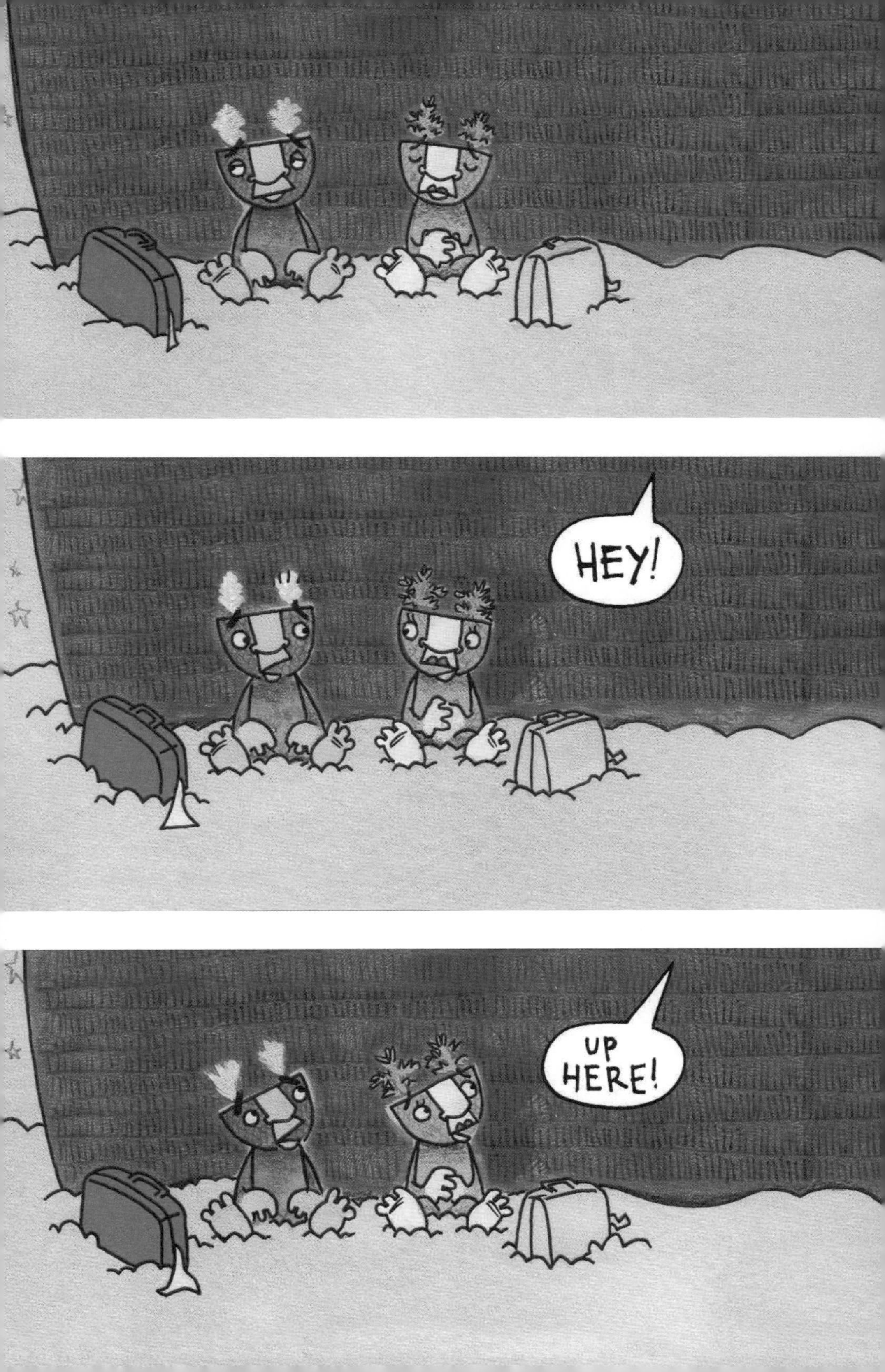
HEY!
UP HERE!

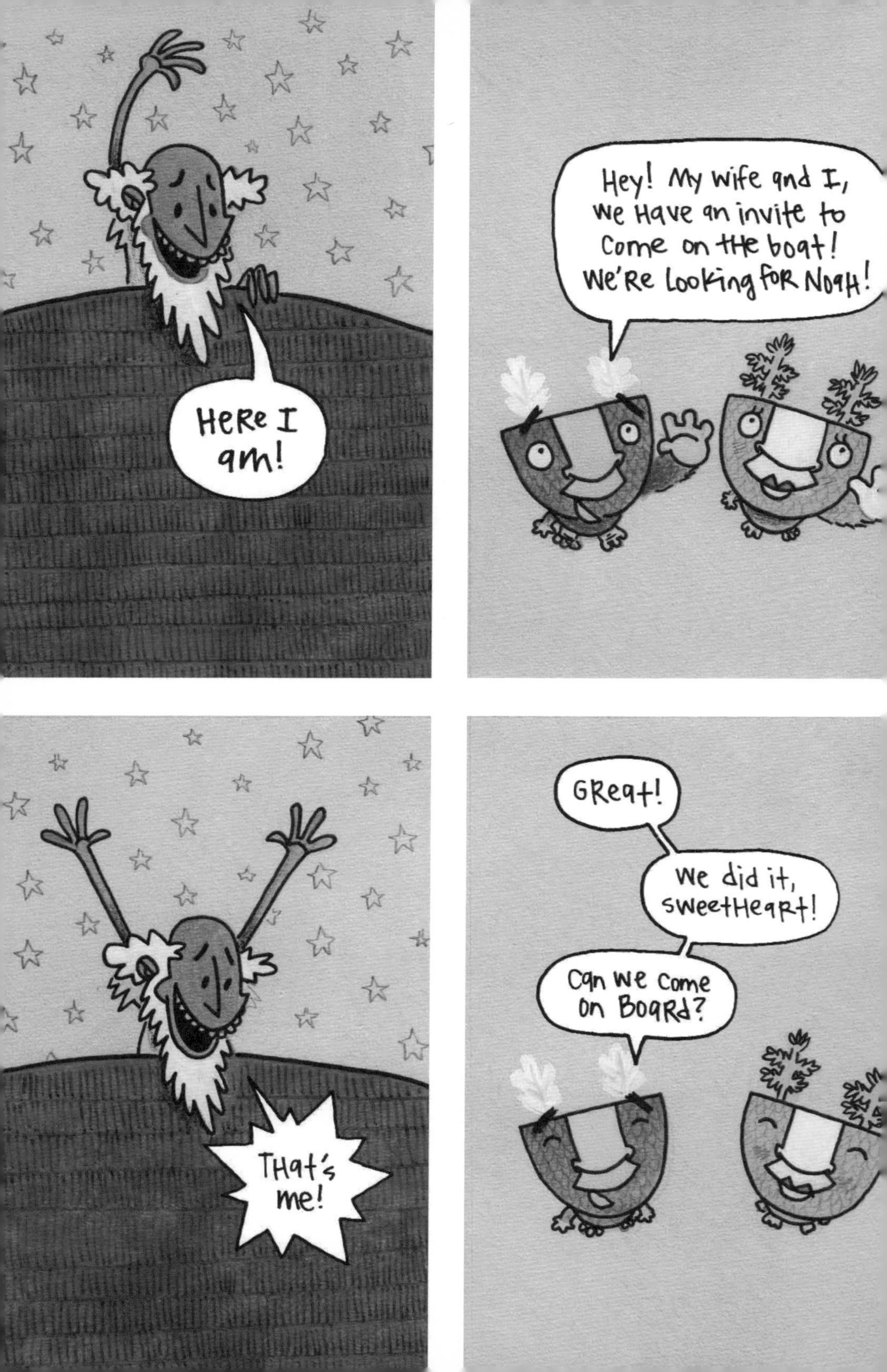
Here I am!
Hey! My wife and I, we have an invite to come on the boat! We're looking for Noah!
That's me!
Great!
We did it, sweetheart!
Can we come on board?

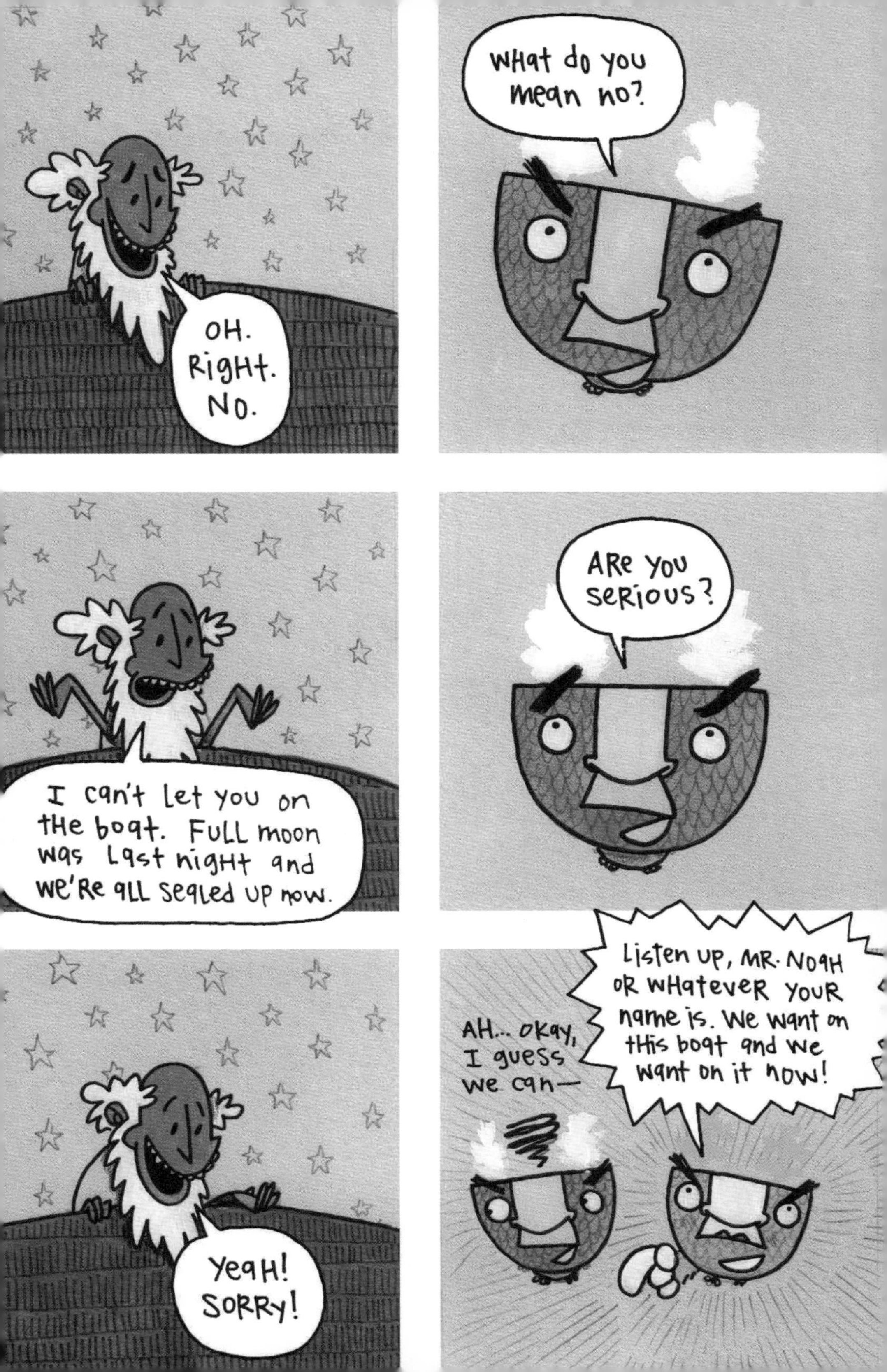
OH. RIGHT. NO.
WHAT do you mean no?
I can't let you on tHe boat. FULL moon was last night and we're all sealed up now.
ARe you seRious?
YeaH! SORRY!
AH... okay, I guess we can—
Listen up, MR. NOAH OR WHatever YOUR name is. We want on tHis boat and we want on it now!

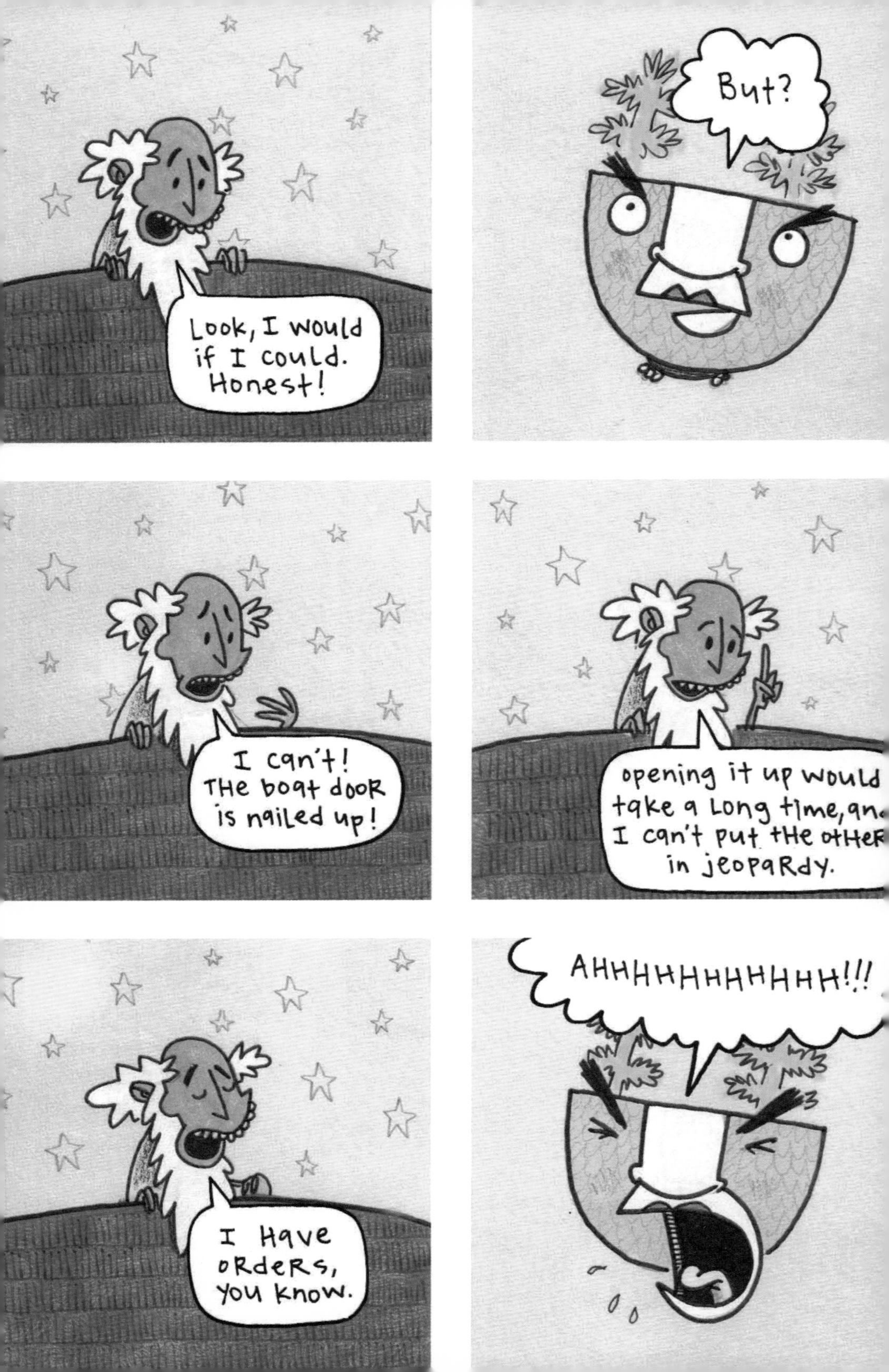
Look, I would if I could. Honest!
But?
I can't! The boat door is nailed up!
opening it up would take a long time, an
I can't put the other
in jeopardy.
I have orders, you know.
AHHHHHHHHHHHH!!!

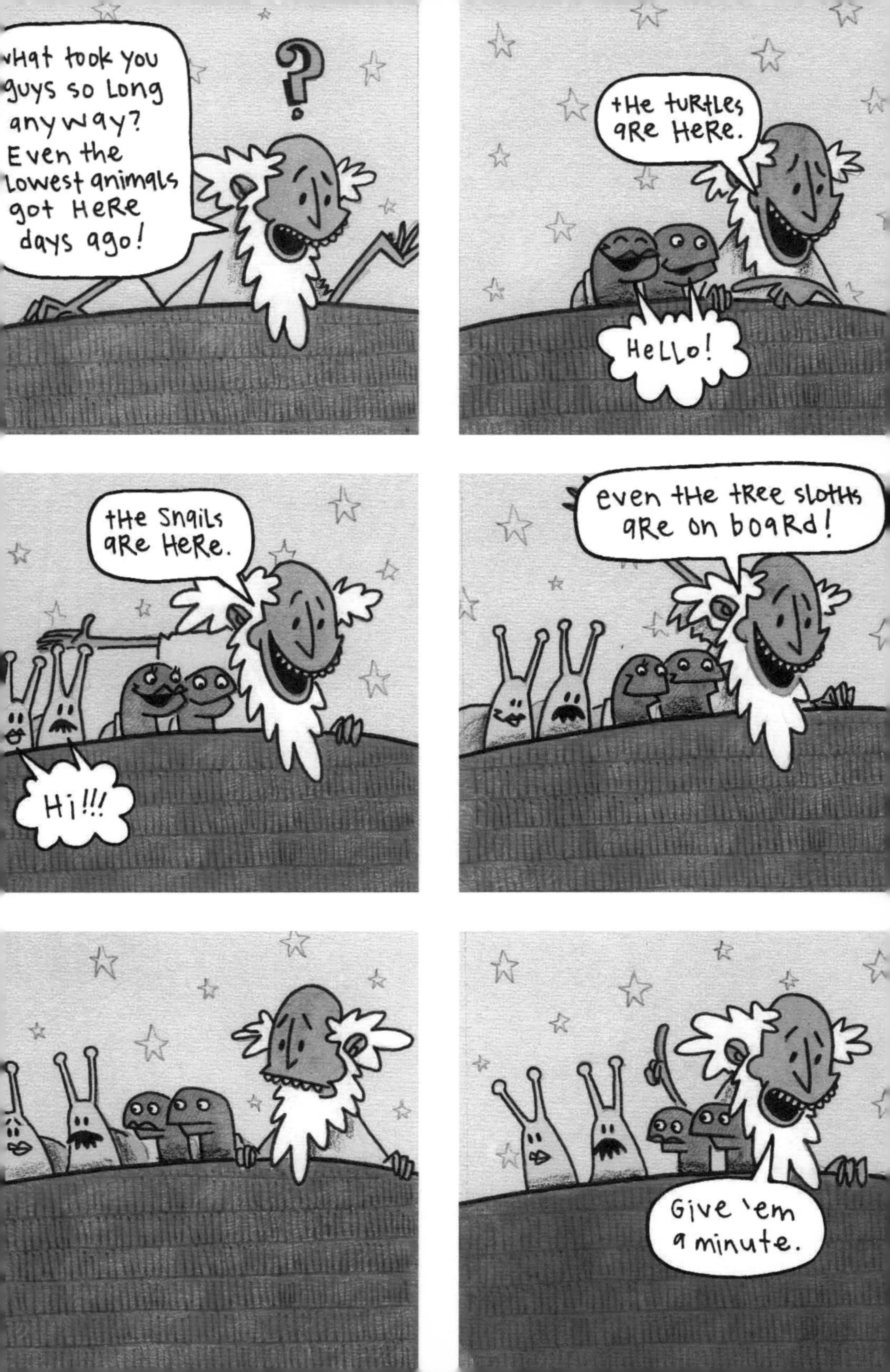
what took you guys so Long anyway? Even the Lowest animals got HERE days ago!
?
tHe turtles are HeRe.
HeLLo!
tHe Snails are HeRe.
Hi!!!
even tHe tree sloths are on board!
Give 'em a minute.

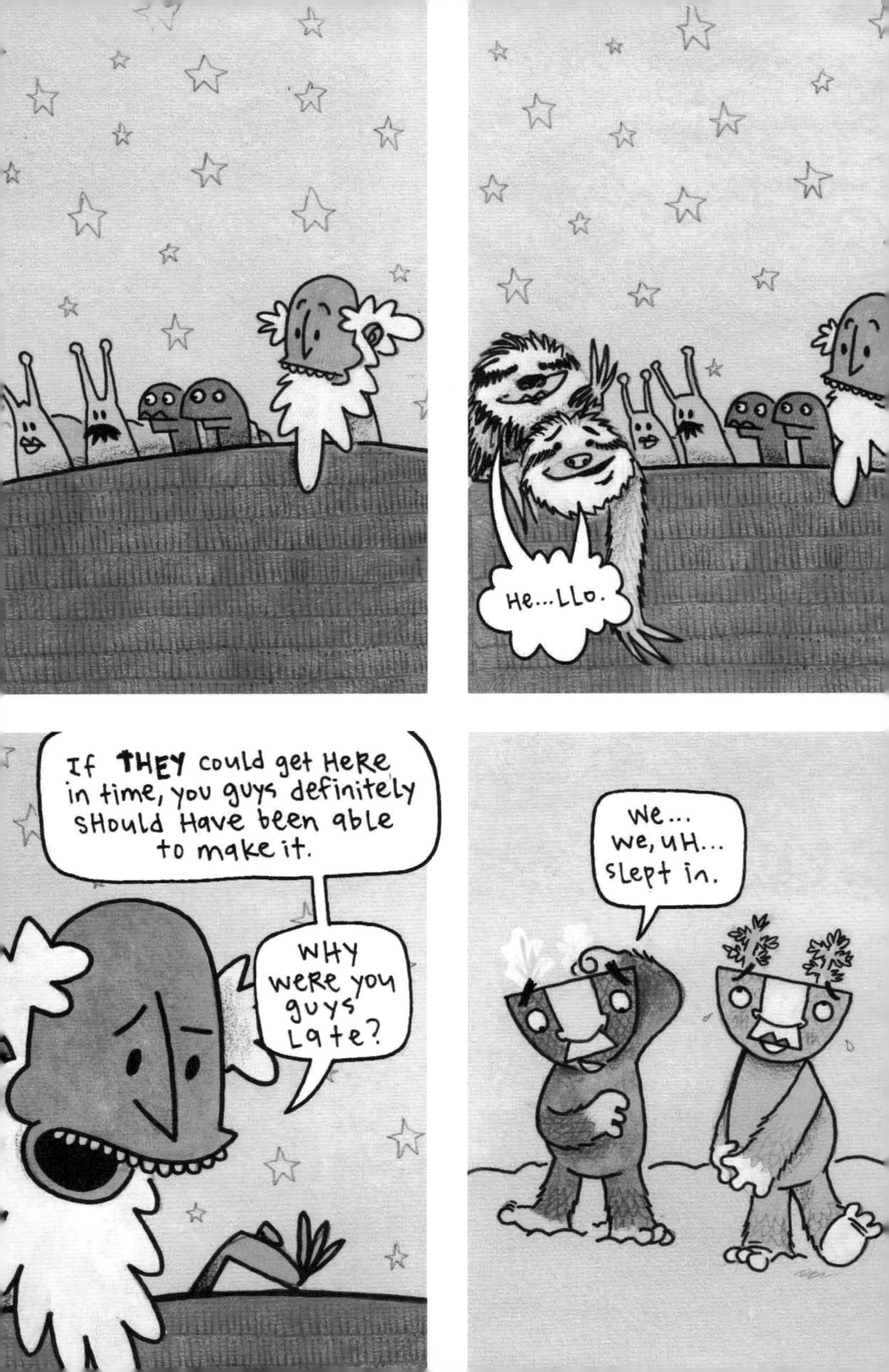
He...LLo.
If THEY could get Here in time, you guys definitely sHould Have been able to make it.
WHY were you guys Late?
We... we, uH... slept in.

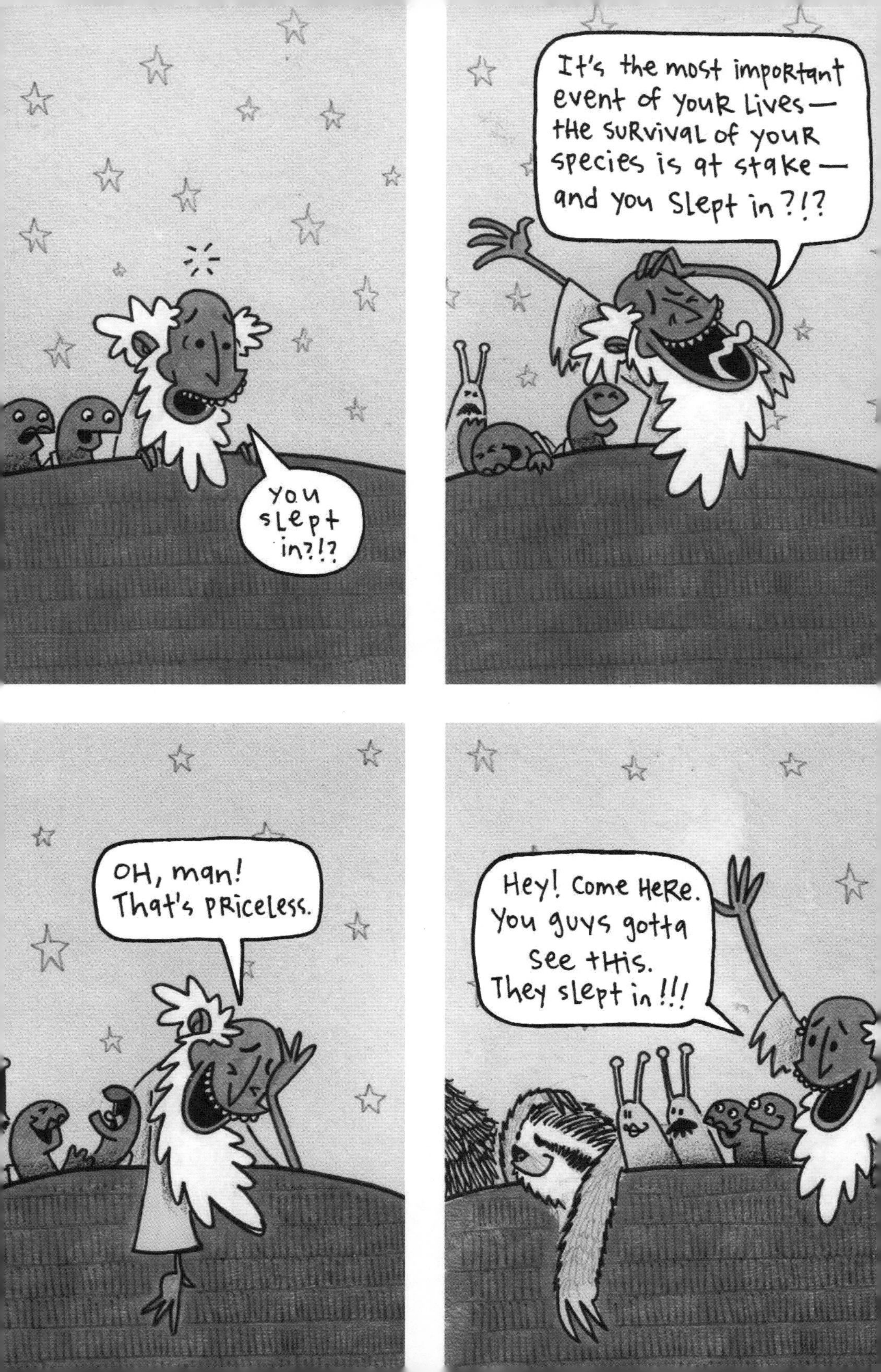
You slept in?!?
It's the most important event of your lives—the survival of your species is at stake—and you slept in?!?
OH, man! That's PRiceless.
Hey! Come HeRe. You guys gotta see tHis. They slept in!!!

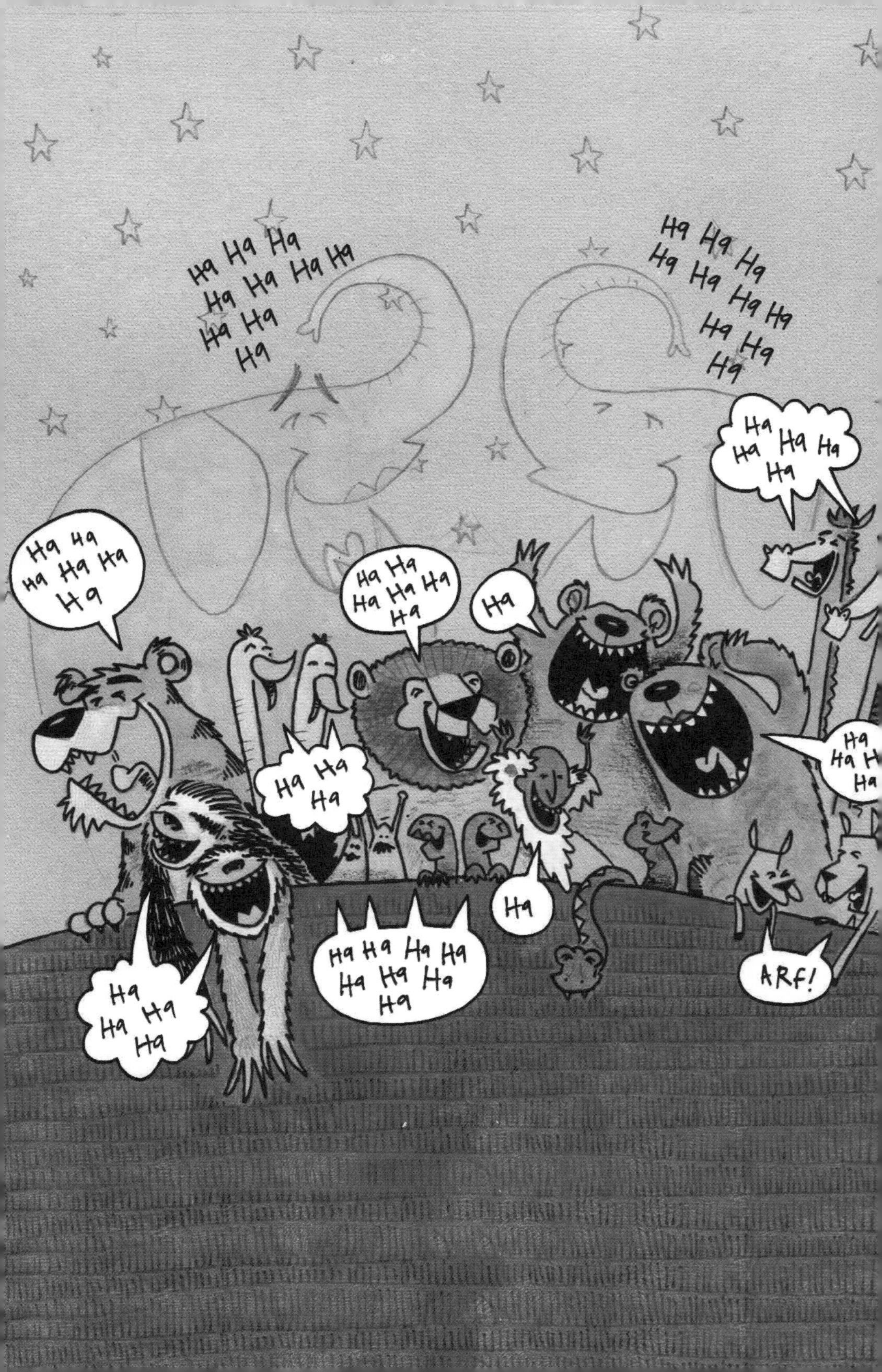
Ha Ha Ha
Ha Ha Ha Ha
Ha Ha
Ha
Ha Ha
Ha Ha Ha
Ha Ha Ha Ha
Ha Ha
Ha
Ha
Ha Ha Ha
Ha
Ha ha
ha Ha Ha
Ha
Ha Ha
Ha Ha Ha
Ha
Ha
Ha Ha
Ha
Ha
Ha Ha Ha Ha
Ha Ha Ha
Ha
Ha
Ha Ha
Ha
Ha Ha Ha Ha
Ha Ha Ha
Ha
ARF!

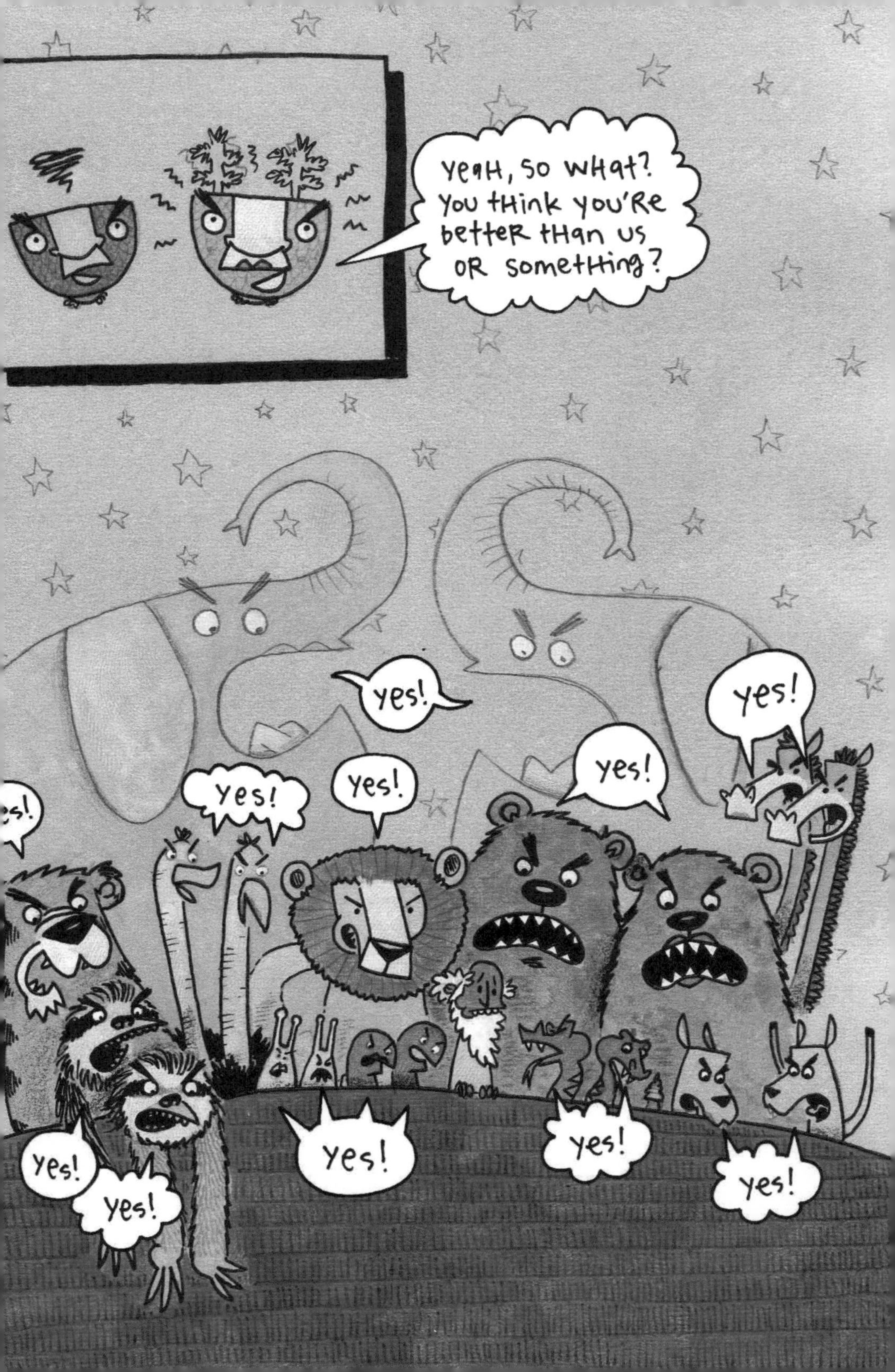

YeaH, so WHat? You tHink you're better tHan us or sometHing?
yes!
yes!
yes!
yes!
yes!
yes!
yes!
yes!
yes!
yes!
yes!

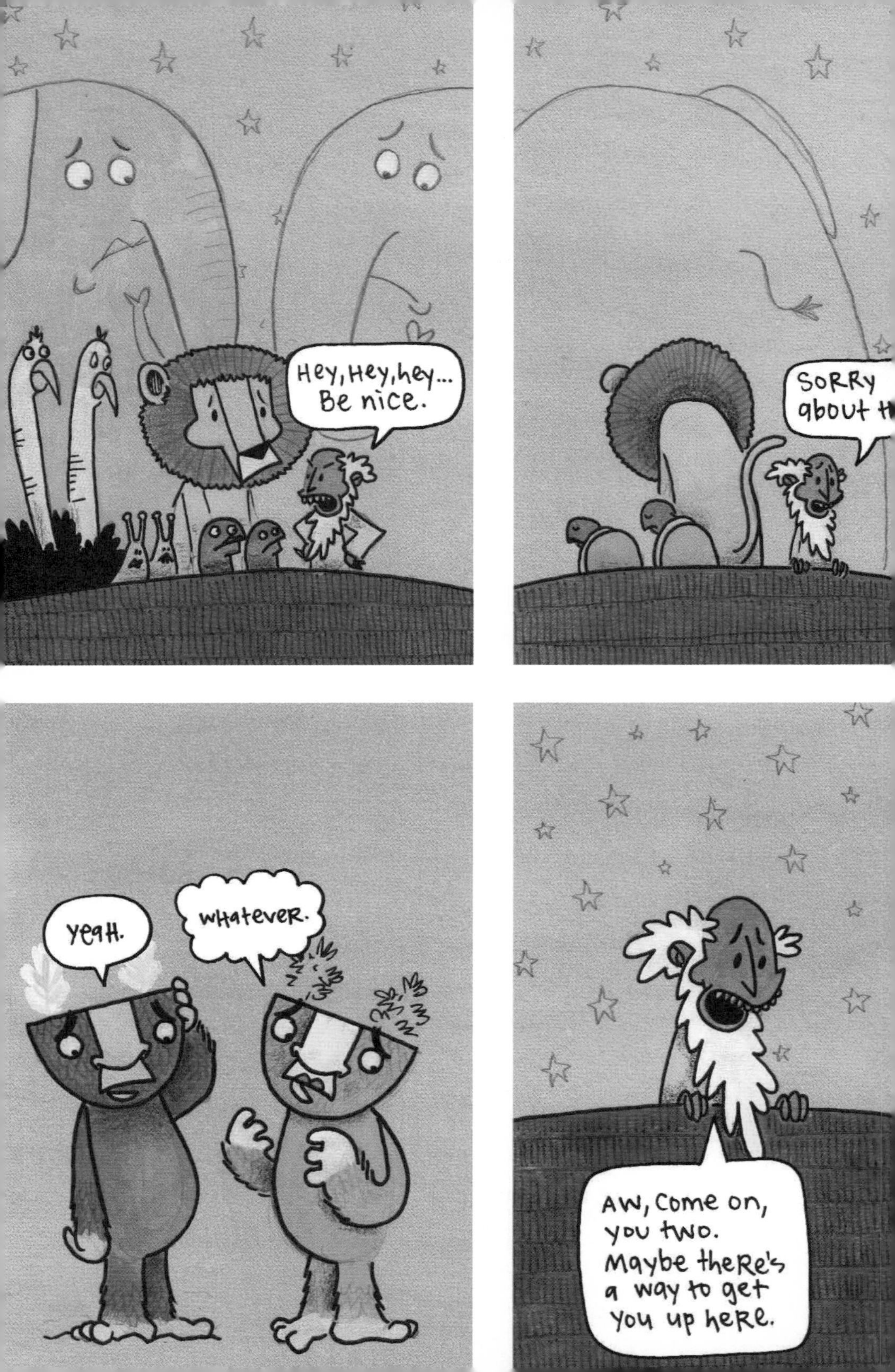
Hey, Hey, hey... Be nice.
SoRRy about t
yeaH.
whatever.
AW, Come on, you two. Maybe theRe's a way to get you up heRe.

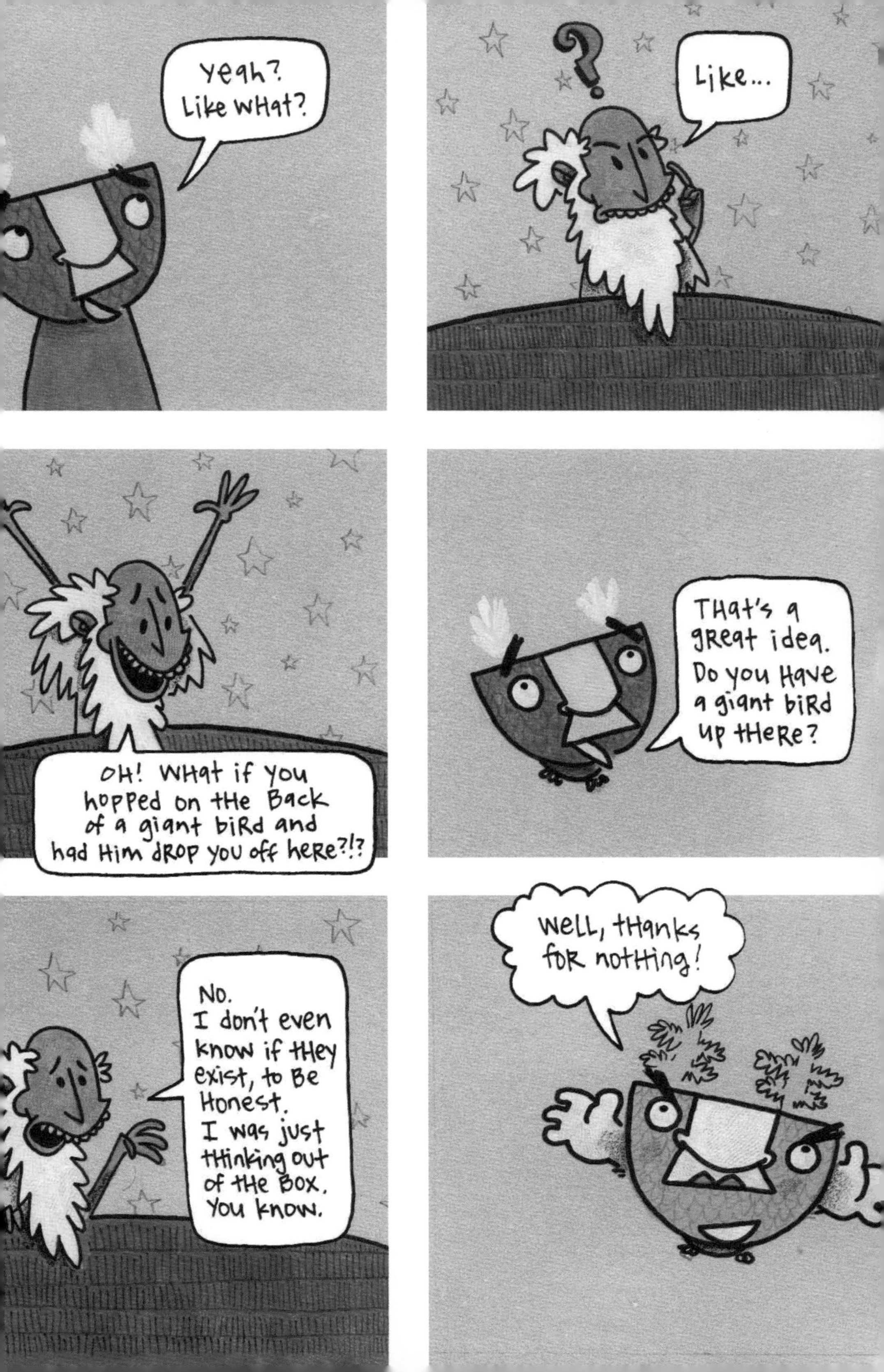
Yeah? Like WHat?
Like...
OH! WHat if you hopped on tHe Back of a giant biRd and had Him dRop you off heRe?!?
THat's a gReat idea. Do you Have a giant biRd up tHeRe?
No. I don't even know if tHey exist, to Be Honest. I was just tHinking out of tHe Box. You know.
WeLL, tHanks foR notHing!

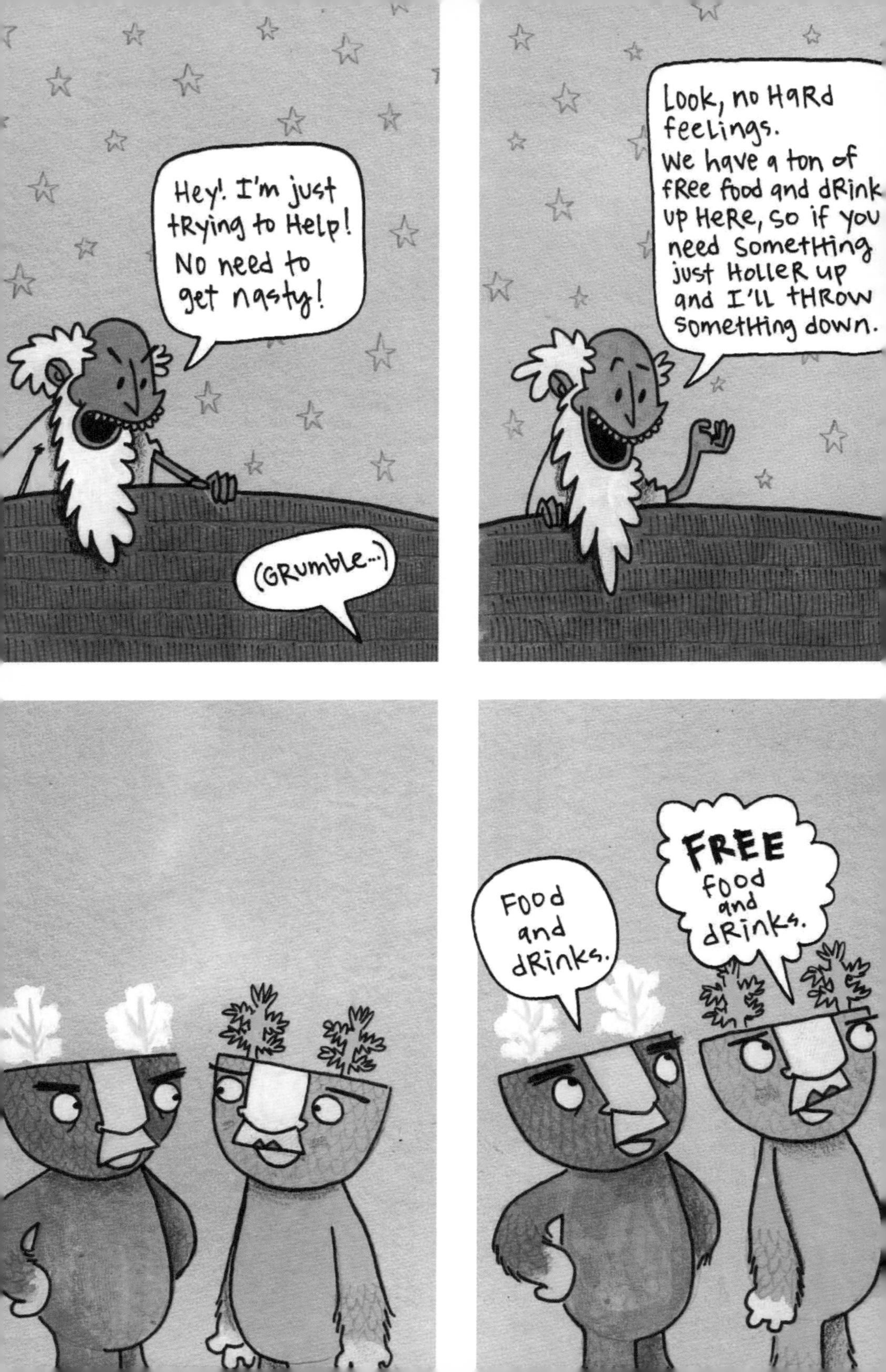
Hey! I'm just tRying to Help! No need to get nasty!
(GRumble...)
Look, no HaRd feelings. We have a ton of fRee food and dRink up HeRe, so if you need Something just HolleR up and I'll tHRow Something down.
Food and dRinks.
FREE food and dRinks.

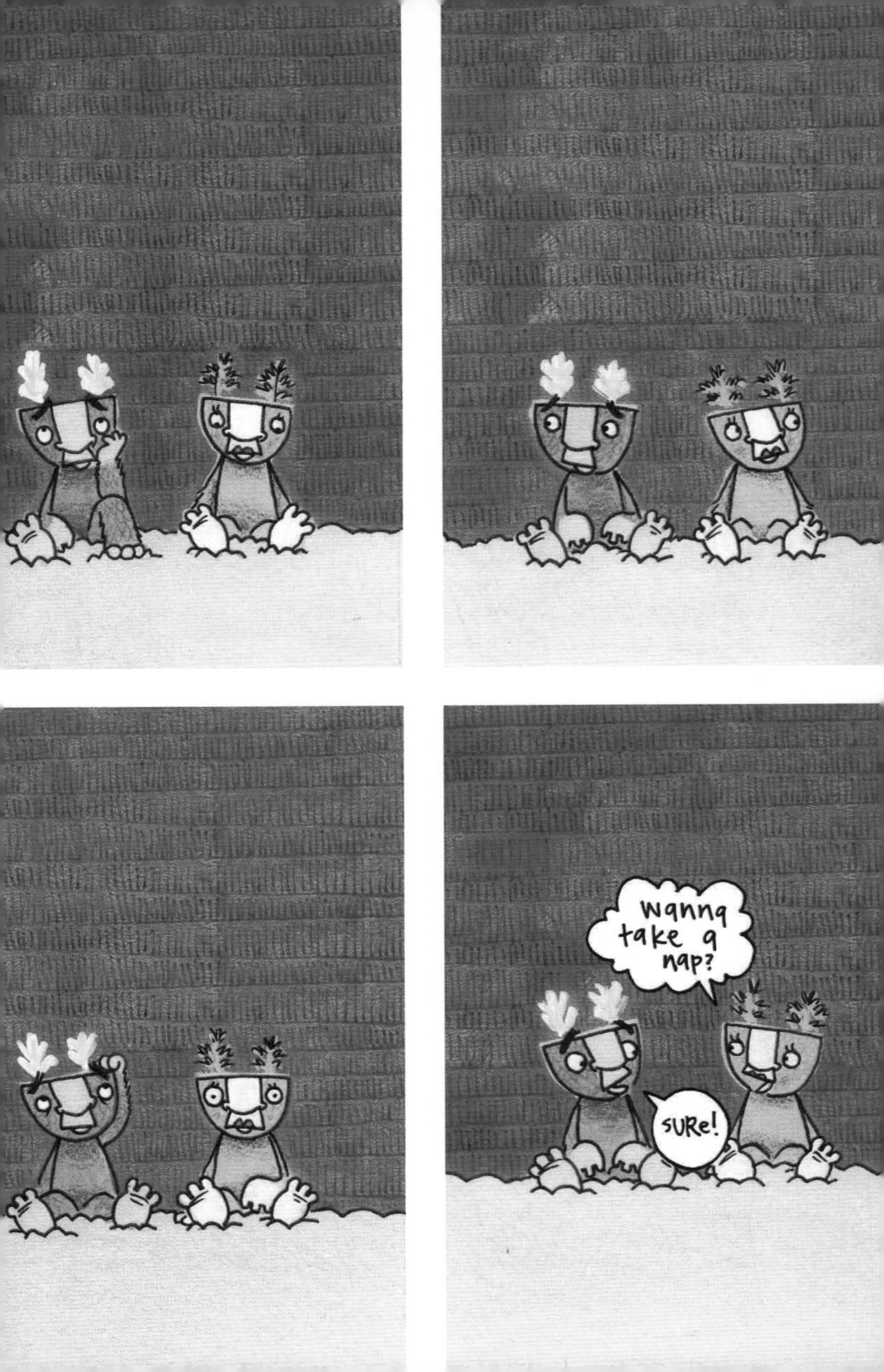
wanna take a nap?
SURe!

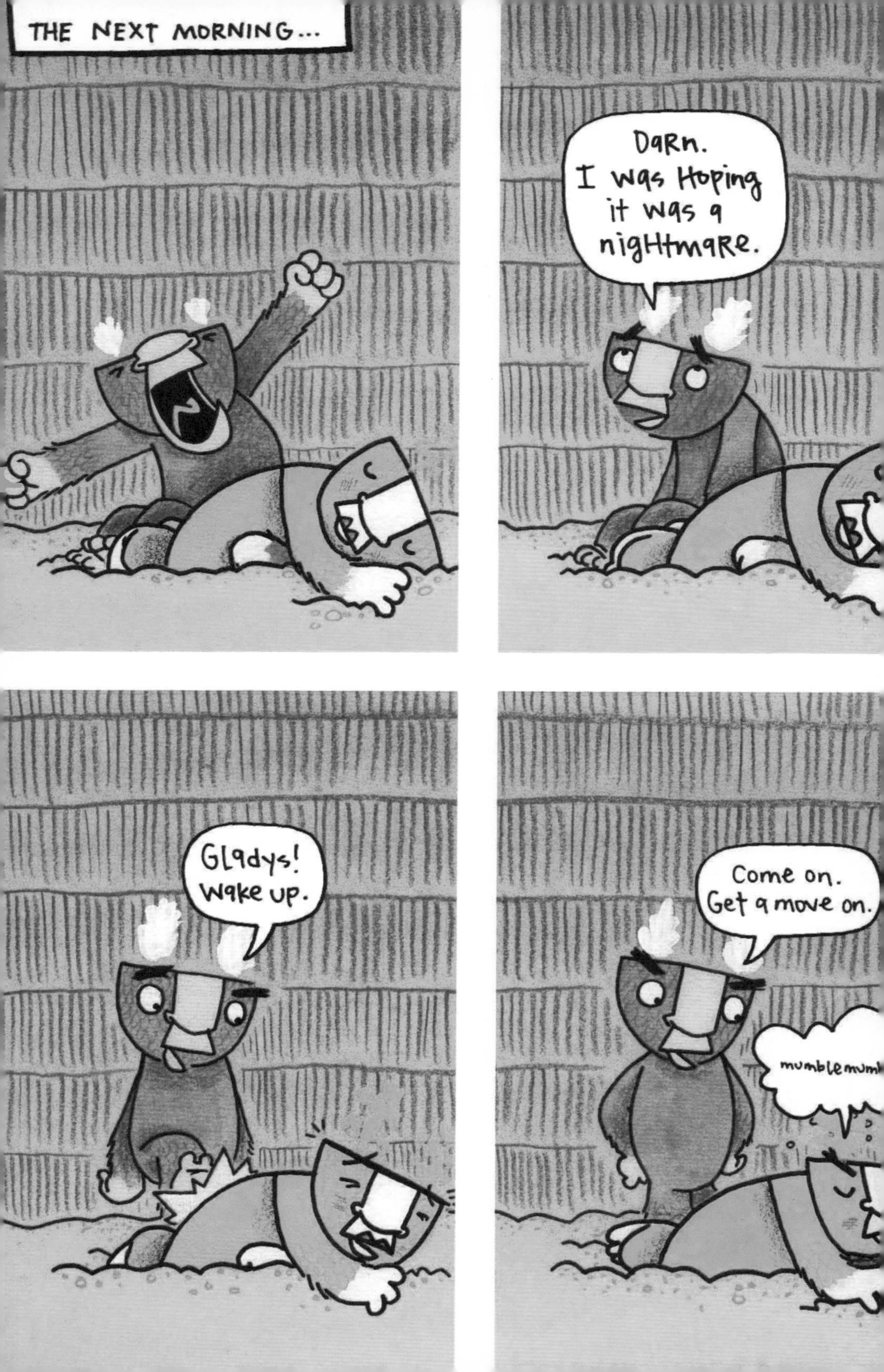
THE NEXT MORNING...
Darn. I was Hoping it was a nightmare.
Gladys! Wake up.
Come on. Get a move on.

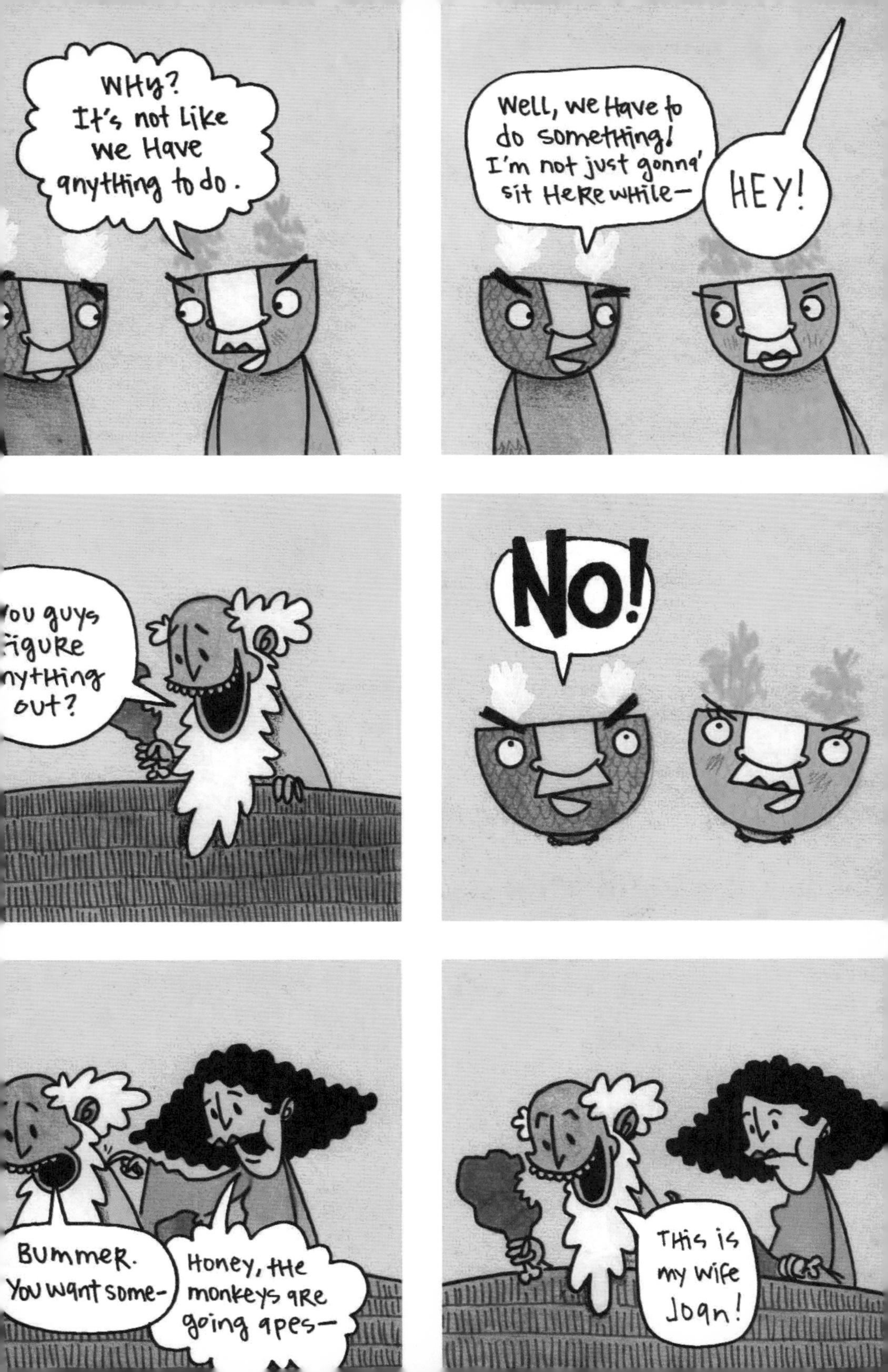
WHY?
It's not Like we Have anything to do.
Well, we Have to do something! I'm not just gonna' sit Here while—
HEY!
You guys figure anything out?
NO!
Bummer. You want some-
Honey, the monkeys are going apes—
This is my wife Joan!

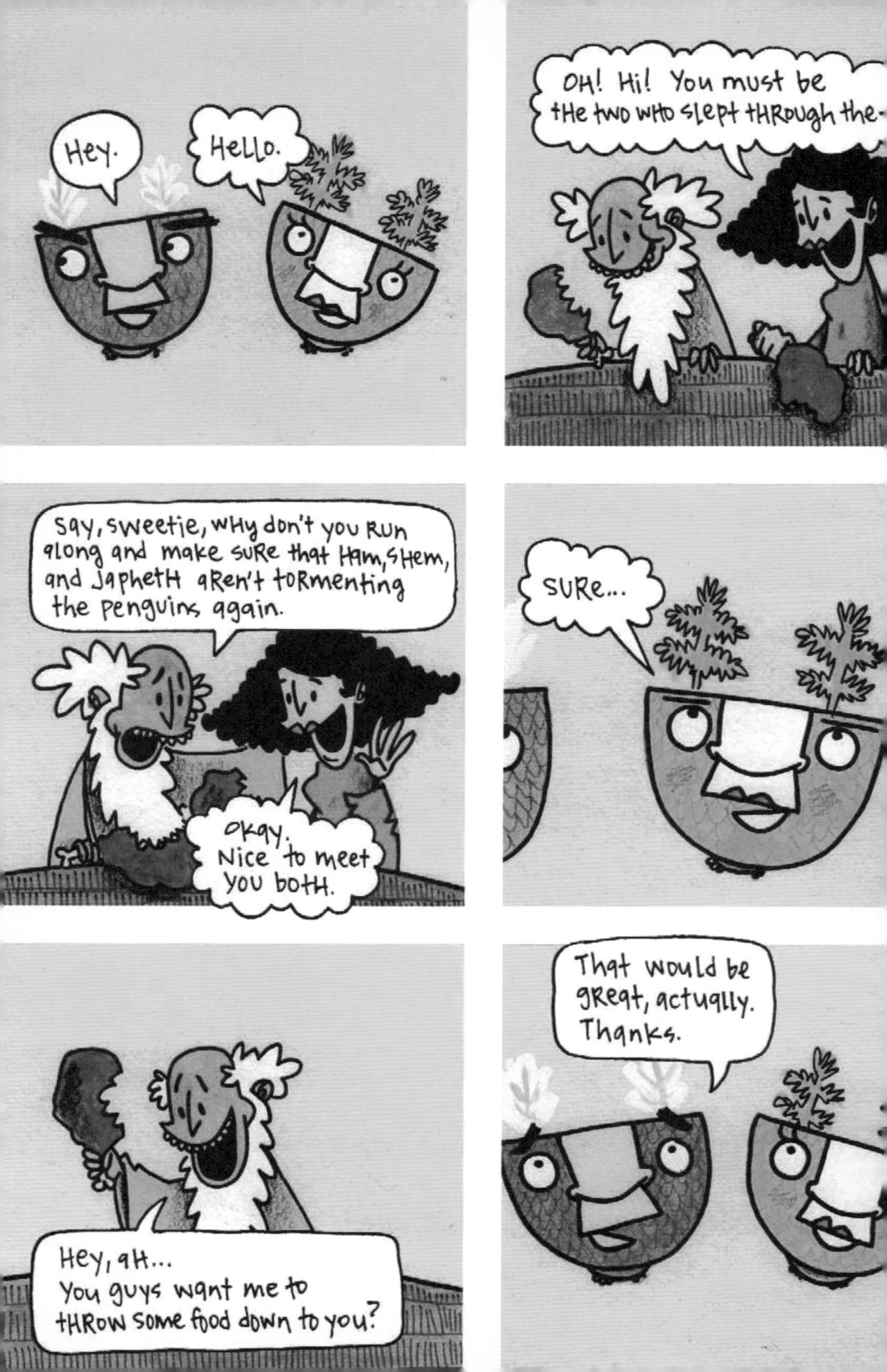
Hey.
Hello.
OH! Hi! You must be tHe two wHo slept tHRough the-
Say, sweetie, wHy don't you Run along and make suRe that Ham, SHem, and JapHetH aRen't toRmenting the penguins again.
Okay. Nice to meet you both.
SuRe...
Hey, aH... You guys want me to tHRow some food down to you?
That would be gReat, actually. Thanks.

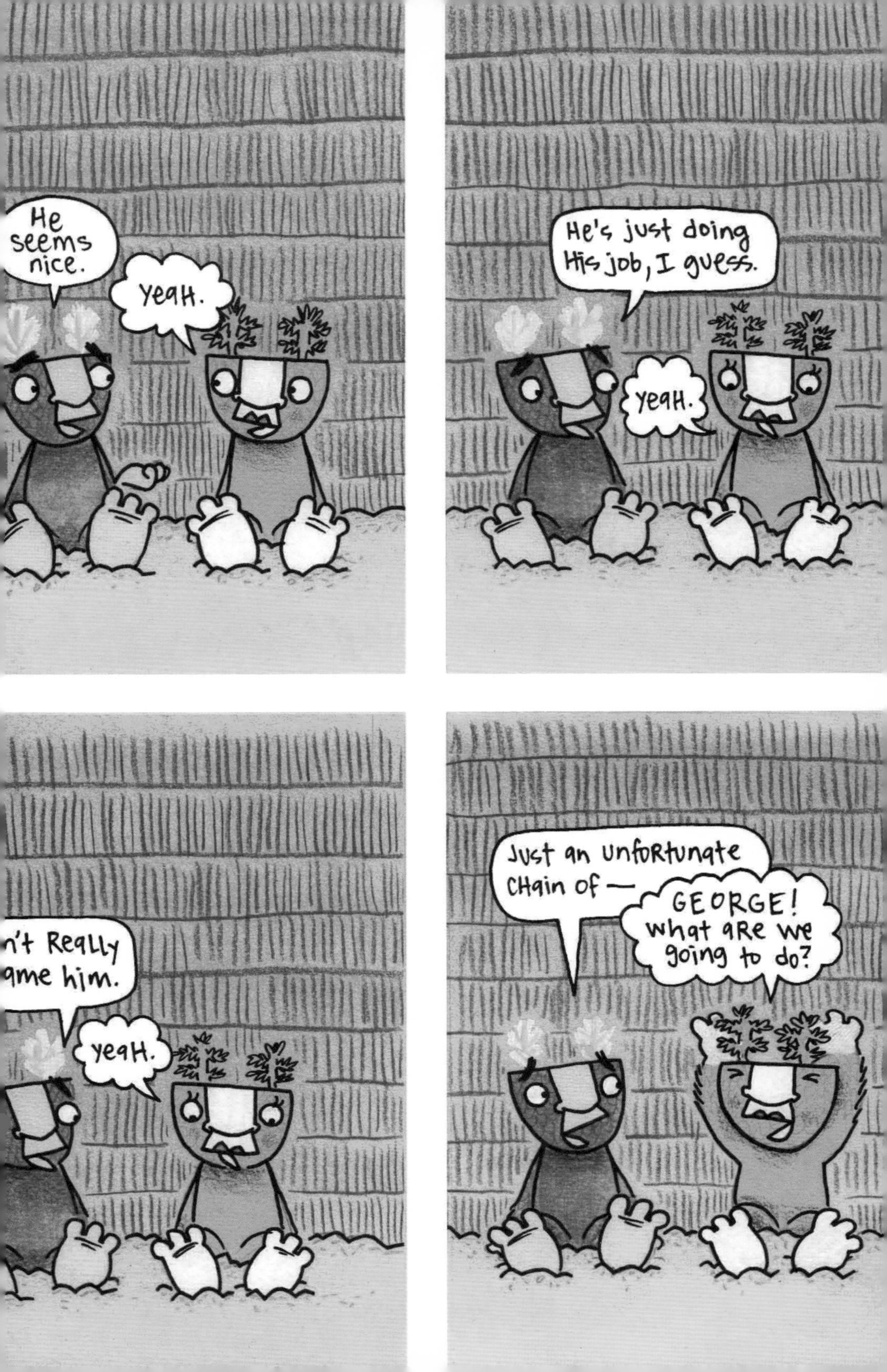
He seems nice.
yeah.
He's just doing His job, I guess.
yeah.
n't Really ame him.
yeah.
Just an unfortunate chain of —
GEORGE! what are we going to do?

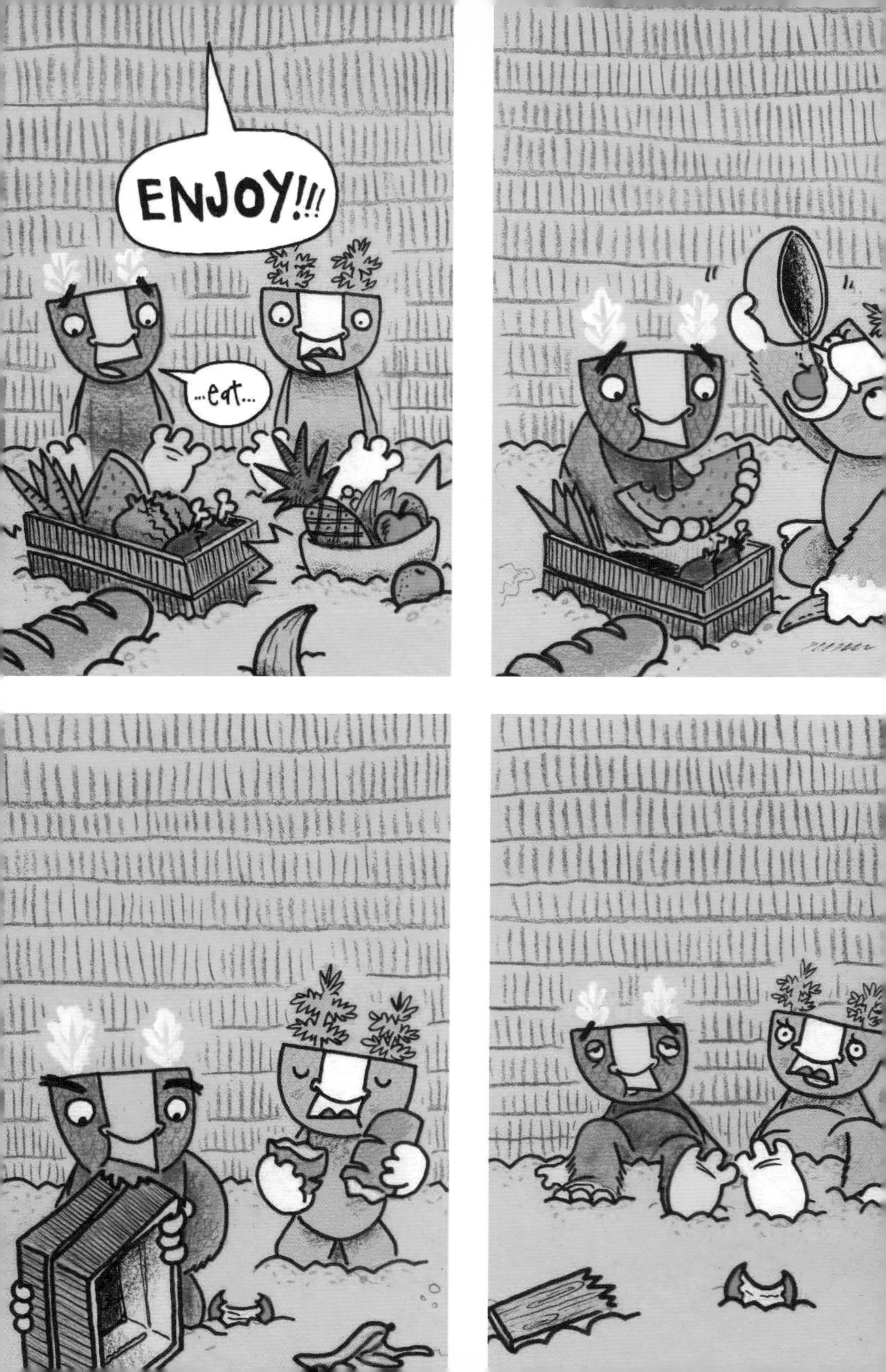
ENJOY!!!
...eat...

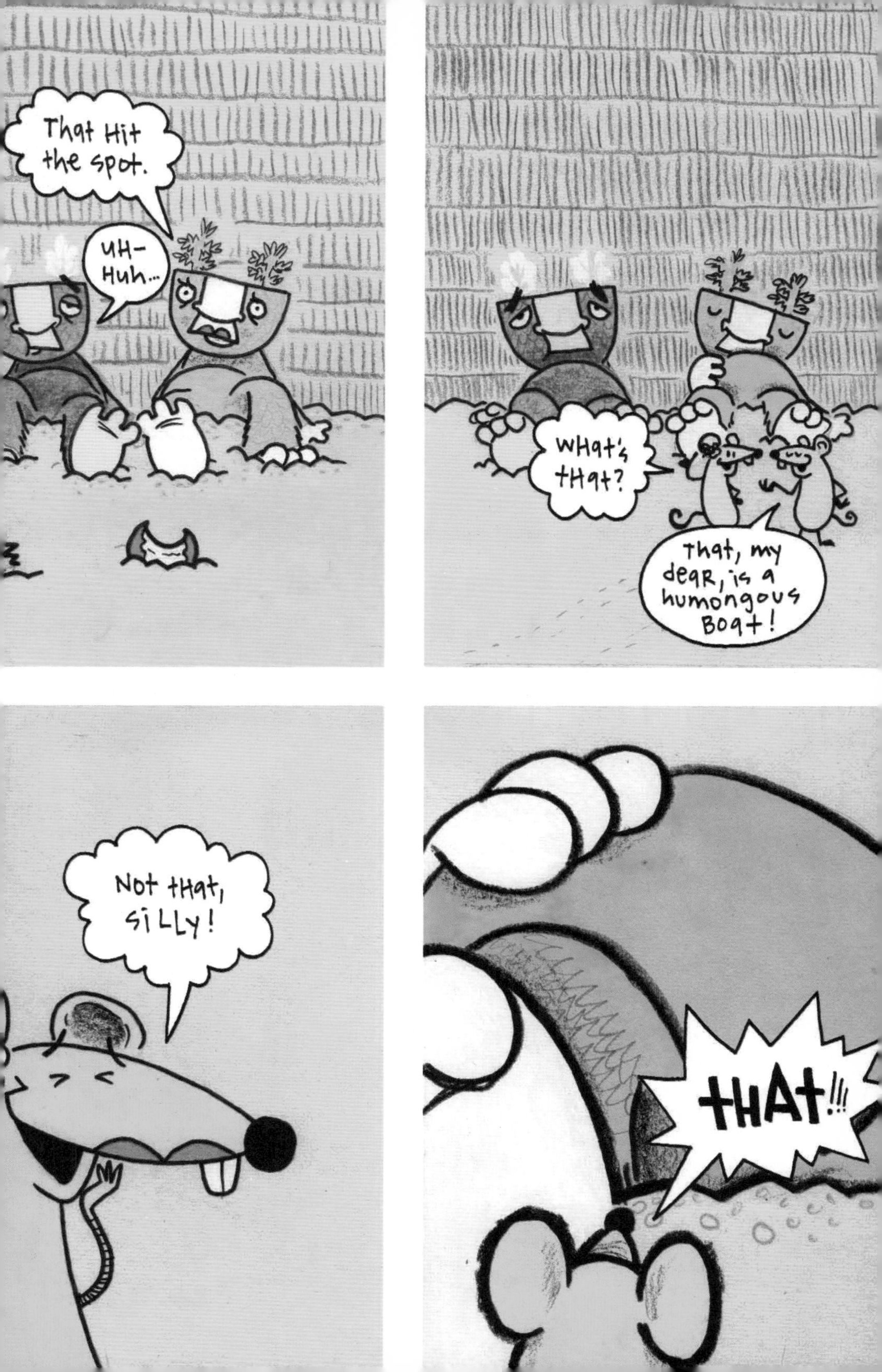
That Hit the spot.
UH-Huh...
WHat's tHat?
That, my dear, is a humongous Boat!
Not tHat, siLLy!
tHAt!!!

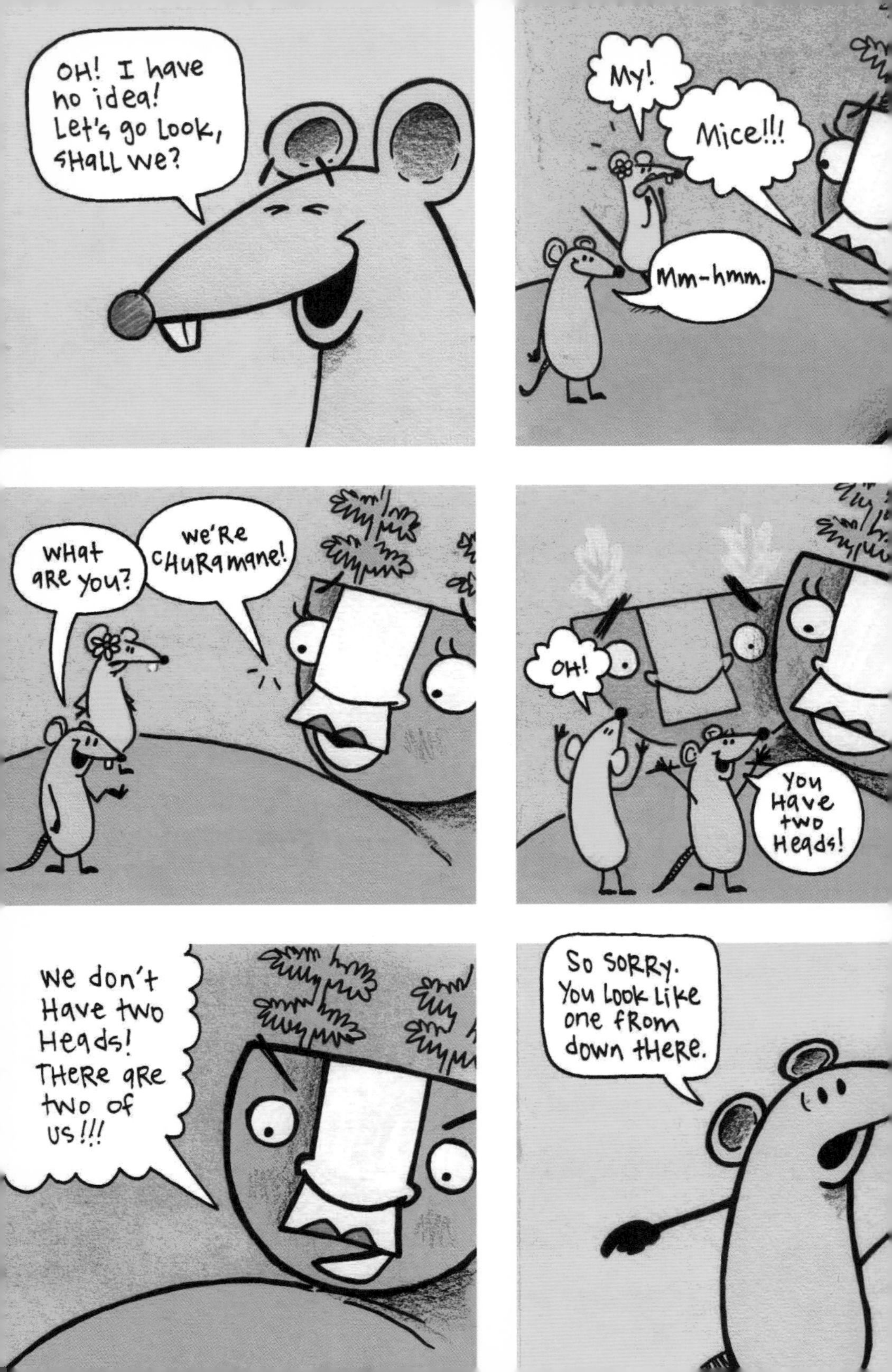
OH! I have no idea! Let's go look, SHALL we?
My!
Mice!!!
Mm-hmm.
WHat are you?
we're CHURamane!
OH!
You Have two Heads!
We don't Have two Heads! THERE are two of US!!!
So SORRY. You Look Like one FRom down THERE.

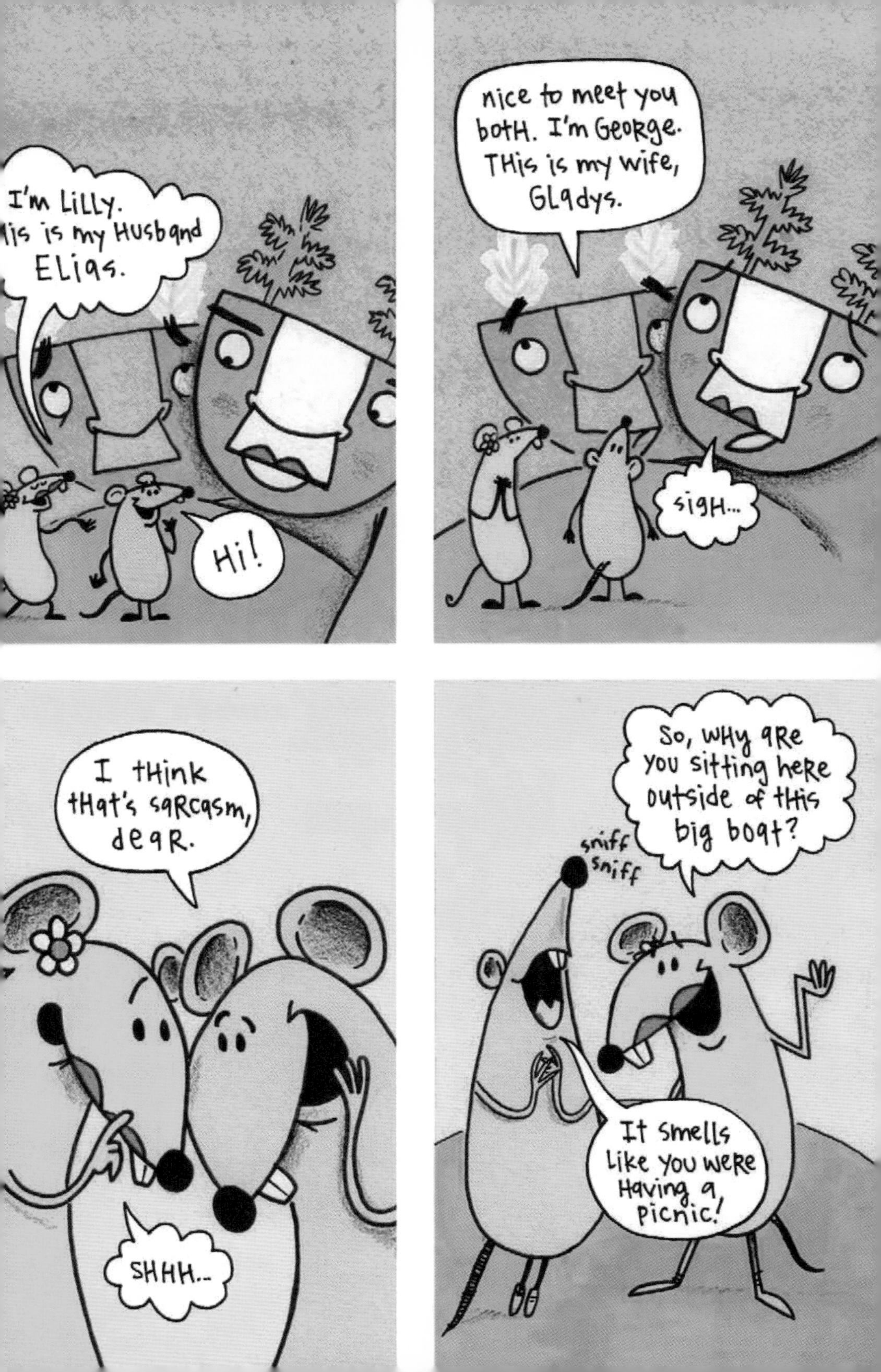

I'm Lilly. This is my Husband Elias.
Hi!
nice to meet you both. I'm George. This is my wife, Gladys.
sigh...
I think that's sarcasm, dear.
SHHH...
sniff sniff
So, why are you sitting here outside of this big boat?
It smells like you were having a picnic!

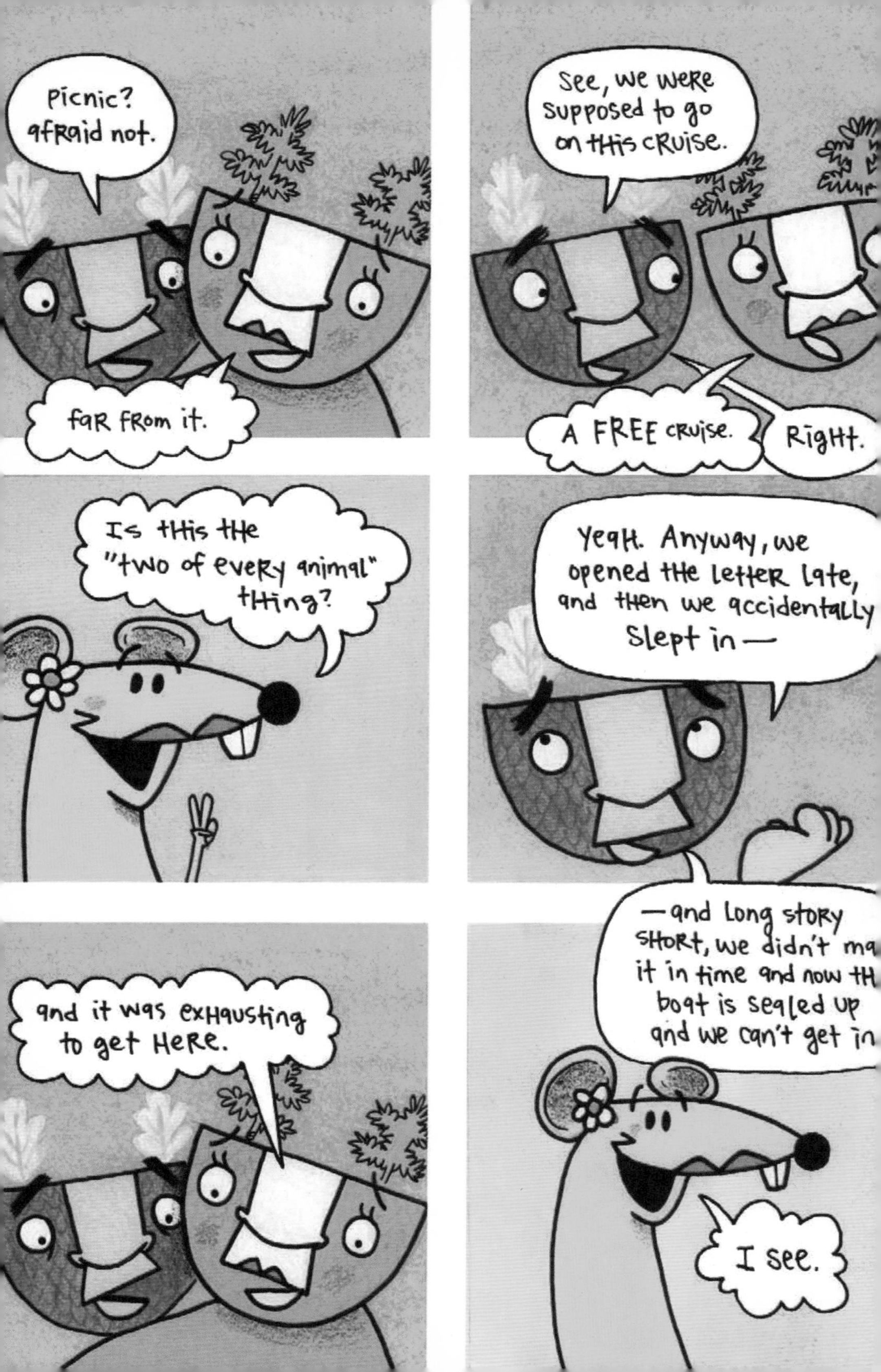
Picnic? afraid not.
far from it.
See, we were supposed to go on this cruise.
A FREE cruise.
Right.
Is this the "two of every animal" thing?
Yeah. Anyway, we opened the letter late, and then we accidentally slept in—
and it was exhausting to get here.
—and long story short, we didn't ma
it in time and now th
boat is sealed up
and we can't get in
I see.

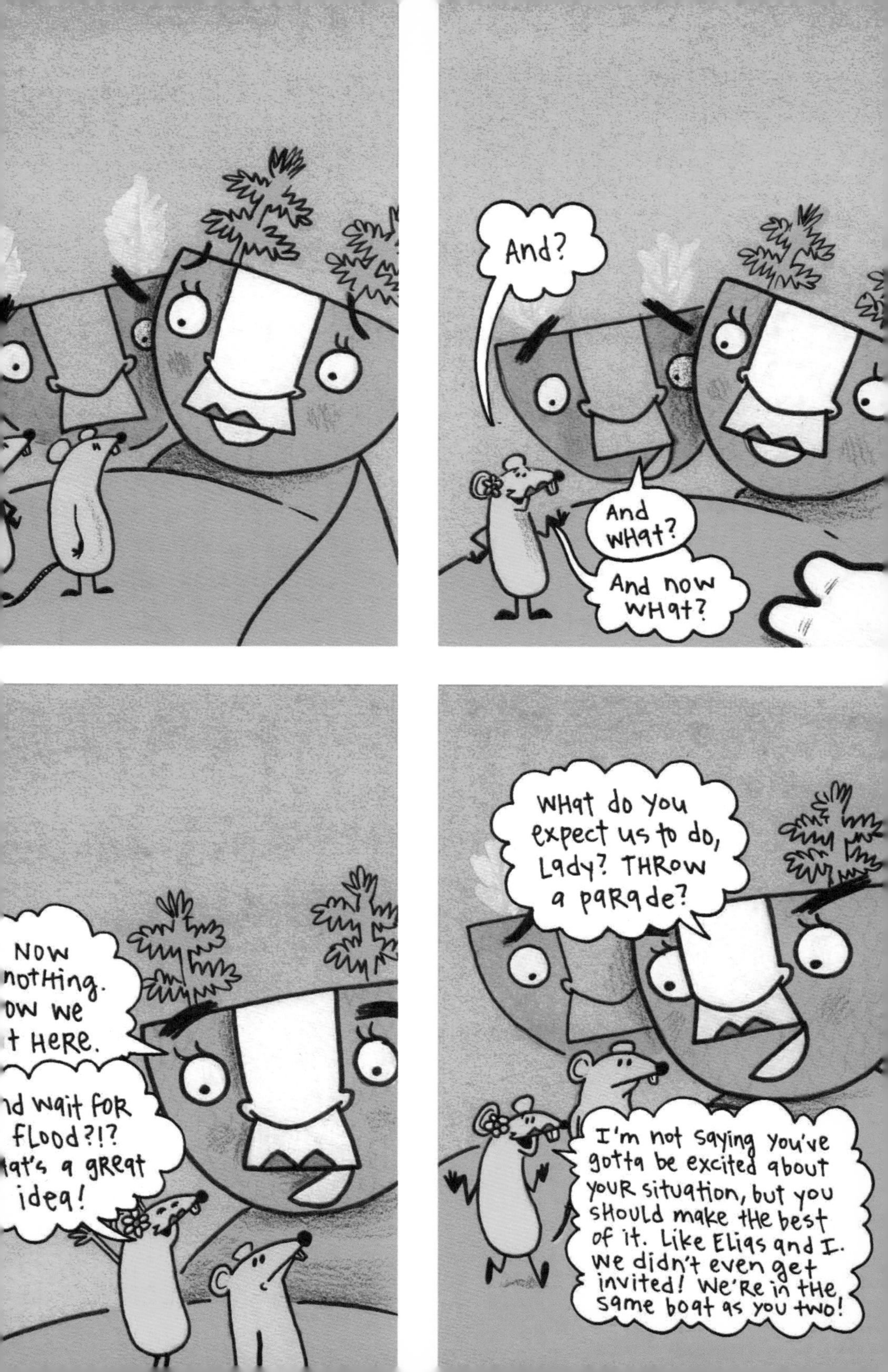
And?
And what?
And now what?
Now nothing. ow we t here.
d wait for flood?!? at's a great idea!
What do you expect us to do, Lady? Throw a parade?
I'm not saying you've gotta be excited about your situation, but you should make the best of it. Like Elias and I. We didn't even get invited! We're in the same boat as you two!

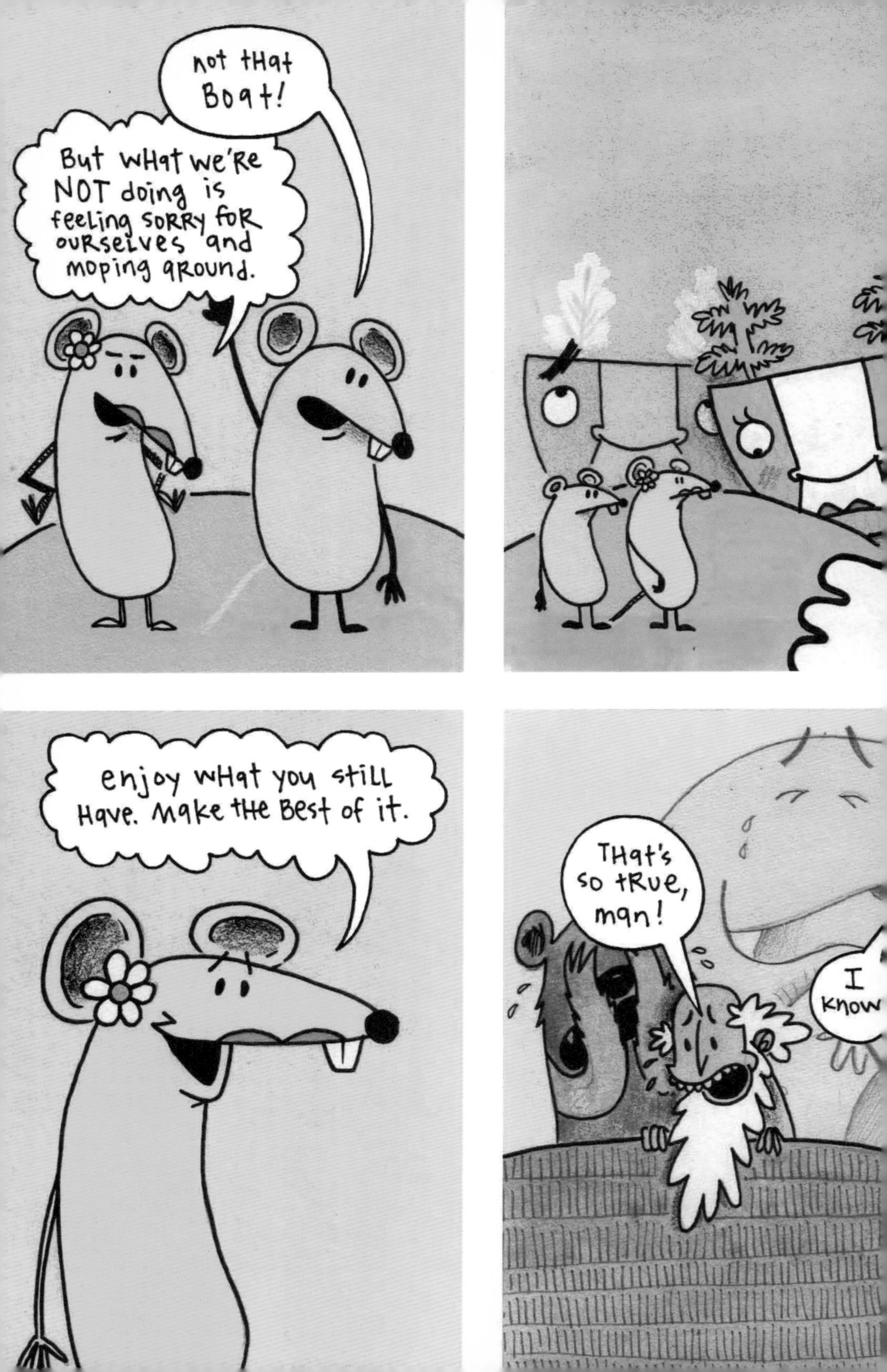
not tHat Boat!
But wHat we're NOT doing is feeling sorry for ourselves and moping around.
enjoy wHat you still Have. Make tHe Best of it.
THat's so tRue, man!
I know

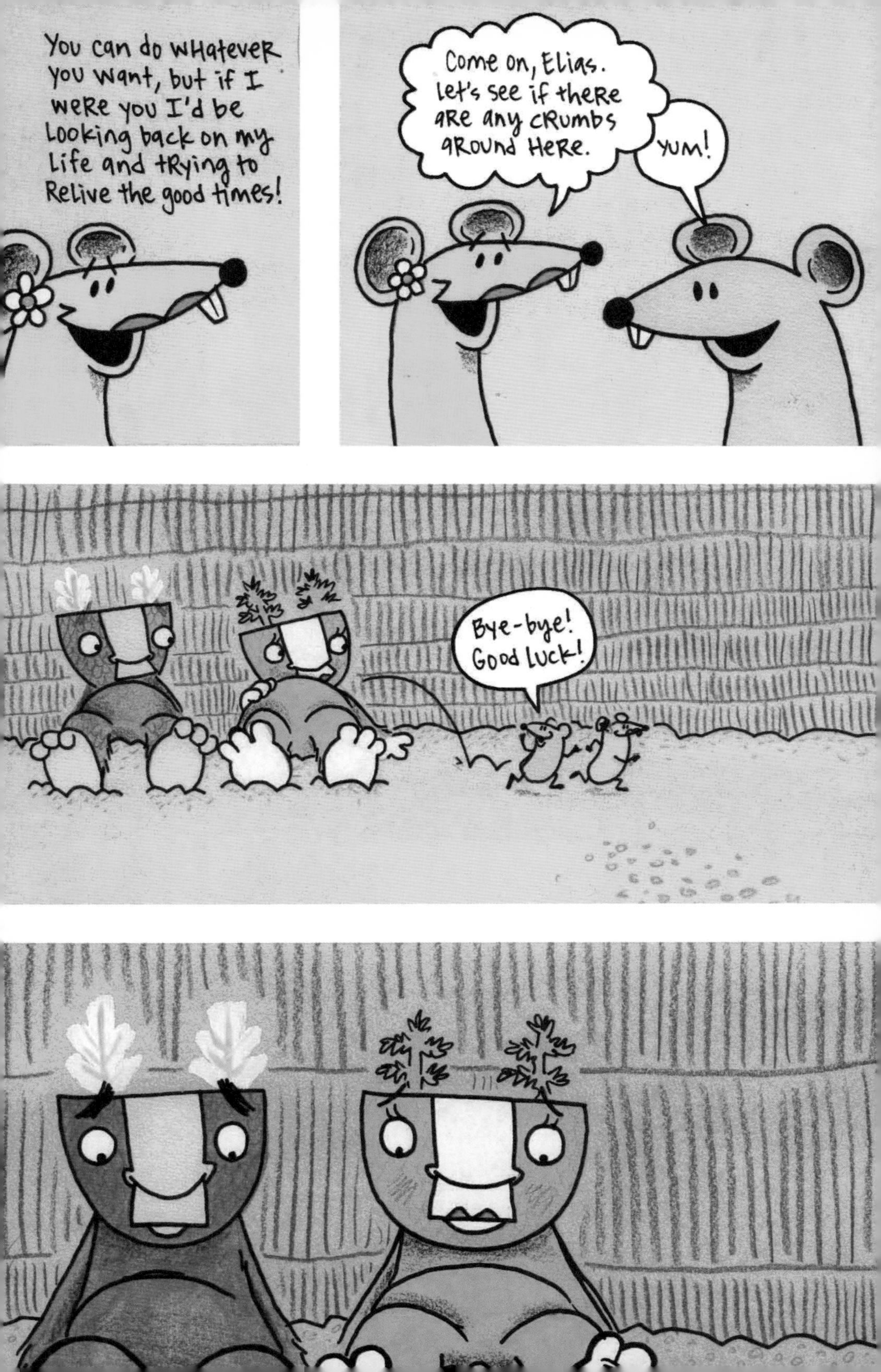
You can do whatever you want, but if I were you I'd be looking back on my life and trying to relive the good times!
Come on, Elias. Let's see if there are any crumbs around here.
YUM!
Bye-bye! Good luck!

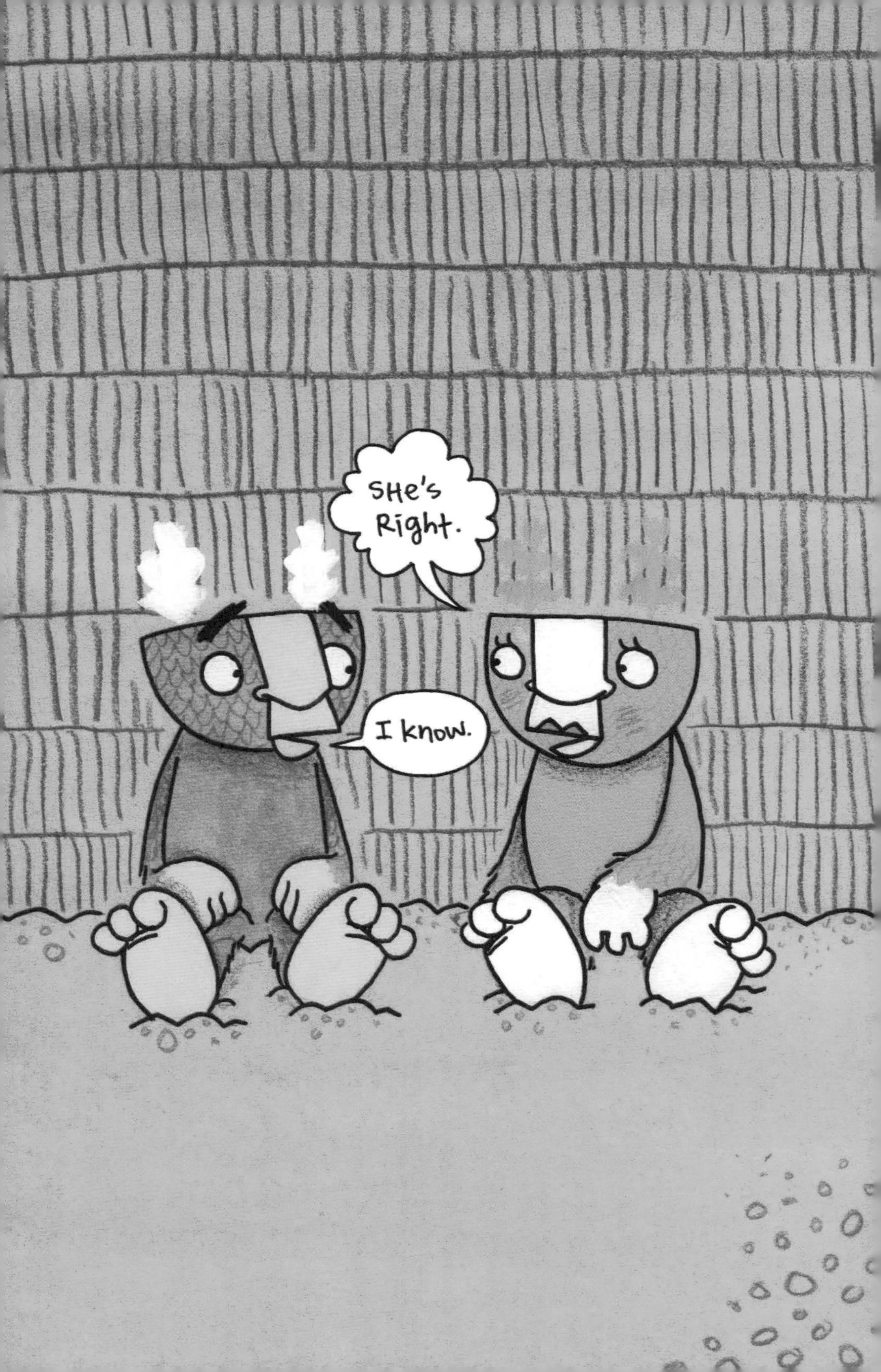
SHe's Right.
I know.

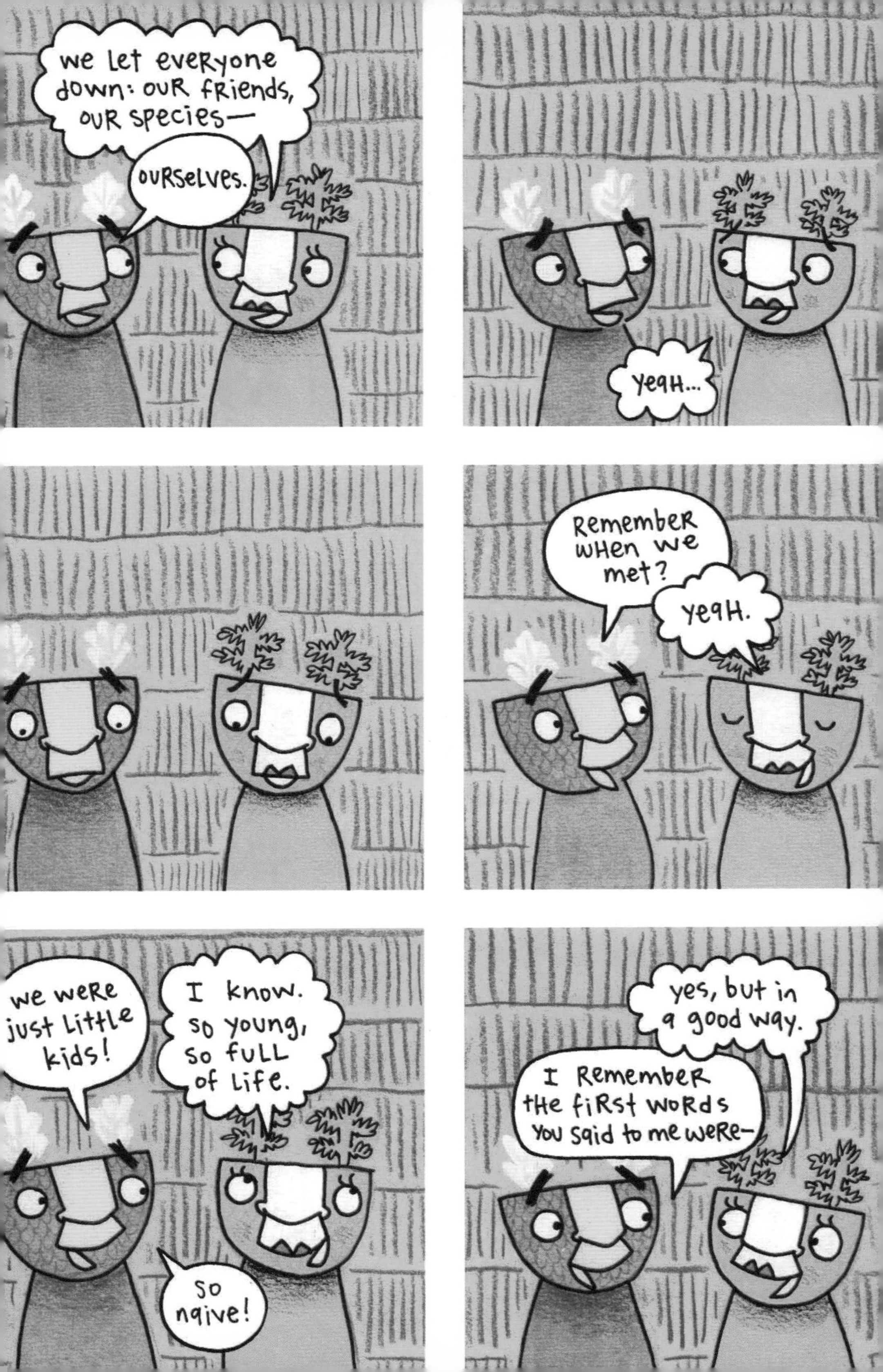
we let everyone down: our friends, our species—
ourselves.
yeah...
Remember when we met?
yeah.
we were just little kids!
I know. so young, so full of life.
so naive!
I Remember the first words you said to me were—
yes, but in a good way.

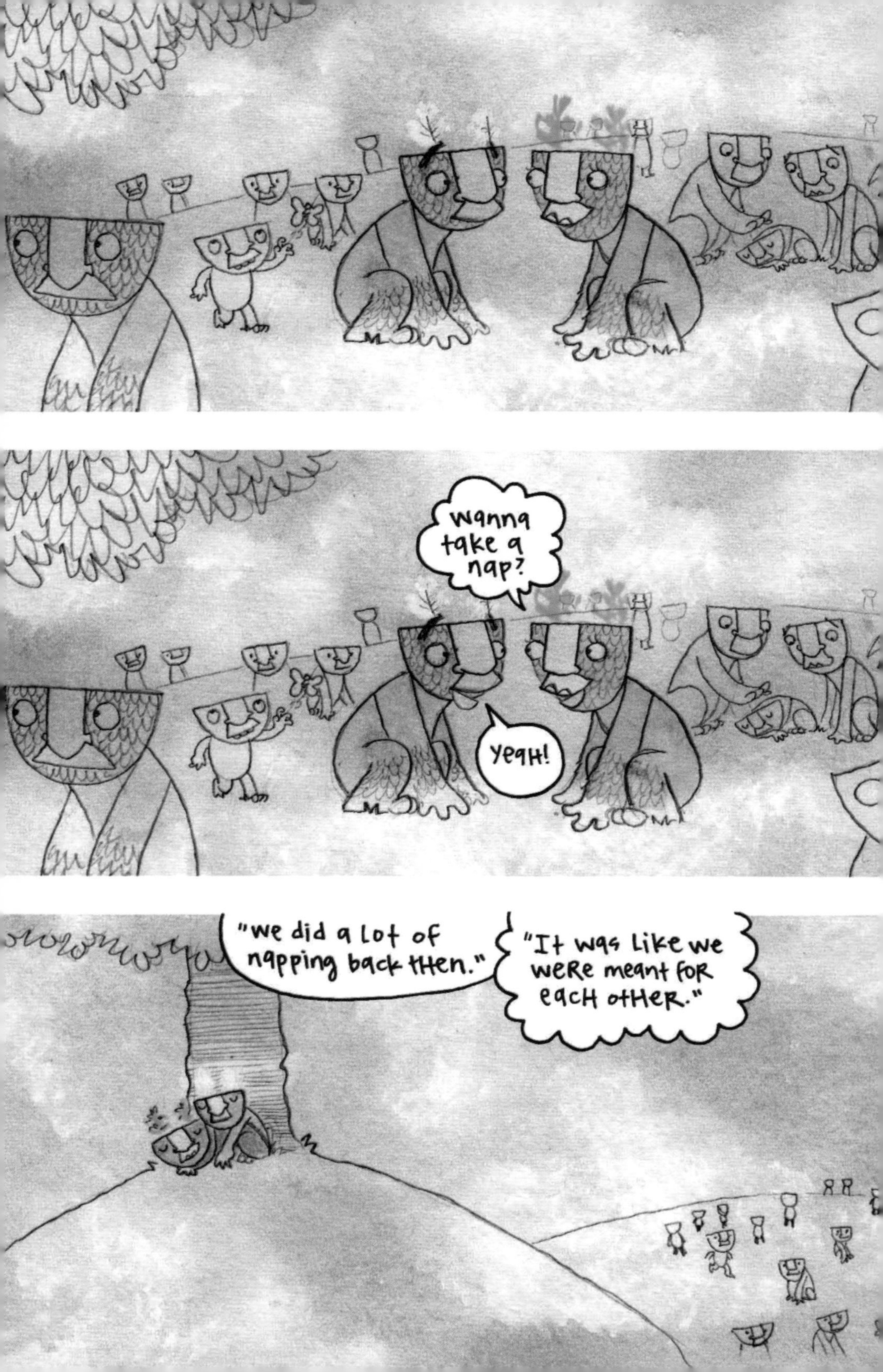
wanna take a nap?
yeah!
"we did a lot of napping back then."
"It was like we were meant for each other."

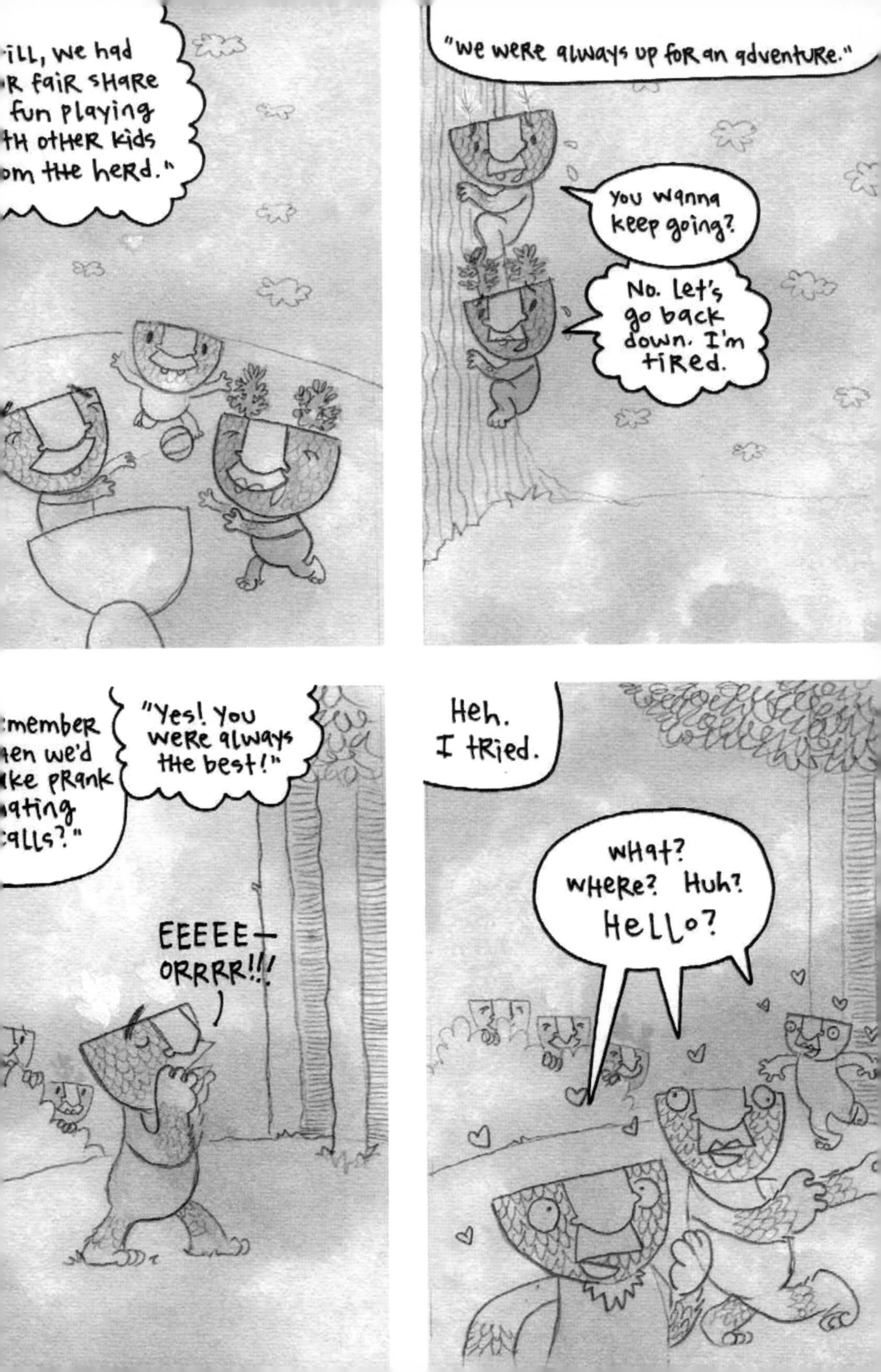
ILL, WE HAD
R FAIR SHARE
FUN PLAYING
TH OTHER KIDS
OM THE HERD."
"WE WERE ALWAYS UP FOR AN ADVENTURE."
YOU WANNA KEEP GOING?
NO. LET'S GO BACK DOWN. I'M TIRED.
MEMBER
EN WE'D
KE PRANK
ATING
ALLS?"
"YES! YOU WERE ALWAYS THE BEST!"
EEEEE—ORRRR!!!
HEH. I TRIED.
WHAT? WHERE? HUH? HELLO?

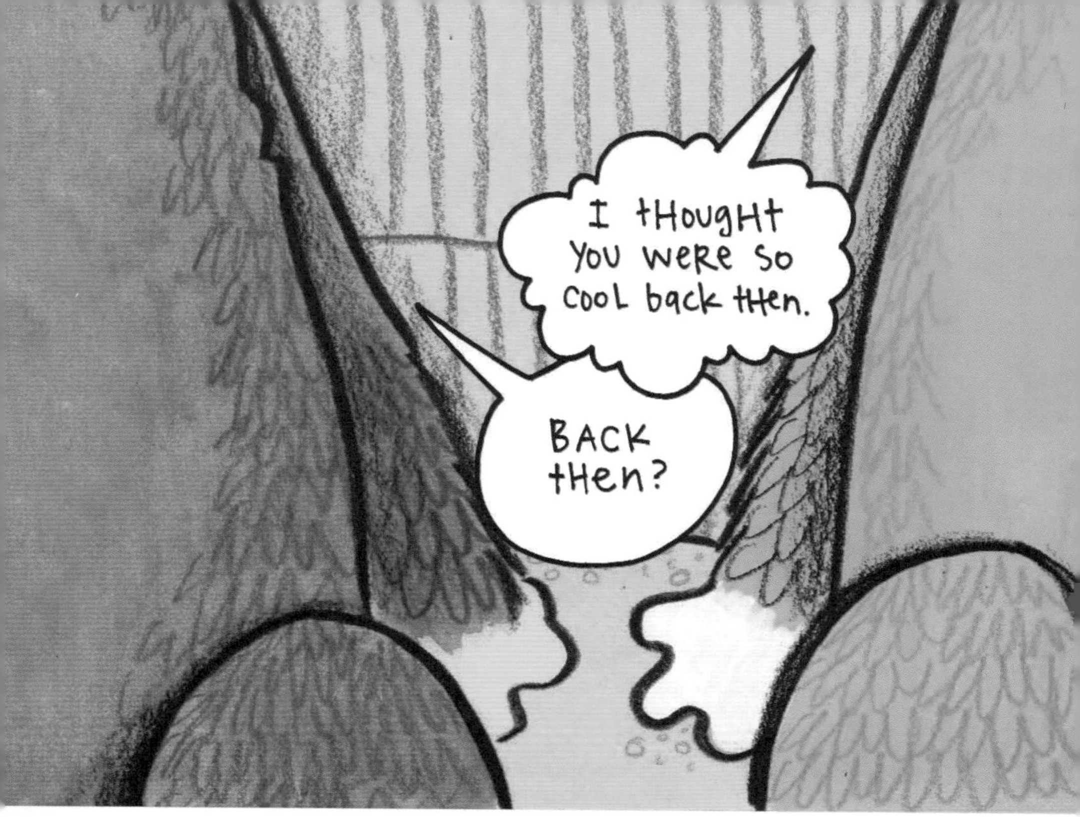
I thought you were so cool back then.
BACK then?

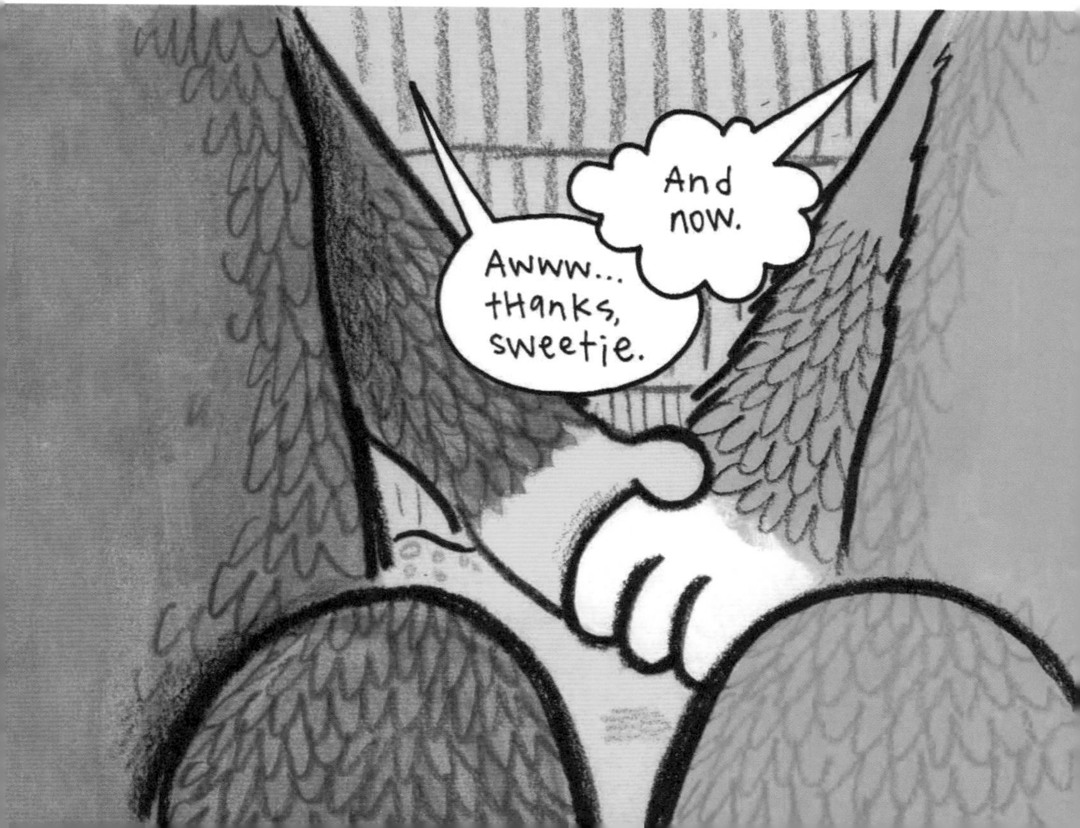
And now.
Awww... thanks, sweetie.

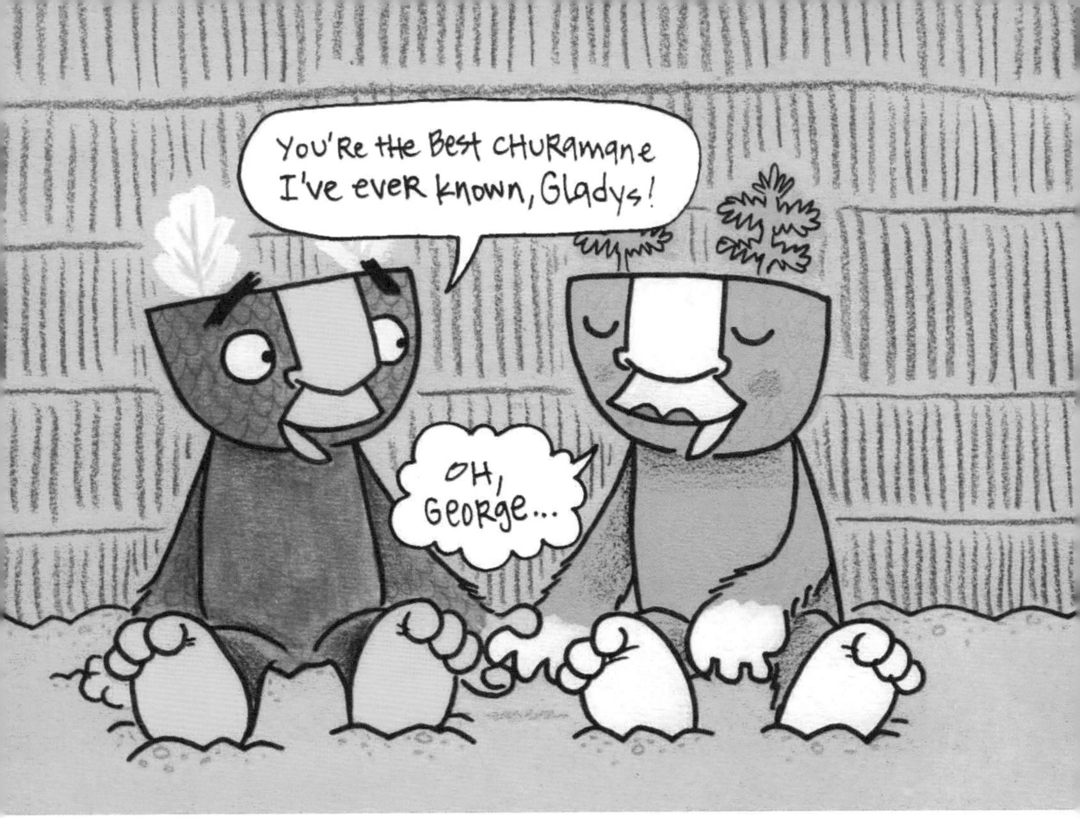
You're the Best CHURamane I've ever known, Gladys!
OH, George...

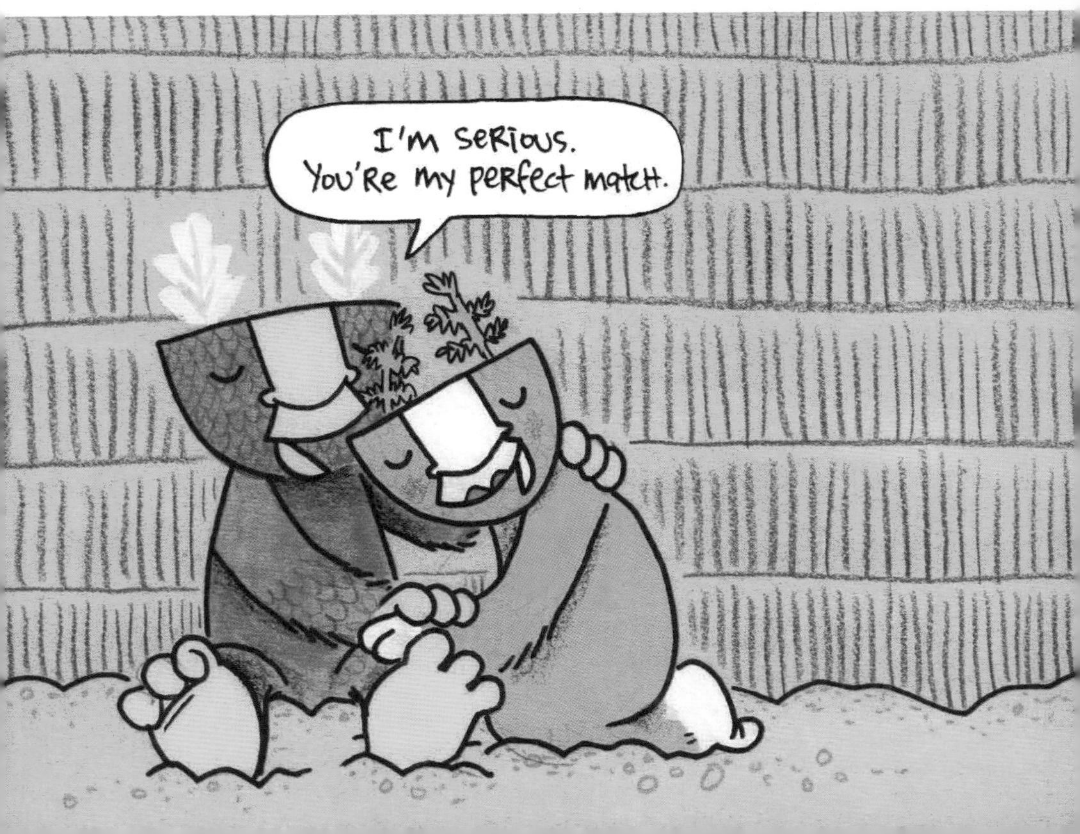
I'm SeRious. You're my perfect match.

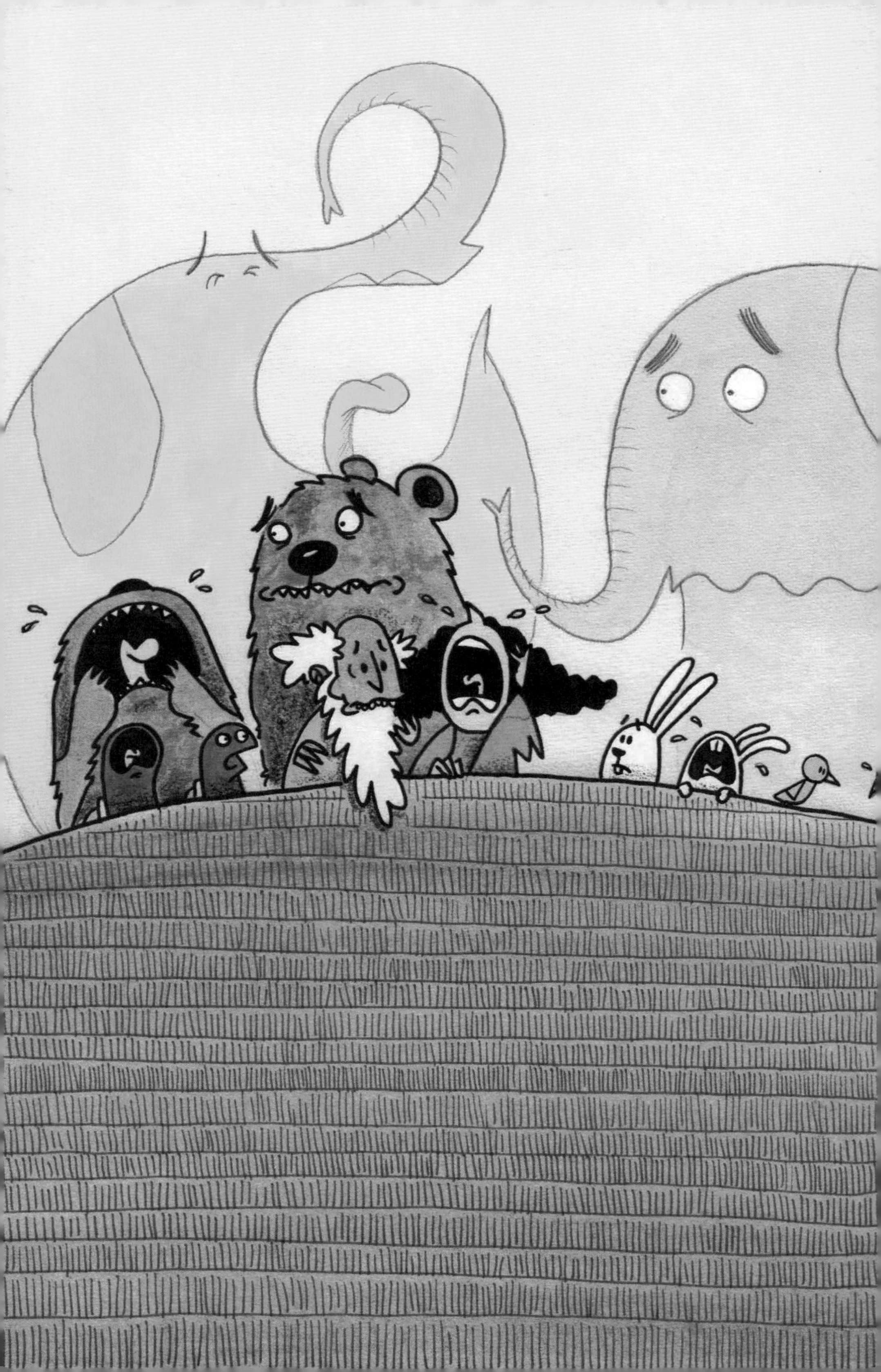

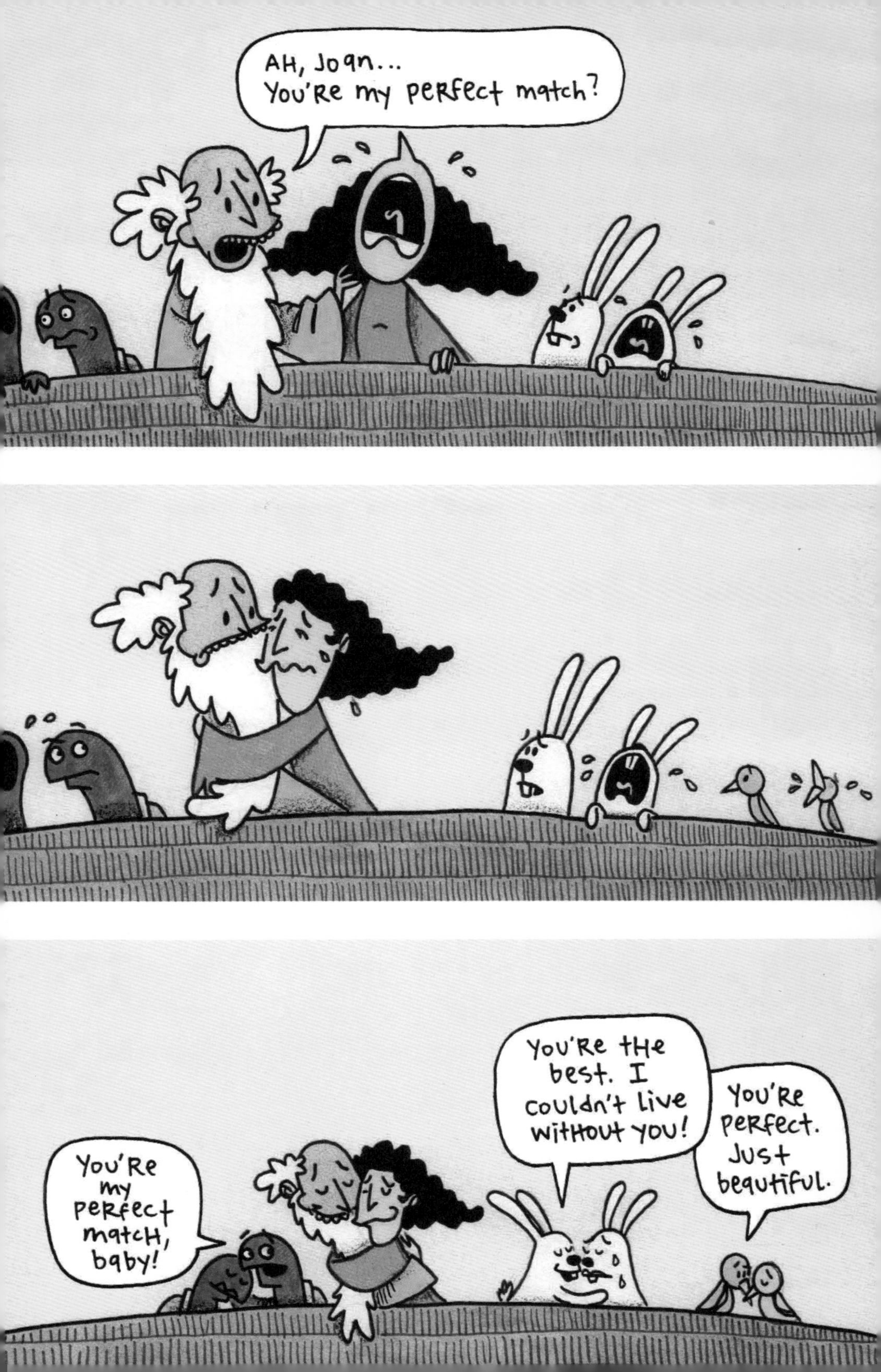
AH, Joan...
You're my perfect match?
You're my perfect match, baby!
You're the best. I couldn't live without you!
You're perfect. Just beautiful.

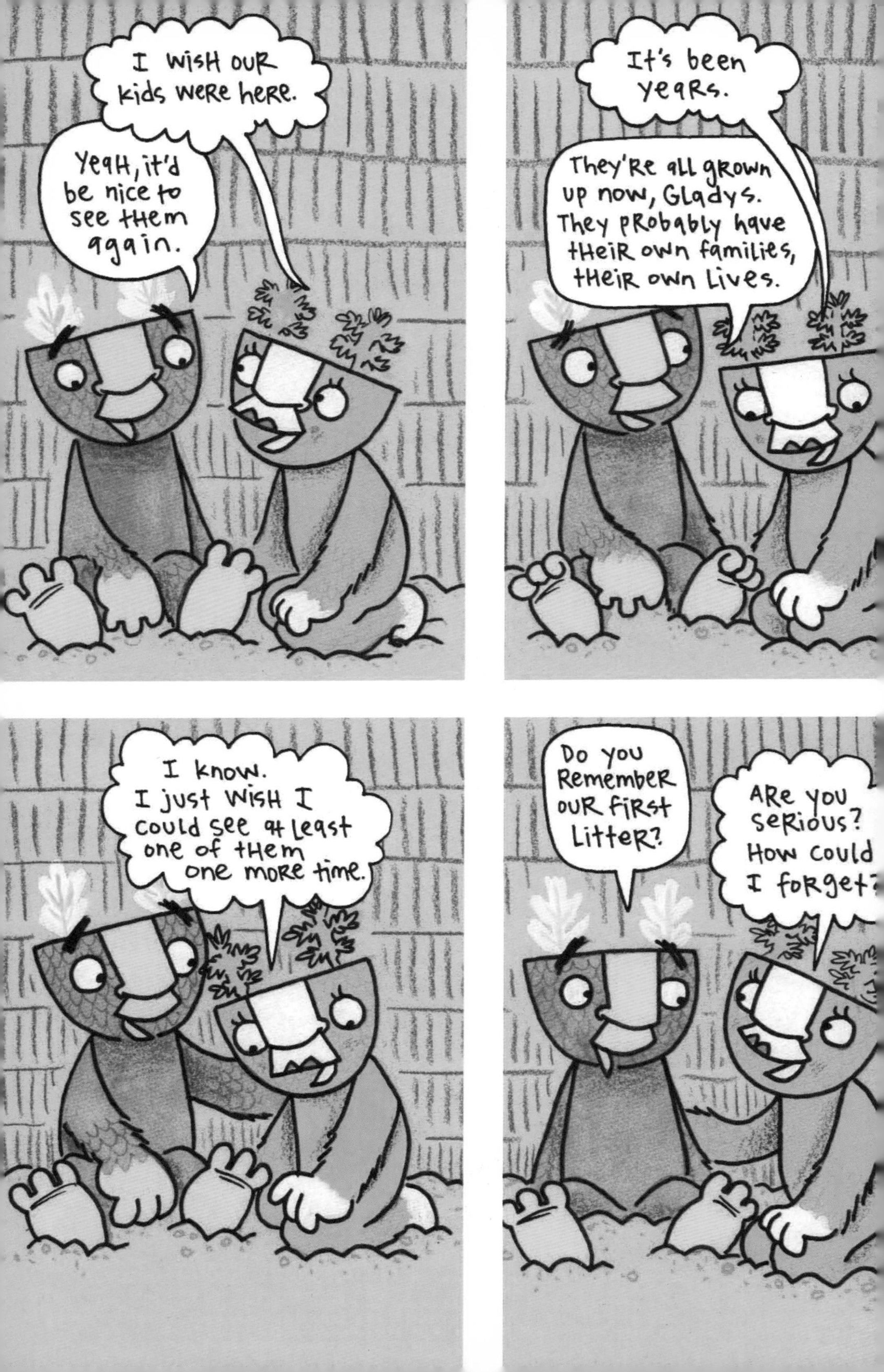
I WISH OUR kids WERE here.
YeaH, it'd be nice to see tHem again.
It's been years.
They're all grown up now, Gladys. They probably have tHeir own families, tHeir own Lives.
I know. I just WISH I could see at Least one of tHem one more time.
Do you Remember our first Litter?
Are you serious? How could I forget?

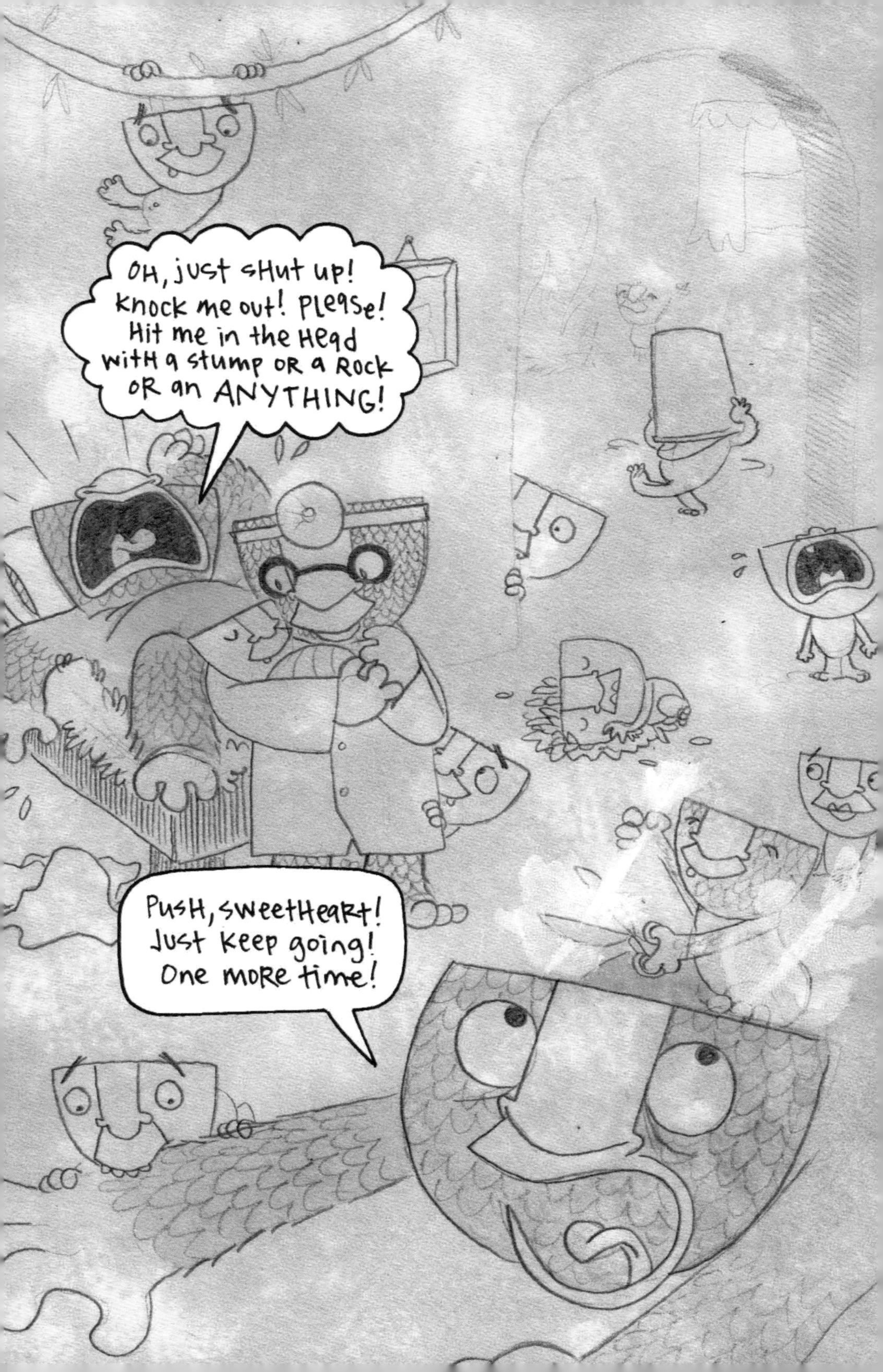
OH, JUST SHUT UP! KNOCK ME OUT! PLEASE! HIT ME IN THE HEAD WITH A STUMP OR A ROCK OR AN ANYTHING!
PUSH, SWEETHEART! JUST KEEP GOING! ONE MORE TIME!

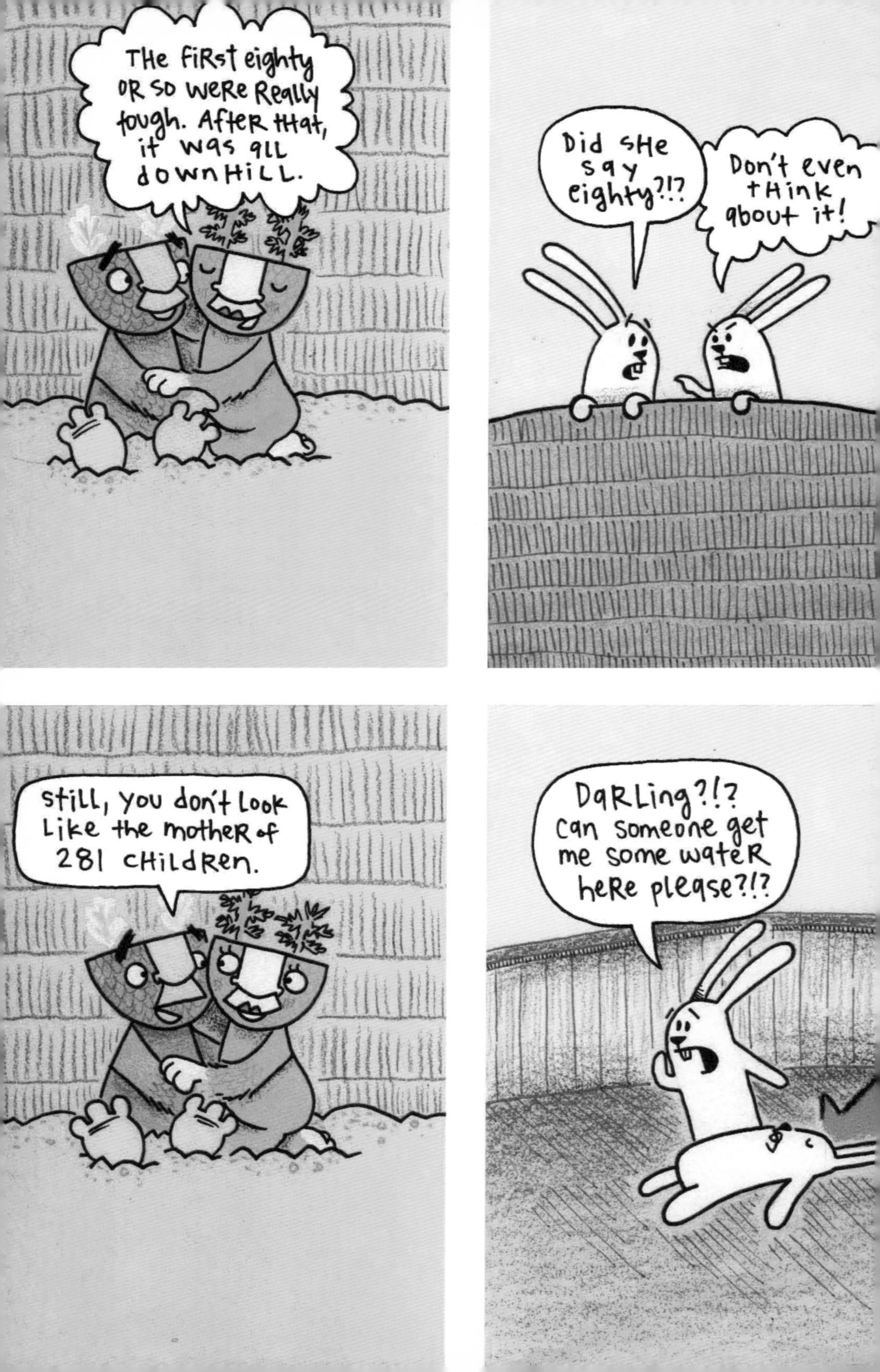
THE FIRst eighty OR SO WERE Really tough. After that, it was all downHILL.
Did sHe say eighty?!?
Don't even tHink about it!
still, you don't Look Like the mother of 281 CHildRen.
DaRLing?!? can someone get me some water here please?!?

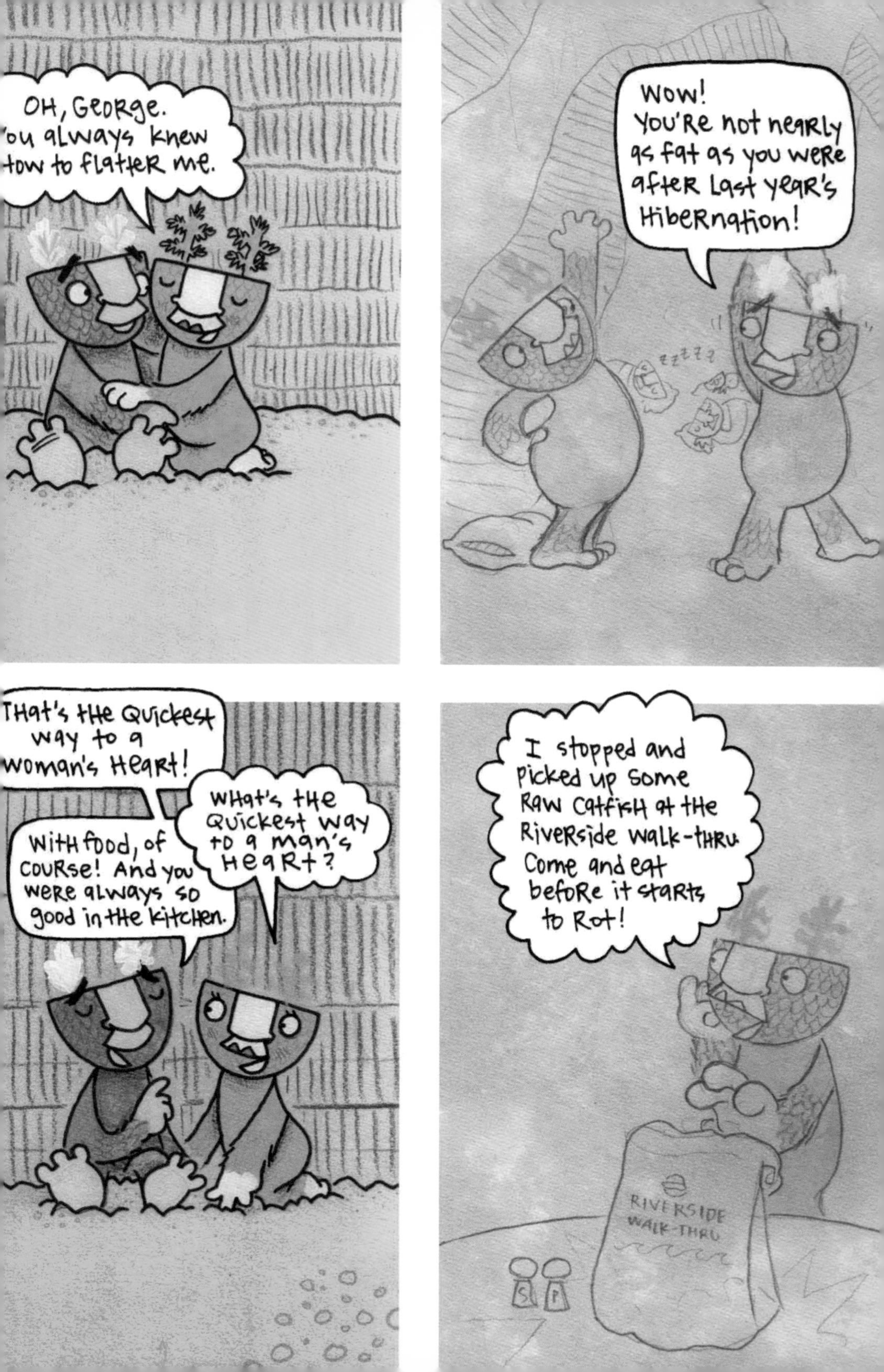
OH, GEORGE. 'OU ALWAYS KNEW HOW TO FLATTER ME.
WOW! YOU'RE NOT NEARLY AS FAT AS YOU WERE AFTER LAST YEAR'S HIBERNATION!
THAT'S THE QUICKEST WAY TO A WOMAN'S HEART!
WHAT'S THE QUICKEST WAY TO A MAN'S HEART?
WITH FOOD, OF COURSE! AND YOU WERE ALWAYS SO GOOD IN THE KITCHEN.
I STOPPED AND PICKED UP SOME RAW CATFISH AT THE RIVERSIDE WALK-THRU. COME AND EAT BEFORE IT STARTS TO ROT!
RIVERSIDE WALK-THRU
S
P

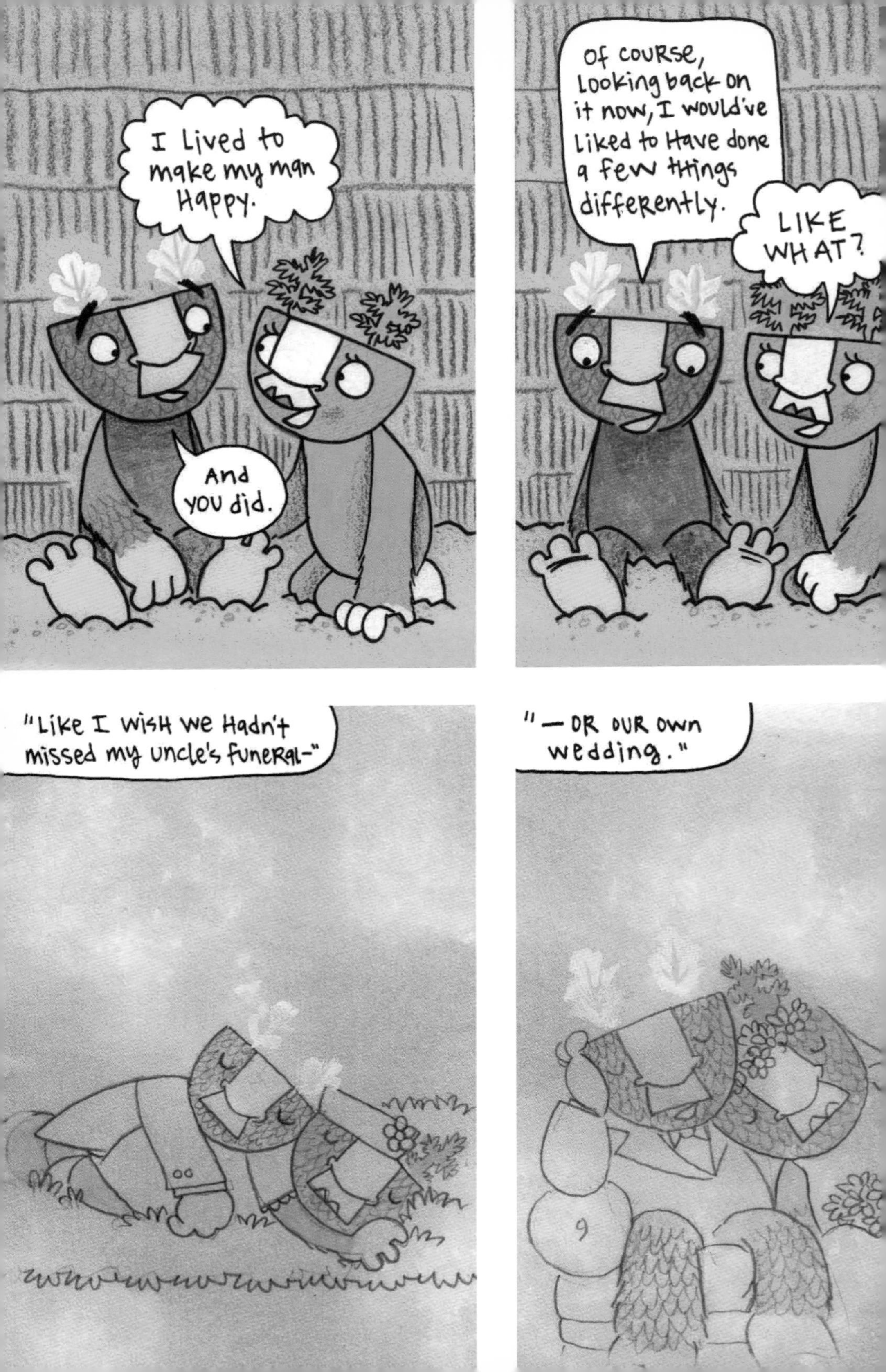
I lived to make my man Happy.
And you did.
Of course, looking back on it now, I would've liked to have done a few things differently.
LIKE WHAT?
"Like I wish we hadn't missed my uncle's funeral-"
"—or our own wedding."

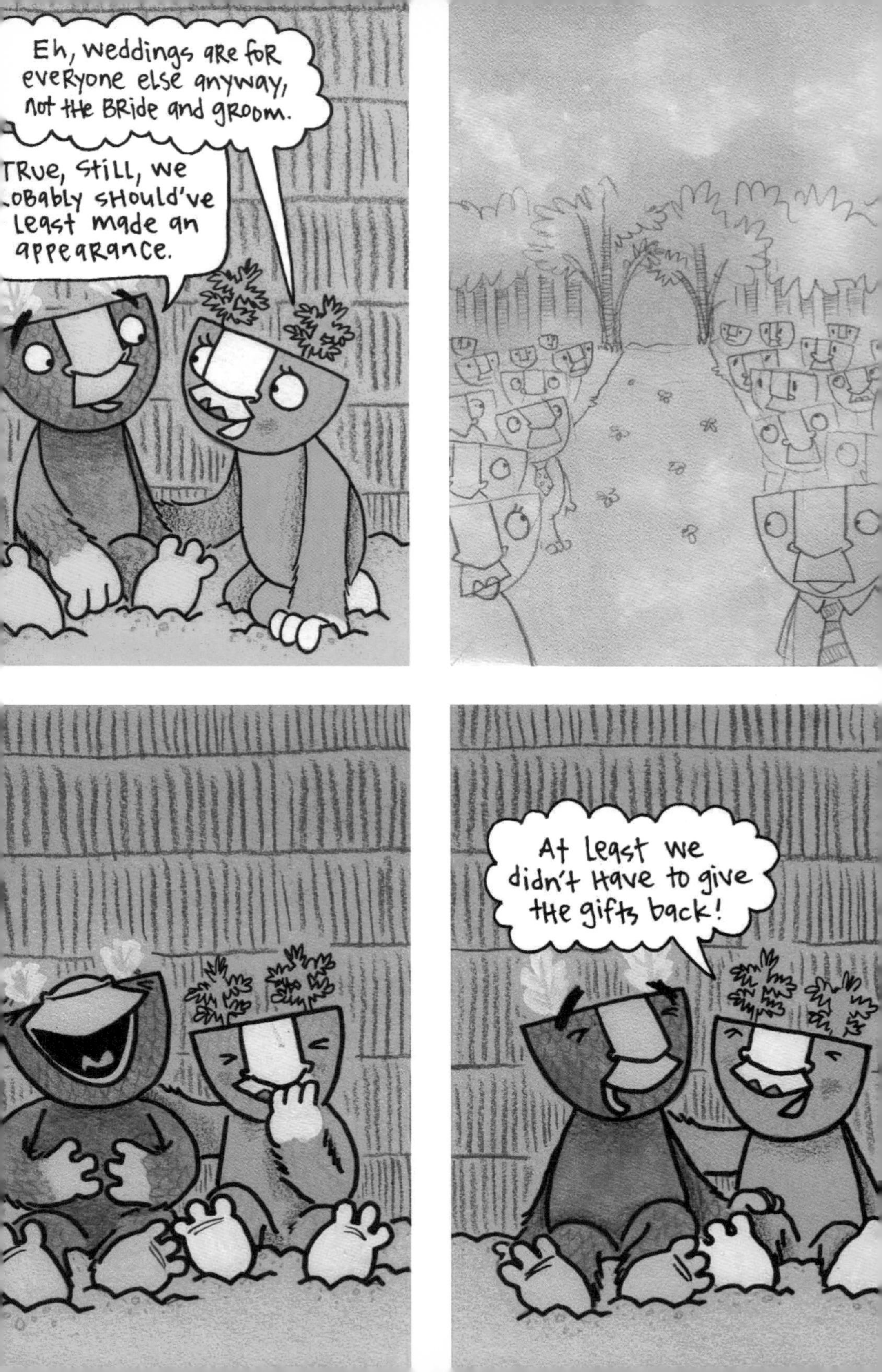
Eh, weddings are for everyone else anyway, not the bride and groom.
True, still, we ...obably should've ... least made an appearance.
At least we didn't have to give the gifts back!

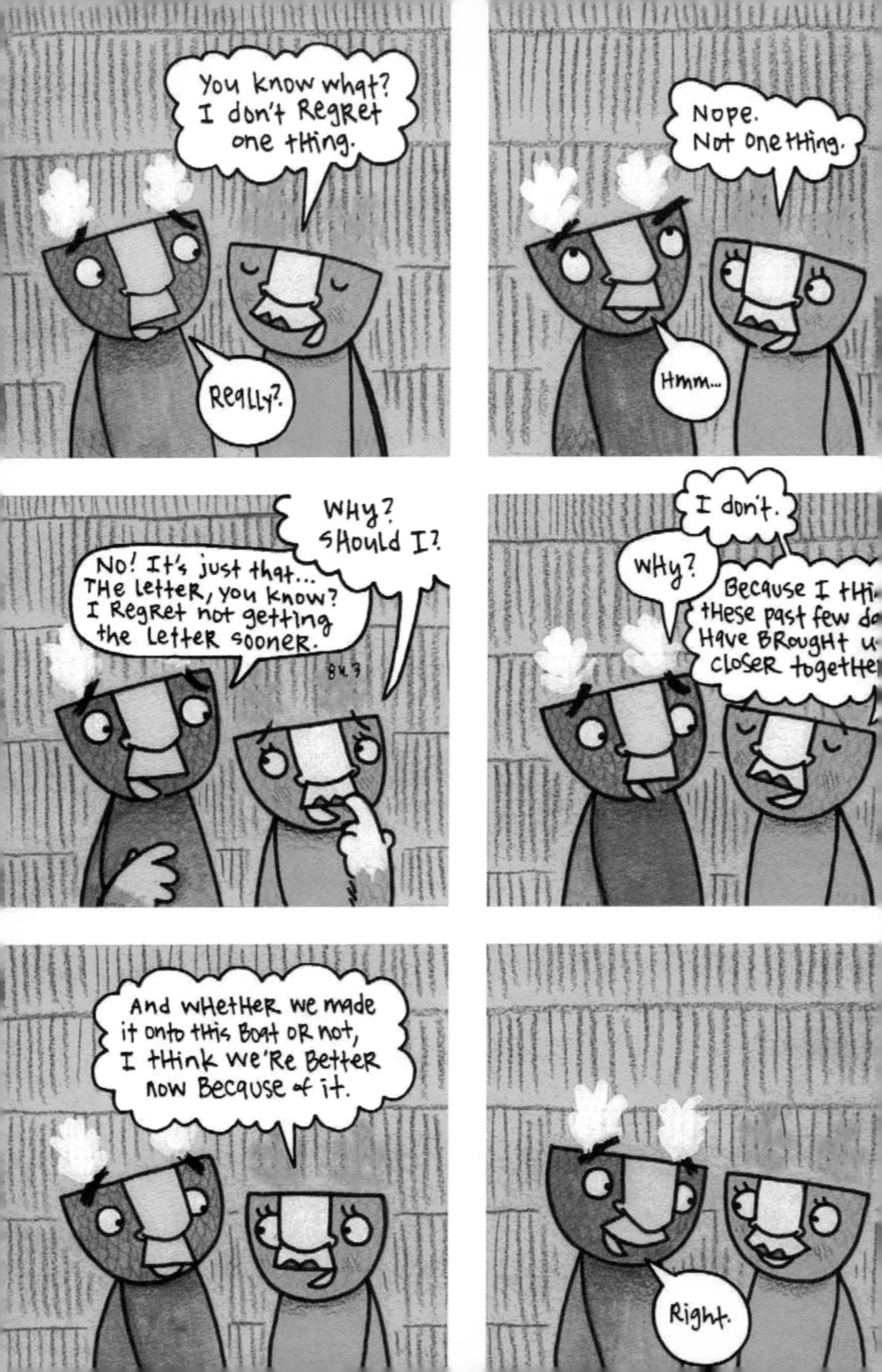
You know what? I don't Regret one thing.
Really?
Nope. Not one thing.
Hmm...
Why? Should I?
No! It's just that... The letter, you know? I Regret not getting the letter sooner.
I don't.
Why?
Because I thi these past few da Have Brought u closer togethe
And whether we made it onto this Boat or not, I think we're Better now Because of it.
Right.

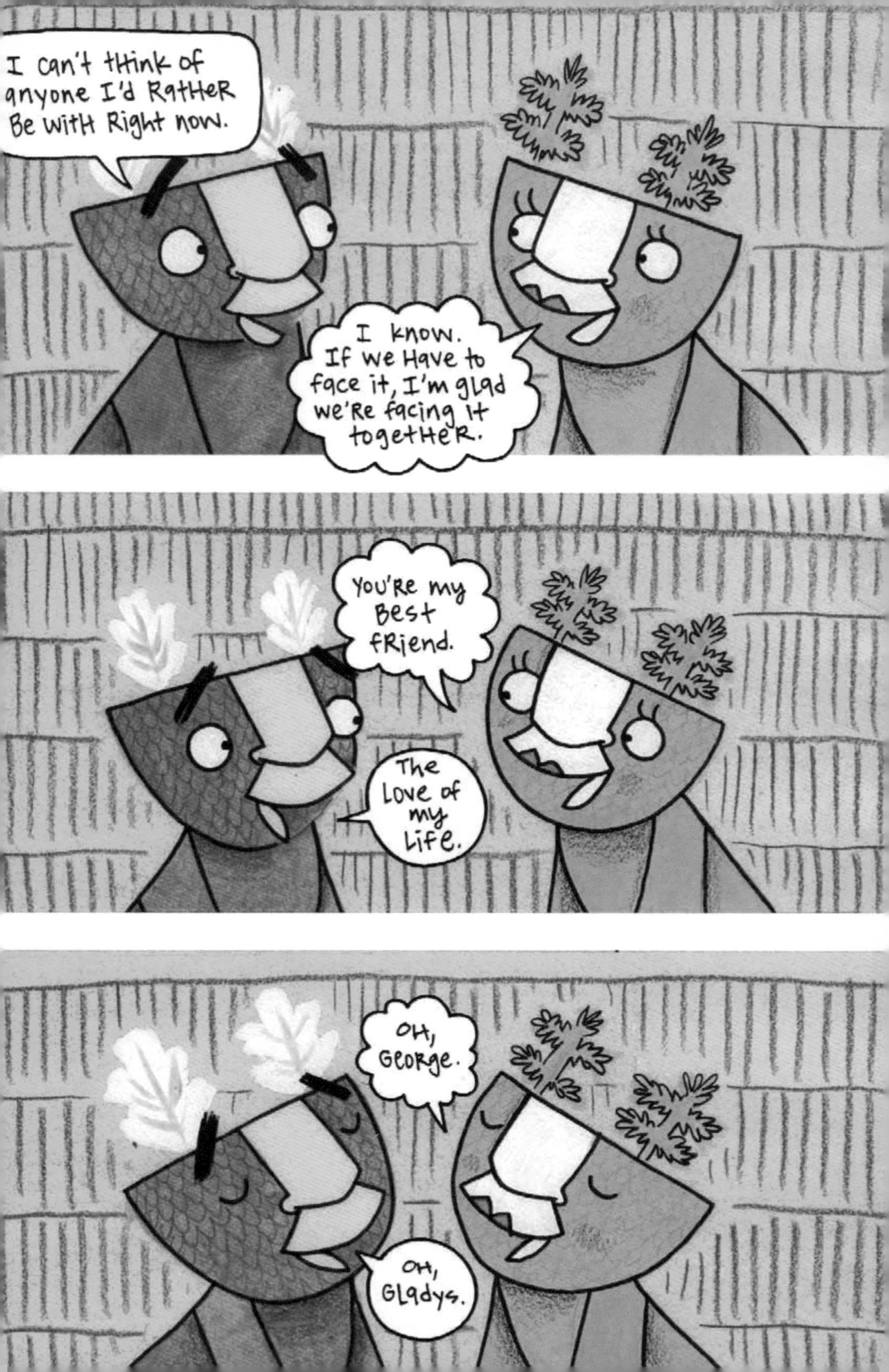
I can't think of anyone I'd rather be with right now.
I know. If we have to face it, I'm glad we're facing it together.
You're my best friend.
The love of my life.
Oh, George.
Oh, Gladys.

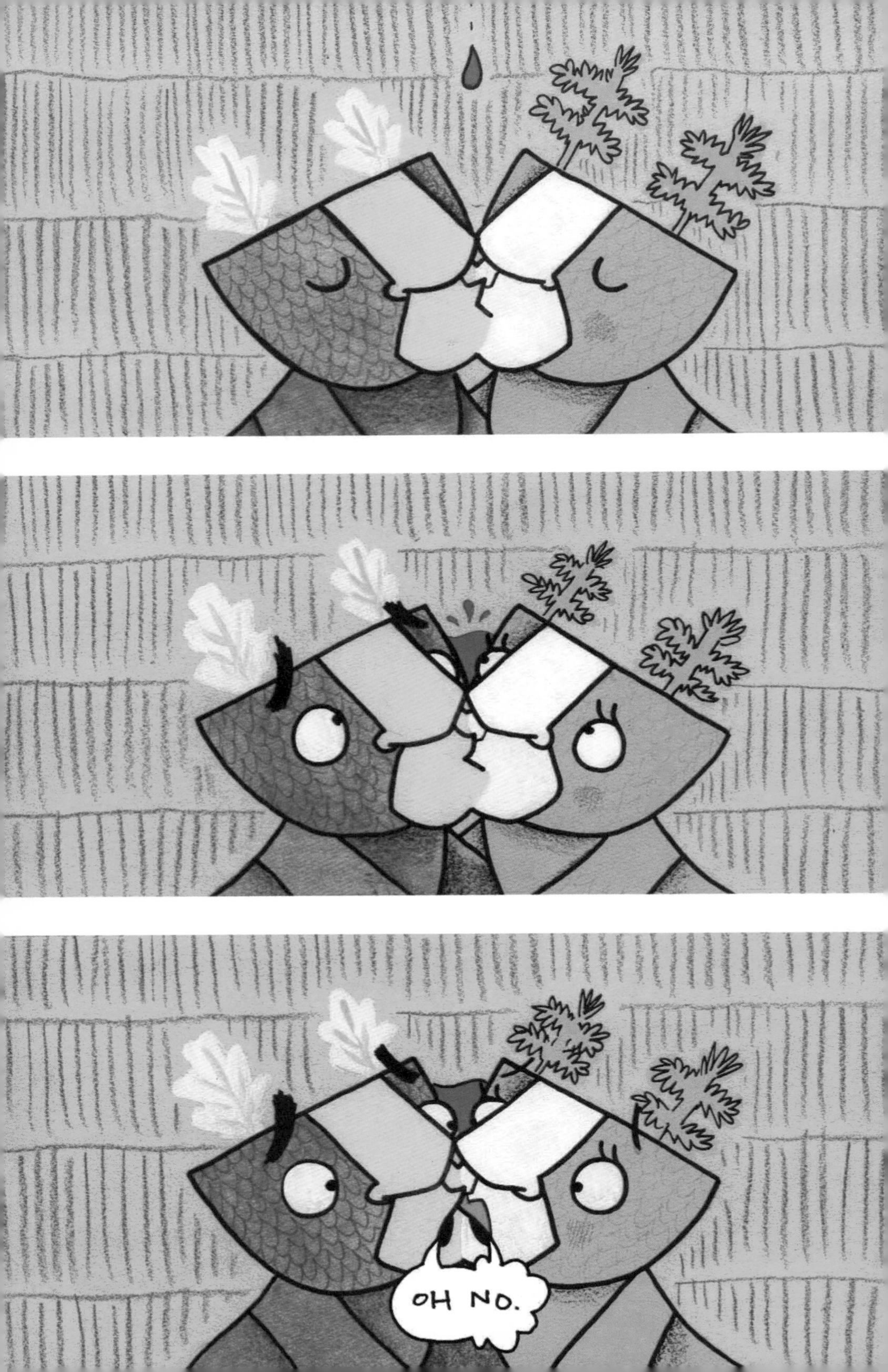
OH NO.

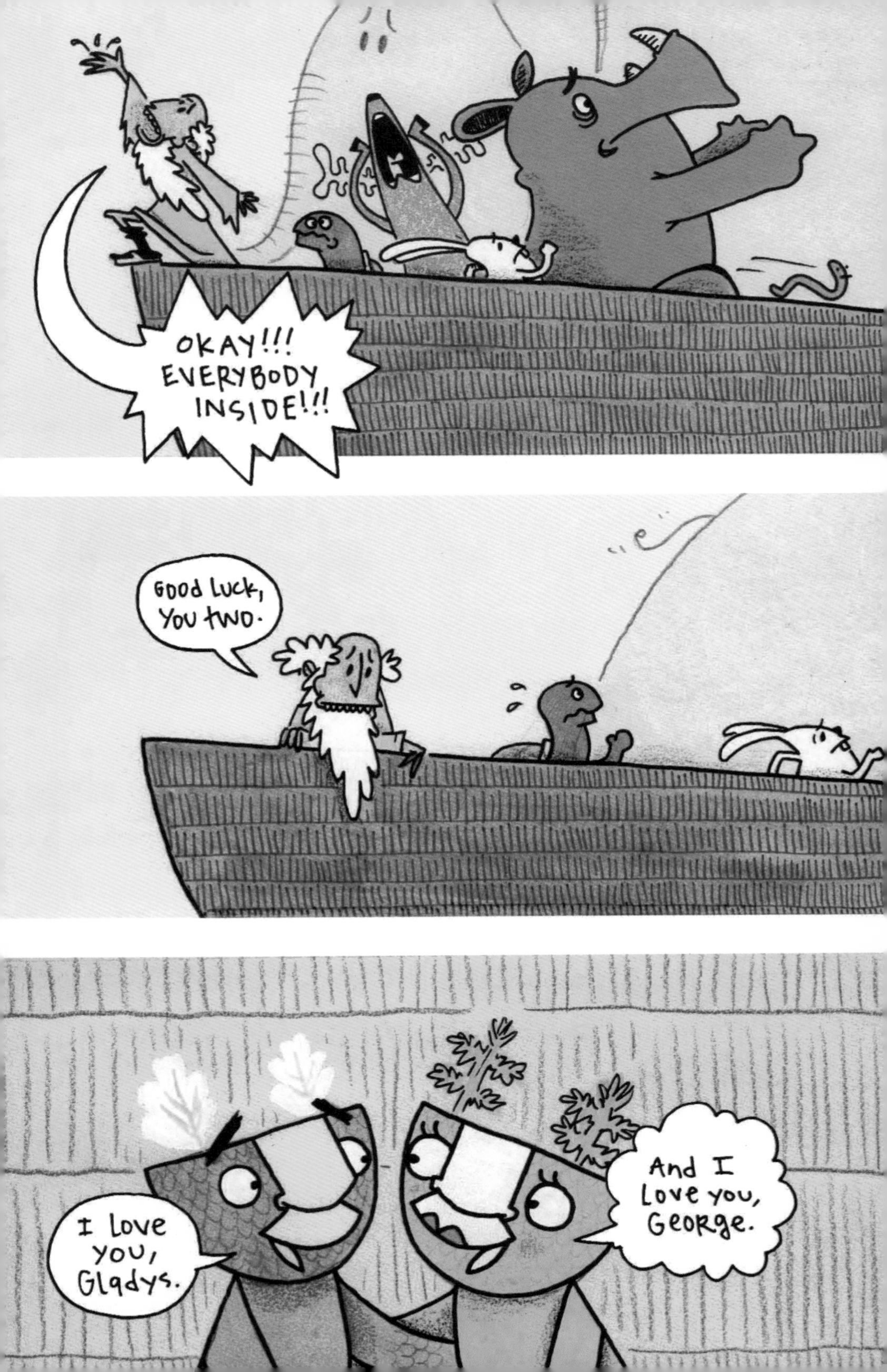
OKAY!!! EVERYBODY INSIDE!!!
Good Luck, You two.
I love you, Gladys.
And I Love you, George.

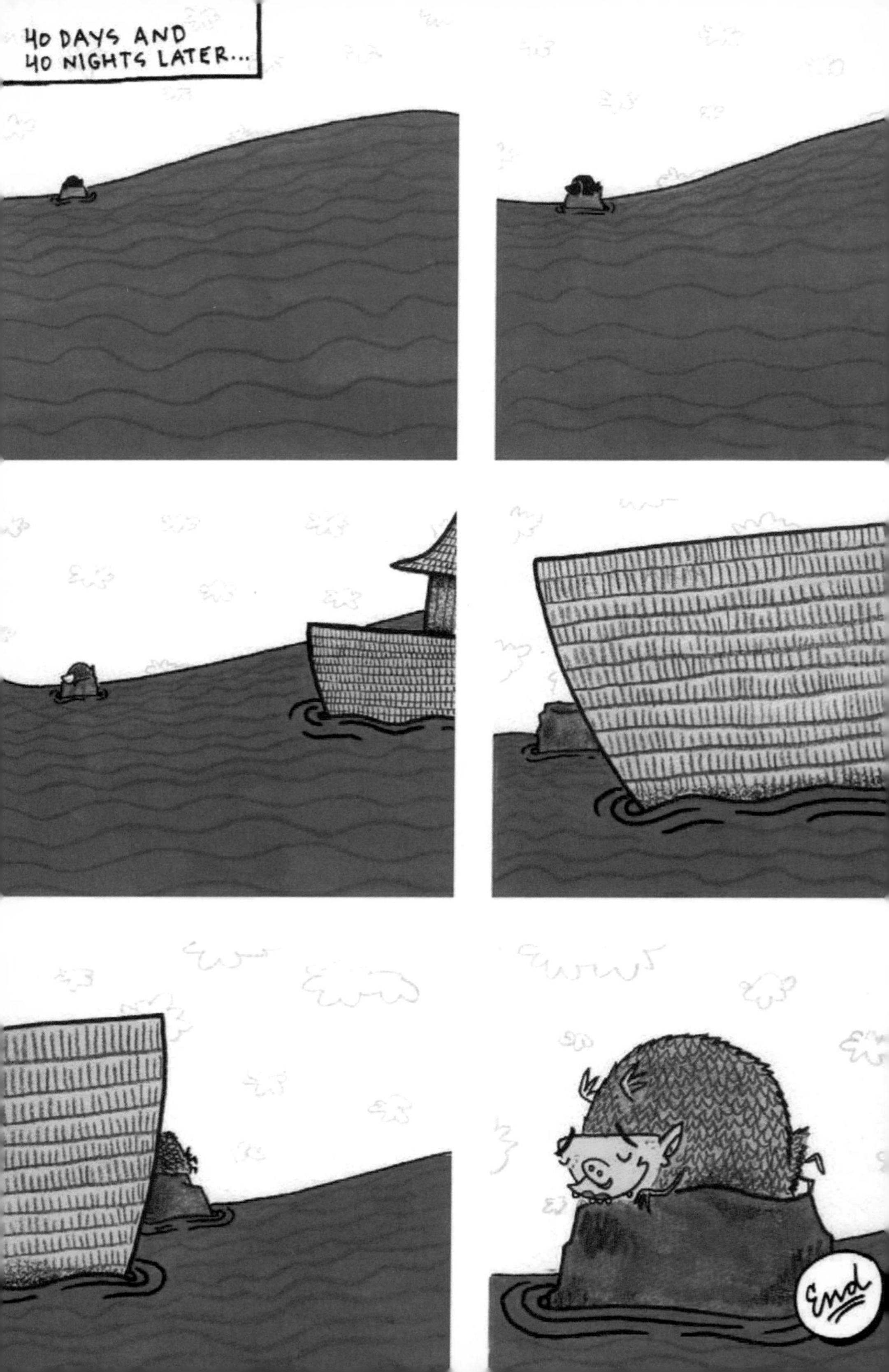
40 DAYS AND
40 NIGHTS LATER...
End

(the original cover idea for "Missing the Boat.")

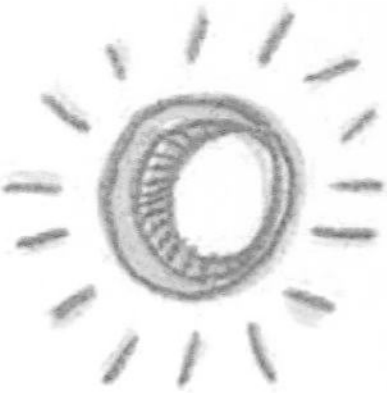

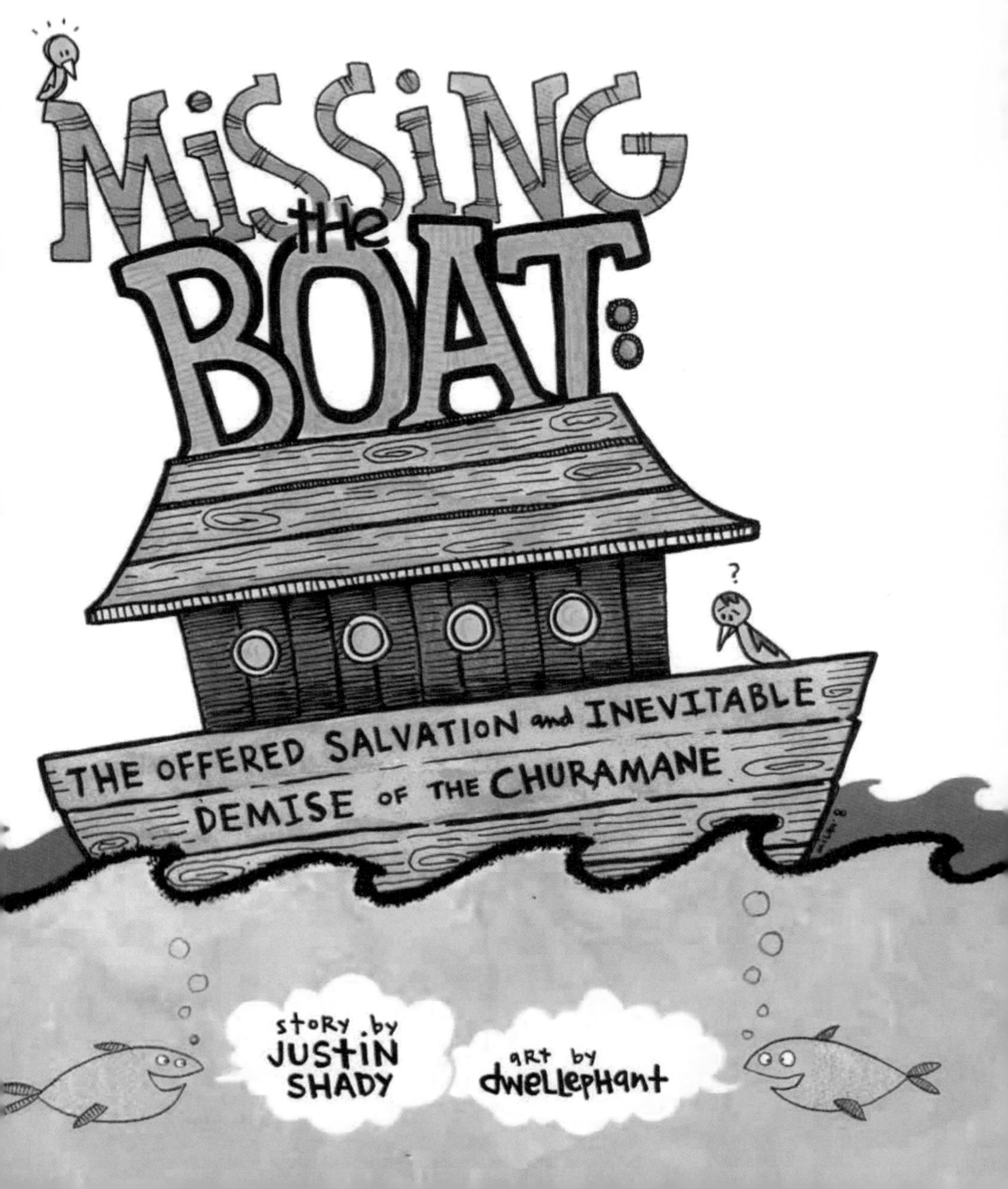

MISSING the BOAT:
THE OFFERED SALVATION and INEVITABLE DEMISE OF THE CHURAMANE
story by JUSTIN SHADY
art by dwellephant

Silverline

B O O K S

Dedicated to publishing quality, family-friendly books that are uplifting and bridge the gap betwee traditional story books and graphic novels. Available in hardcover and softcover.

For more information, please visit us at:

www.silverlinebooks.com

A division of

Shadowline™ image®

GRAPHIC NOVELS FOR THE YOUNGER READER...

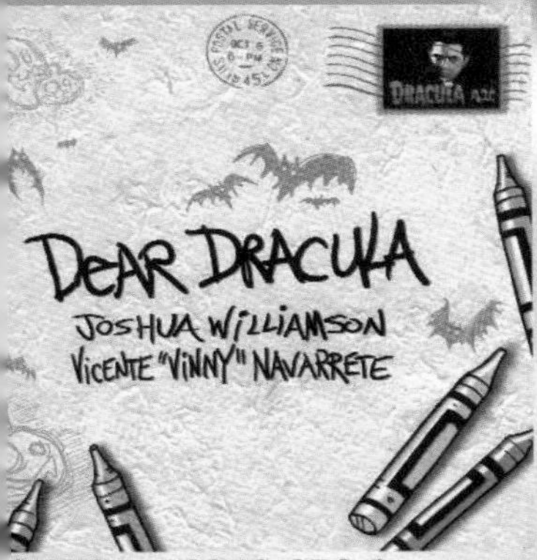
DRACULA
DEAR DRACULA
JOSHUA WILLIAMSON
VICENTE "VINNY" NAVARRETE

N: 978-1-58240-970-2

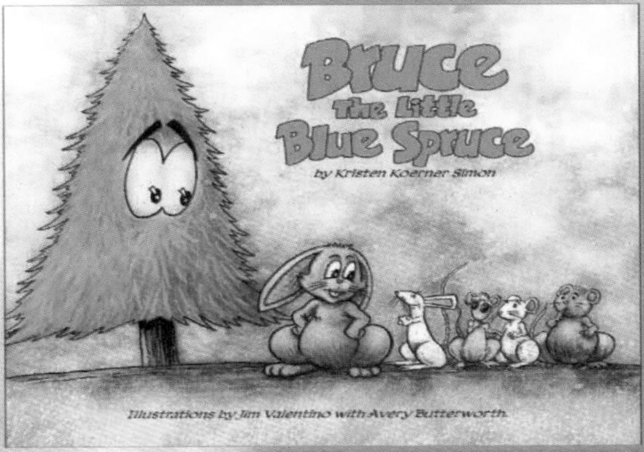
Bruce The Little Blue Spruce
by Kristen Koerner Simon
Illustrations by Jim Valentino with Avery Butterworth

ISBN: 978-1-58240-008-6

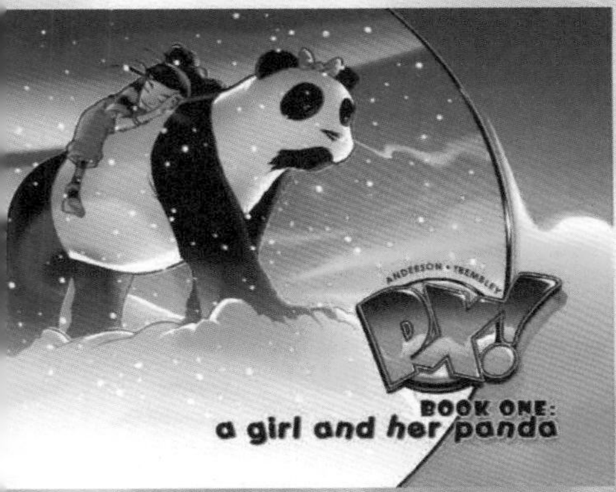
ANDERSON • TREMBLEY
PX!
BOOK ONE:
a girl and her panda

N: 978-1-58240-820-0

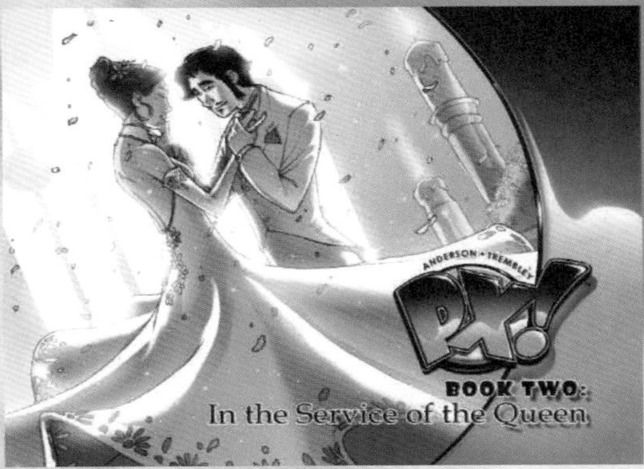
ANDERSON • TREMBLEY
PX!
BOOK TWO:
In the Service of the Queen

ISBN: 978-1-58240-018-5

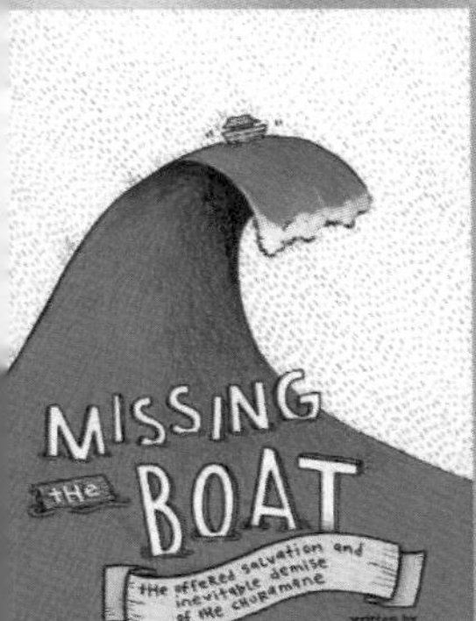
MISSING the BOAT

N: 978-1-58240-015-4

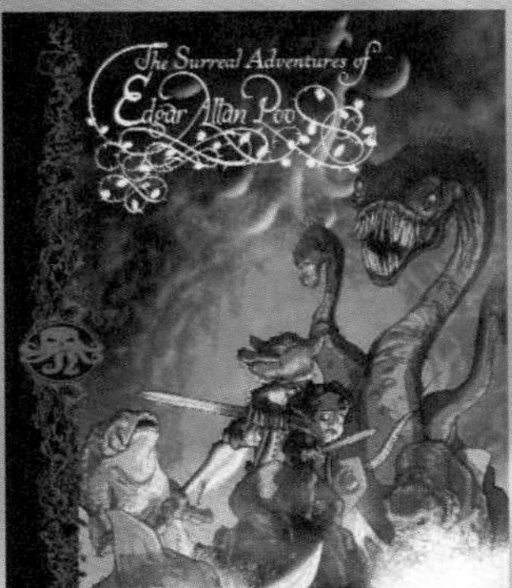
The Surreal Adventures of
Edgar Allan Poo

ISBN: 978-1-58240-816-3

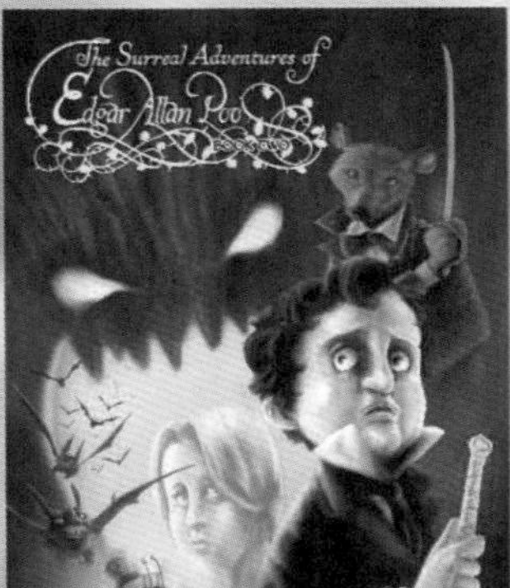
The Surreal Adventures of
Edgar Allan Poo

ISBN: 978-1-58240-975-7

WWW.SILVERLINEBOOKS.COM

Silverline™ BOOKS *Because every cloud has one*

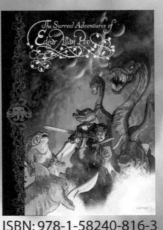

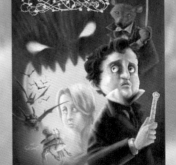

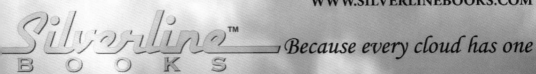

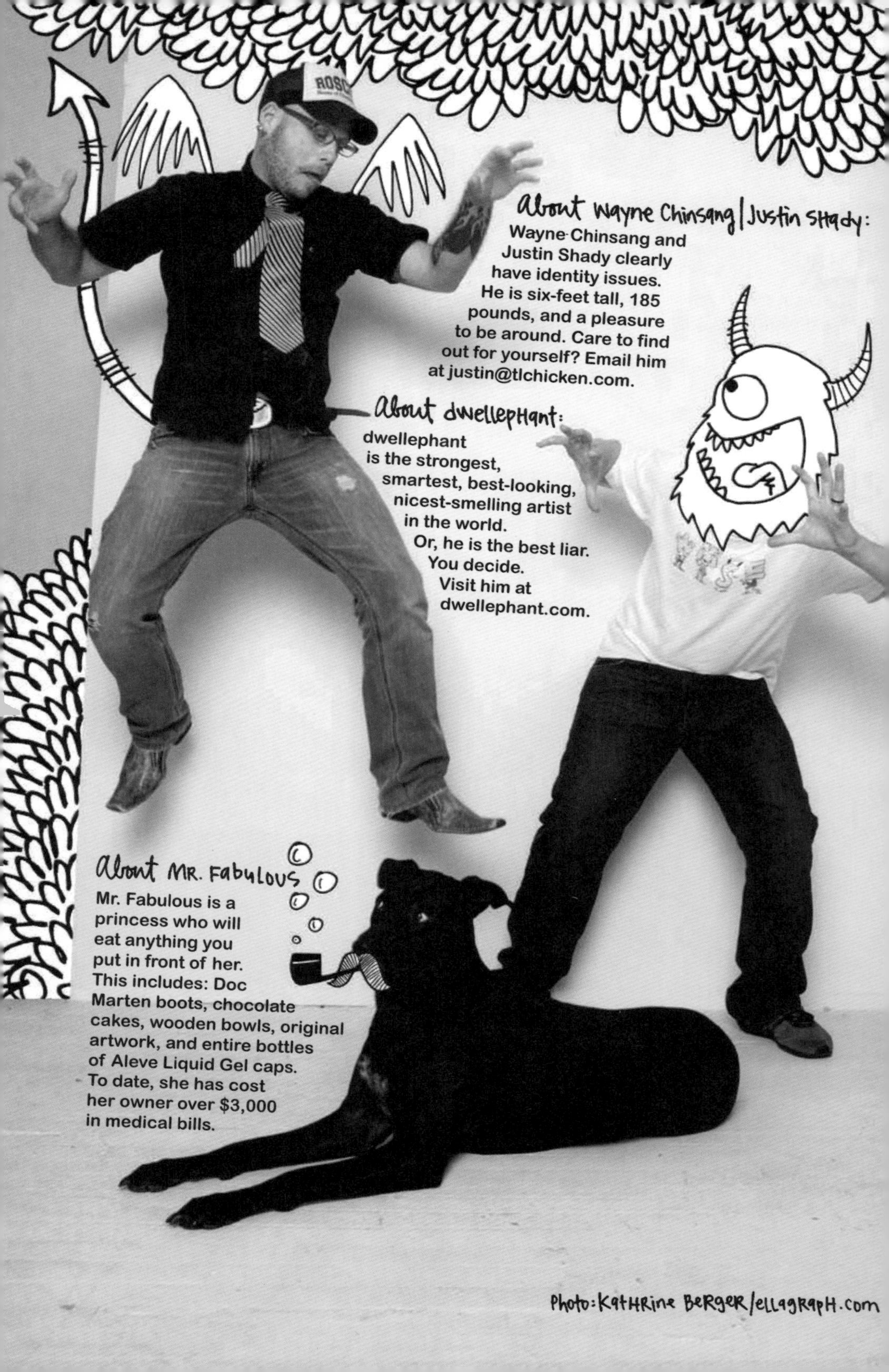

About Wayne Chinsang/Justin Shady:

Wayne Chinsang and Justin Shady clearly have identity issues. He is six-feet tall, 185 pounds, and a pleasure to be around. Care to find out for yourself? Email him at justin@tlchicken.com.

About dwellephant:

dwellephant is the strongest, smartest, best-looking, nicest-smelling artist in the world. Or, he is the best liar. You decide. Visit him at dwellephant.com.

About Mr. Fabulous

Mr. Fabulous is a princess who will eat anything you put in front of her. This includes: Doc Marten boots, chocolate cakes, wooden bowls, original artwork, and entire bottles of Aleve Liquid Gel caps. To date, she has cost her owner over $3,000 in medical bills.

Photo: Kathrine Berger/ellagraph.com